The Fake Out

DANICA FLYNN

THE FAKE OUT

A PHILADELPHIA BULLDOGS BOOK

DANICA FLYNN

The FAKE OUT

This is a work of fiction. Names, characters, businesses, places, events, and incidents are either products of the author's imagination or used in a fictitious manner. Any resemblance to actual persons, living or dead, or actual events is purely coincidental.

ISBN: 978-1-957494-25-8
Cover Art: Qamber Designs
Editor: Charlie Knight

AUTHOR'S NOTE

Blaise's sister Maja's name is pronounced like Maya. My-uh, not Ma-ja.

For Zach Sullivan of the Manchester Storm for being his true self. I think Blaise would appreciate you!

PLAYLIST

"Caught in a Blonde" By HorrorPops
"Howling for You" By The Black Keys
"Ain't No Rest for The Wicked" By Cage the Elephant
"Bad Things" By Jace Everett
"Tortured" By Devil Doll
"I Will Possess Your Heart" By Death Cab for Cutie
"Help I'm Alive" By Metric
"Hornylovesickmess" By Girl In Red
"Bandages" By Hot Hot Heat
"Baby Lou Tattoo" By Horrorpops
"Zombie" By The Cranberries
"Meet Me In The Bathroom" By The Strokes
"Gimme Sympathy" By Metric
"Misery Business" By Paramore
"Fade Into You" By Mazzy Star

CHAPTER ONE

BLAISE

JULY

I leaned against the bar and tried to drown out the noise of the sports network blaring above my head. Working at Dad's bar hadn't been my off-season plan, but ending my season with my career in the toilet hadn't been ideal either. So here I was.

I sighed and ran a hand through my short hair. The first thing I did when my long-distance girlfriend of ten years broke up with me was chop off my hockey flow. My baby sister Maja was the only one who recognized it as a cry for help and told me to go home to Philly. I didn't think going home meant I'd be living with my dad and working at his bar.

I looked up at the TV screen with a scowl.

"What about Blaise Holmstrom? He had a bad season this year, but Toronto could get a good deal with him from a team looking to fill their blueline."

"Well, he's got good hockey sense. He's a solid D. Buffalo, Pittsburgh, or Philly could get a good deal on him."

Pittsburgh? No way I'd ever play for the Miners. That was practically illegal when you grew up a Bulldogs fan. I already told my agent Pittsburgh was a 'hard no' if given the choice. But if the Wolves traded me, I didn't have a choice because I didn't have a no-move clause in my contract. I tried to ignore trade rumors, but after having a shitty season, I had my doubts. Being back home in Philly, under the scrutiny of my dad, didn't help assuage that anxiety.

On TV, the analysts droned on about me being a good fit in Philly. They said I had that gritty Broad Street Bullies style to my play. That shouldn't be a shock to any of these bozos since I learned to skate at the Bulldogs arena when my dad was the captain of the team back in the day.

My scowl returned when the pundits started comparing me to my dad and then to my oldest brother, Eli, who played for Montreal. If you were from a hockey dynasty family, it was inevitable you got compared to your family. Especially when you were coming off the worst season of your entire career. The kind of season that could kill the career of a lesser player.

Dad looked up at the TV at the mention of his name. Across the screen flashed old footage of him on the ice, but he turned away when the conversation got morose about why he hung up his skates.

That had been right before Mom died.

Dad raised a blonde eyebrow at me. "You think you're getting traded?" he asked in his native Swedish.

I knitted my brows together as I processed his question. Despite my dad and my ex-girlfriend both being Swedish, my grasp of the language was horrendous.

"Why do you even care?" I snarled in English instead and stomped off to go bus a couple of tables.

That was childish, but every time I spoke with my dad, all that teen angst came barreling back at me. When the Toronto Wolves drafted me, I thought for sure I had gained Dad's approval. But I couldn't help but feel like no matter what, I was always going to be the troublemaker kid Dad felt like he had to rein in.

I was the fuck up Holmstrom, and he never let me forget it.

I aggressively cleared one of the tables, slamming plates down into the bucket until my little brother Ayden came over to me.

Ayden was the reason I was working at the bar tonight. He was a shift manager, hoping to take over once Dad finally retired, even though that wasn't anytime soon. When one of the bartenders called out, Ayden pulled me out of my bed at Dad's house and told me to make myself useful instead of wallowing in self-pity.

He was a dickhead like that.

Ayden ran a hand over his shaved head. "Dude, you need to smile a little more. No one wants to tip the surly bartender."

"Good, because I'm not a bartender," I snapped and fixed him with a piercing glare. The kind I'd give in the face-off zone. Ayden knew that stare meant to back off.

"Dude, don't be like Dad," Ayden sighed under his breath.

We both took a second and glanced over at Dad. He stood behind the bar mixing drinks for an attractive older woman. He was giving her that signature Holmstrom smile, but his flirting was all for show. Dad still wore his wedding ring and never got over Mom.

"I'm not like him," I said and nearly broke a dish when I slammed it down into the bucket.

Ayden raised an eyebrow at me. "Bro, get over her! She broke up with you over video chat. She couldn't even bother to tell you in person. I know Astrid was your first love, but you got together when you were fifteen! You were kids and—"

"And what?" I snarled.

"Look, you can't have a good relationship when you live in separate countries, especially when she didn't want to move for you."

"I would have gone to her," I admitted.

"What? To play in Europe? Your place is in the big league."

I snorted. "Sure, if my team still wants me."

His gaze clouded as he stared at me. "Are you getting traded?"

I pointed to the TV where the sports network was still on. "They seem to think so. I don't want to play for the Miners."

Ayden chewed on his lip in thought. "At least you'd be closer to home."

I fixed him with an annoyed glare. "Fuck that! The Miners suck!"

He laughed. "Not if they're paying you millions of dollars."

"Maja would disown me if I was wearing the black and yellow sweater."

Ayden laughed. We all knew our baby sis. Being the only girl in a family of five hockey-playing brothers, she fit right in. She was the most rabid hockey fan of us all, and she lived by the Philly-Pittsburgh rivalry. She could be intense, but she was my favorite sibling, and I loved her despite her chaotic energy.

"You'll figure it out. Hey, if Philly's interested, maybe you could move back home," Ayden suggested.

I grumbled a noncommittal noise.

"Stop scowling and get back to work."

I wanted to give him the finger, but a few customers were watching us, so I shook my head instead.

After I finished busing tables, I saw my buddy TJ sitting at the bar with his teammate, Benny. They both played for the Bulldogs, but I became friends with TJ last season after his girlfriend Maxine introduced us. We were old classmates from high school. It was funny that not much had changed since then; she was as shy as ever.

"Oh, woof, you look like hell!" TJ said with a laugh.

Last night, I hit up TJ to go out drinking. Probably not the best idea since he and his twin sister Rox drank like fish. TJ kept trying to tell me I needed to bang a couple of bunnies to get Astrid out of my system. While Rox egged me on and kept pointing out the cute guy who had been eyeing me up all night. We had bonded over being bisexual hockey players, and I snorted when she said she thought an out bisexual hockey player in the league didn't exist.

I got a lot of heat when I came out, and it hadn't been easy. As much as the league talked a big game about hockey being for everyone, that wasn't necessarily true. But tough guys shut up real quick when I checked their biphobic asses into the boards.

Despite the twins' encouragement last night, I wasn't much for one-night stands. I had been with the same person since I was fifteen, and the hookup scene wasn't for me. I had to admit, the guy last night was hot, and he slipped me his number, but I wasn't sure I was ready to date again.

"How do you look like you didn't even drink a beer last night?" I grumbled at TJ.

He grinned. "It's a gift!"

Benny shook his head. He hadn't bothered keeping up with the twins last night. He obviously knew better. "The twins are like that. It's annoying as hell."

"What do you two assholes want, anyway?" I asked.

"Don't be rude to the customers," Ayden snapped at me as he set a beer down for the pretty blonde sitting a couple seats away.

I waved him off. He could go be a micromanager somewhere else.

"Lagers," Benny said, cutting off TJ before he tried to order a round of shots.

I went over to the taps and filled beer into glasses, only half-listening to their conversation. I set down their beers and walked away to get another beer for the lone guy at the other end of the bar.

Next to me, Dad poured a beer into a glass and handed it to Ayden. "Go take this to Veronica. On the house."

Ayden rolled his eyes, but I watched him walk over to a table where a pale woman dressed in all black sat with a pissed-off look on her face. She had black hair that turned into blue at the tips and a sleeve of colorful tattoos down one of her arms.

That piqued my interest. Tattoos were hot.

"Who's that?" I asked.

"Hmm? Oh, that's Veronica. She's a regular," Dad explained with a shrug.

I cocked an eyebrow at him, like that explained anything at all. "So you're giving her a beer for free...why?"

Dad fixed me with a glare. "Because it's my bar, and I

can do what I want. Go see what that pretty brunette down at the bar wants."

I rolled my eyes at him but did as he asked.

I smiled at the pretty brunette, who was clearly interested by the way she looked at my forearms and the sultry smile she flashed. But my eyes drifted over to the mysterious woman Ayden was talking to. Damn. From here, she looked gorgeous, and my curiosity wanted to get a better look at her tattoos up close.

"Blaise? Go ask Veronica if she needs a ride home," Dad said while he fixed another drink.

Ayden came back around to the bar, printed out a check from the register, and then shoved it at me. "Go deliver this."

I reluctantly took it. "Why me?" I asked Dad.

He fixed me with a blue-eyed glare that mirrored my own. "Just do it. I need Ayden here to manage the bar. Make sure she gets home safe."

I felt like this was some sort of setup. Who was this woman? And why did my dad want me to make sure she got home safe?

Maybe if she wasn't so hot, I would have questioned my dad's motives. But it got me out of working the rest of the night, so I didn't care.

CHAPTER TWO

VERONICA

My ex was a hockey fan. Like hardcore, bled black and red for the Philadelphia Bulldogs. I'd watch games with him, but sports were never my thing. I'd sketch or paint while he had the game on, tuning it out while I worked on my art.

So why did I spend a lot of time at the hockey-themed sports bar we used to frequent? Probably to torture myself. But also because I had a soft spot for the owner Hal.

Hal was an ex-Bulldog—hence his bar being hockey-themed. Come to think of it, it wasn't just hockey-themed; it was Bulldogs-themed. On the wall hung one of his game-worn jerseys and memorabilia from when the team won the Cup back in the eighties. Even the decor was black and red. Not to mention, it was the local after-game hangout for the current team.

The real reason I came here was because I felt safe at the bar. Hal always told me he was watching over me, and since my dad passed a few years ago, I craved that fatherly protection.

Tonight I was on another date, but unfortunately, it was yet another bust in a series of busts.

The bald-headed bartender with skin that might be whiter than mine put a beer down in front of me. I squinted up at Ayden Holmstrom. "I didn't order this."

Ayden jerked his thumb to the bar where Hal was laughing with another big blonde dude that looked just like him. I had to assume it was one of Ayden's brothers.

"My dad thinks you need it. Did the guy bail?" Ayden asked.

Ayden was kind of douchey but hot. I may have aggressively hit on him before when I was drunk, but he claimed Hal said I was off-limits. I think that was his way of letting me down easily. It wasn't my fault the entire family was hot. I probably would have hit on Hal, too, if not for the fact he still wore his wedding ring.

I dropped my head to the table and pretended to bang it against the wood. "He said tattoos on women were ugly, and then I told him to eat a dick."

Ayden laughed while he cleared the plates. My date had bailed as soon as I said that last part. He said he had to go to the bathroom and never came back. That was ten minutes ago, and now I was stuck with the check for both of us.

"You're an asshole, V!" Ayden teased.

"Duh!" I agreed and sipped my lager.

I eyed the mysterious blonde guy at the bar. He leaned over it, laughing while he flirted with a pretty brunette. The two of them were all coy smiles.

"Who's that?" I asked.

Ayden rolled his eyes. "My pathetic brother."

"Which one?"

He shook his head at me and walked back to the bar, leaving my question unanswered.

The mysterious Holmstrom brother locked eyes with me. He gave me a small wave, and I noted one of his arms was covered in tattoos as colorful as mine. Oh yes, I wanted to get a better look at those. Preferably while wearing little to no clothing.

I finished my beer, and I perked up when I saw the mysterious hottie walking over toward me with the check.

"My dad wants to know if you need a ride home," he grumbled.

I shook my head. "No need for that. You play hockey, right?"

"Yeah, for Toronto. I hate coming home."

I racked my brain for information. Hal said two of his sons were in the league playing for Canadian cities, but I couldn't remember either of their names. Neither of them came home that often, so I'd never met them.

"What's your name, again?" I asked.

"Blaise."

"I'm Veronica."

I held out my hand, offering it to him. His grip was firm, and it sent a warm sensation down my body. Holy shit, he had nice forearms. They were so huge and veiny...

Okay, I really need to get laid.

"Nice to meet you, Veronica," he said, and then he walked off.

I totally didn't stare at his hockey butt while he walked away. Just kidding! I totally did.

And hockey butt was real. Oh boy, was it real. I always forgot hockey players were massive dudes with trim waists and big asses. Seriously, that hockey butt commercial one of the Detroit players did a while back was such a thirst trap. But accurate.

My libido wondered how I could get that man on top of me. Or behind me. I was horny tonight, especially since I thought I was going to get laid before my date bailed. Wasn't that the only reason people used those apps? I wasn't looking for something long-term. I had that before, and he left. Everyone would abandon me someday, so I might as well enjoy the ride on my own terms.

Blaise came back to take my credit card. He looked annoyed. "Dad said I *have* to drive you home."

I sent a glare to the older man at the bar, who gave me that 'stern dad' look in return.

I sighed. "I live out in the suburbs. You really don't have to."

"Dad will take you himself if you don't let me."

I rolled my eyes. Hal was a teddy bear but also super over-protective.

"Fine," I said and handed Blaise my credit card so I could pay my bill.

He took it and was back seconds later with the receipt for me to sign. I signed it quickly, leaving a nice tip for Ayden, and then I stood. I grabbed my purse off the back of the chair while Blaise waited for me.

I followed him to his car and watched Blaise's tight ass on the way. His six-foot-three height towered over me. I wasn't tiny, I clocked in at five-foot-seven, but this man was like a mountain next to me. Hmm. Maybe I could find myself beneath this hunky man tonight. If I played my cards right.

"You didn't have to drive me home. It's kinda far," I admitted after we had been driving for a couple of minutes.

Blaise shrugged. "It's not a problem. Besides, my dad likes you. Surprisingly."

"What does that mean?" I snapped.

He sighed and pointed to my tattooed arm. "Dad always gives me shit about my tattoos."

I laughed. "Oh, yeah, he gave me hell too, but I'm an artist, so..."

I peered at his sleeve. He had some blank canvas in spots that I thought needed to be filled in, but nothing too out of place. I would have loved to get my hands and my tattoo machine on him. More than anything, I wanted to get my mouth on his skin. I'd kiss my way down those colorful tattoos as I marveled at his incredible body.

So sue me, Blaise Holmstrom was one of the hottest men I'd ever seen.

"Where do you live again?" he asked, pulling me away from my horny thoughts.

"Drakesville."

I had typed my address into the GPS when we got into his car, but he clearly hadn't spent much time in the suburbs. Even though I worked on South Street, I liked living in my small town. The only downside was the forty-five-minute to an hour commute, but I did my best sketching and sometimes reading on the train or the bus; sometimes I drove if I knew I was going to be in the city too late to grab the train home in time. I tried not to do that because parking in the city was such an expensive pain in the ass.

I directed him where to park, in the side alley two houses away from the duplex apartment I lived in.

"Do you want to come inside? It's a long drive back. I could make you a coffee," I offered with a sly smile.

He gave me a shy smile in return, which seemed odd to me. An attractive man like him had to know 'coffee' was code for, 'Hey, do you want to put your cock inside me?' He had to know what I was really asking. Hockey players got around; I was sure he knew what I meant.

He cut the engine. "Sure. Lead the way, sweets."

I rolled my eyes at the pet name but led the way a block up the street to the twin home on the corner. I walked up the porch and stopped at my door, noticing the heavy package on my doorstep. I forgot the canvases I ordered were supposed to come in the mail today.

"Hey, let me get that," Blaise offered while I dug into my purse for my keys.

I didn't argue and let him take the package from me. We walked up the steps to my second-floor apartment, where he gingerly placed the package on my kitchen table.

It was hot as balls in my apartment. I didn't have A/C, only a window unit, and I didn't leave it on while I was gone. I couldn't afford that electric bill.

Blaise removed his beanie and ran a hand through his short blonde hair. I dropped my purse on the table, but my mind wondered what my hands would feel like threading their way through those locks while he was on his knees between my thighs.

Okay, libido, settle down.

"Sorry it's hot in here. I only have a window unit, but it's in my bedroom," I told him.

"Oh. That's fine," he said, but he still had that shy look on his face.

I walked down the narrow hallway toward my bedroom in the back of the apartment. I turned the air on high blast, and when I spun around, I saw Blaise standing in the doorway, shoes off and looking like he was waiting for an invitation. I sat on the edge of my bed and toed off my Doc Martens. I patted the spot beside me.

"Close the door, will you?" I asked.

He did as he was told, and the bed sunk down under his weight.

"Thanks for driving me home. I know it's pretty out of the way. You could've driven me to the train station instead."

I wasn't sure why he decided to drive me all the way home to Drakesville. But now that he was in my bedroom, I had plans for the rest of the night. Preferably with me beneath him.

Blaise shook his head. "No worries."

I ran my hand through my hair and gave him a sly smile.

He reached up and brushed a strand of my black-to-blue ombré styled hair behind my ear. "I like your hair."

"Thanks. I like to change it up."

His big hand lingered on my jaw, his thumb caressing my cheek. I bridged the gap between us, leaning over and pressing my mouth to his. He froze at first, but then he snaked his hands into my hair as we kissed.

He kissed like a man starved, moaning into my mouth when I parted my lips to let him inside. He sucked on my tongue and tilted my head to get a better angle. He might have been nervous, but this man knew how to kiss—and how to hold a woman in place. Mmm, I loved a demanding alpha male in bed.

I straddled his thighs, and his hands danced down my back until he gripped my ass. He had thick, manly thighs and big hands, and I wondered what it would be like if he took me over his knee and used those hands to spank my ass.

Just thinking about it made me wet. I ground myself against the hard bulge in his jeans. He actually growled while I did it. I kissed from his lips to his jaw and down his neck, hitting that spot below his ear, and nipped at his earlobe.

"Fuck, " he moaned. "Wait, wait. Veronica, stop."

I pulled back and looked into his eyes. They were wide with desire, his arousal evident as much in his gaze as in his cock pressing hard against me. "What's wrong?" I asked.

He sighed. "Um...I don't really do this."

"What? Sex?"

"No, I love sex. But I just got out of a long-term relationship. I can't—"

"Dude, I'm looking for a good time, not a long time."

"I don't do one-night stands."

"Blaise, do you want to fuck me or not?"

"Oh, God, yes..."

I climbed off his lap and stood up in front of him. "Tonight's just some fun; no strings. Now, take off your shirt."

He didn't need to be told twice. He stripped himself of his tight black t-shirt, and a gasp came out of my mouth. He had muscles on top of his muscles. I saw the rest of his sleeve tattoo, and my eyes zeroed in on the phoenix on his shoulder and upper bicep. I traced it slowly with my finger.

"I have a phoenix, too," I said.

"Show me," he demanded, his voice husky with lust.

"Later," I whispered and dropped to my knees on the floor.

My hands went to his belt buckle, and he helped me relieve him of his jeans and boxers. His cock sprung up, and there was a bead of pre-cum waiting to be licked...so I did. His hips jerked up at the sensation, and he let out a moan. I looked up at him while I licked around the head of his cock.

"Fuck, V, that feels good."

Shit, when was the last time this man had a blow job?

I kept eye contact when I slid my lips down his length. He tipped his head back and moaned again. I closed my eyes as I slid my hand and lips up and down his cock. He gripped my hair and bunched it up on the top of my head so it was out of my way. Though I was sure he only did that so he could watch me slide his cock in and out of my mouth—and it turned me on that he wanted to see me at work. I put one hand on his muscular thigh to steady myself while the other stroked his cock.

"Fuck, fuck, you better..." He trailed off, but he bucked his hips against my mouth, and his cock bumped the back of my throat.

I moaned as warm, salty liquid hit my tastebuds, and then I sucked until it was all gone. I released his cock with a loud pop and daintily wiped at my mouth. I peered up at him through my lashes. He towered over me as he sat on the bed while I was on my knees before him, waiting for him to give me a command.

His gaze was so heated, it was like he lit me aflame.

"Strip," he growled.

Oh, hellllooo! That's what I was talking about.

I stood up and stripped off my tank top. I then slid my jeans off, leaving me in my matching black lacy bra and thong.

"C'mere," he demanded. His gaze seared across my body, and a tingle went down my spine at the sound of his deep voice ordering me around.

I stepped forward and straddled him again. I kissed his neck and felt him shudder as I stayed there, sucking on his skin until my lips were on his ear. "What do you want to do to me, Blaise?"

His hands dug into the flesh of my exposed ass. He gripped me like he wanted to possess me, and I wanted him to take me, control me, make me come until I saw stars. "Bad things."

"What kind of bad things?" I whispered into his ear, then continued the descent of my lips on his neck.

"I want to spank you for being a bad girl," he growled.

Oh, hell yes!

"I thought I was a good girl, making you come," I argued in-between rough kisses.

He bit my lip and descended on me again, angling my head as he tasted me and gripped the back of my neck as if telling me who was the boss tonight. He could boss me around as much as he wanted.

"I wanted to come inside your pussy, not your mouth," he said when he wrenched his lips from mine. I pouted at the loss, but before I could respond, he flipped me over and had me face-down over his big thighs. His hands rubbed across the exposed skin of my ass. "Such a bad girl. What am I going to do with you, huh?"

I bit my lip. How did he know I was into that? I looked over my shoulder at him. "Fuck me hard?"

His hand swatted my ass and then soothed the spot. "Nah."

"Please?" I begged and tried to wriggle out of his grasp, but we both knew I was just trying to goad him into spanking me again. I liked his powerful arms holding me down against the bed and punishing me for being so bad. I wanted to feel the smack of his big hand against my ass again.

He held me down and spanked me again, harder this time, and I bit my lip to keep from moaning. To keep him from knowing how much I liked it.

"I want to punish you with my mouth first. Would you like that?" he asked, giving me another little spank.

I gasped, and then he flipped me over onto my back. His fingers trailed down my floral sleeve tattoo, and he shifted my hip so he could see the massive phoenix tattoo that ran from the top of my hip to mid-thigh.

"Wow," he breathed. "This is gorgeous."

He pressed his lips across the bottom of my tattoo and worked his way up my body. I was buzzing with excitement, and when he pulled down the cups of my bra, I thought I was going to explode. He caressed my nipples with the back of his thumbs and turned them to hardened points while I arched my back to get closer to him. With one hand, he reached around and unclasped my bra, tossing the garment across the room.

"So gorgeous, V," he said before he dipped his head down and his tongue skated circles around my nipple.

He moved to my other breast and repeated the action. My body was on edge with anticipation as he trailed kisses down my torso. I gasped when he pulled my thong off with his teeth and gave me a wicked grin.

I think I died and went to heaven. Who was this guy?

CHAPTER THREE

BLAISE

What the fuck am I doing?

When Dad asked me to take her home, I didn't question why he asked. I definitely didn't think I'd be here, running my fingers through her slickness and about to torture her clit with my mouth.

"You okay, honey?" she asked, looking down at me with a concerned look.

I never slept with anyone other than Astrid. Everyone thought since I was a hockey player, I cheated on my girlfriend by banging as many bunnies as I could, but that wasn't me. Astrid had been my one and only for so long. I never had a one-night stand or was interested in the bunny circuit. Never explored my sexuality either, even though I'd known for a long time I was bi. Astrid had been my person until she wasn't anymore. Until she shattered my heart into a million pieces.

But I was twenty-five, and I didn't have to be tied to one

person anymore. Not when there was a woman spread out before me offering herself up only for tonight. I could do casual. Especially with a woman as hot as Veronica.

I spread her thighs and kissed my way up her center. I parted her with my thumbs and practically moaned at how wet she was.

"Is this all for me, sweets?" I asked. I looked up at her, and she nodded while she closed her eyes in ecstasy.

I hadn't missed the way she moaned when she sucked my dick. That was hot. My ex never even pretended to enjoy giving oral. But this woman seemed like she got off on it, and that made my cock pulse in excitement.

"Please," she begged.

"Please, what?" I asked with a grin.

"Lick my pussy," she moaned and writhed like I was torturing her.

I kissed the inside of her thigh, slowly marking my path toward her core. She held in a breath and let out a whimper when I drawled my tongue across her. I gave her soft, gentle licks, and she pressed herself up against my face. I held her hips down on the bed and explored her with my tongue. My cock was a hard spike against the bed while I held her wide open and feasted on her.

"Oh, right there," she cried out and ground herself against my face when I wrapped my lips around her clit.

I moaned as I got my fill of her taste and licked her through an orgasm. But I didn't stop there. I curled two fingers up inside her and pumped them in and out. She dug her fingers into my short hair and clasped her thighs around my head as she cried out.

I gave her one last lick while she came down off her high. "Good?" I asked while I pressed tiny kisses on her thighs.

Her eyes snapped open, and she yanked lightly on my hair. "C'mere, you sexy beast."

"Wait. I don't have a condom."

"I got it," she said. She opened the drawer of her bedside table, pulled out a condom, and handed it to me.

I unwrapped it from its package and rolled the latex down my throbbing cock while she shifted onto her stomach and got on all fours. I situated myself behind her and spread her knees apart. I ran the head of my cock across her entrance, teasing her but not quite giving what she wanted.

"Blaise," she whined and pressed her ass back against me.

I slid her hair off her shoulder and kissed her neck. "You want my cock, huh?"

"Please."

I found her entrance and groaned when I finally slid all the way inside. I pulled out and then slid back in slowly, setting the pace as I filled her up.

She dropped her head down and moaned into the bed. One of her hands played with her clit, and I felt her pussy squeeze around my cock like a vise. I reached around to place my hand on hers. "Let me do that."

"S'okay," she moaned. "I got it."

"You sure?" I whispered in her ear.

She nodded. "You can go hard. You don't have to be gentle."

I slapped her ass again. "Prepare for it to be rough, then."

"I like it rough," she confessed.

"Fuck yeah, you do," I growled. I quickened the pace of my thrusts, slamming into her as hard as I could. I swatted her perfect ass again. "You want me to take you hard, huh?"

She stifled a moan into her pillow. "Yes, please."

She ground back against me, shamelessly thrusting back into me as I snapped my hips and took her deep. I grabbed her hair in my fist and fucked her with reckless abandon while she clutched at the sheets and moaned my name.

I moved inside her more urgently as my abs tightened and a sheen of sweat dripped down my back. I watched my dick sliding in and out of her sweet pussy, watching how I filled her up so good, she cried out in ecstasy.

"Blaise," she moaned. I felt her clench around me as she came all over my dick.

She slumped onto her stomach in a melted puddle of satisfaction while I slammed back into her. The bed shook beneath her, and I filled her again and again until I tipped back my head and roared out my release.

"Fuck..." she moaned and looked at me from over her shoulder.

I took a beat to catch my breath before I pulled out of her. I didn't realize how much I needed that. How much losing myself in her felt like all the pressure was off my shoulders. That should make me feel like an asshole, but she didn't seem to mind.

I ran my hand down Veronica's ass and smoothed it across her alabaster skin, now tinted pink from being spanked. "You okay?" I asked.

She nodded and looked like she wanted to get up, but I tipped her head up toward me and crashed my lips onto hers. She didn't let me linger and broke the kiss quickly to get up and go into her bathroom.

I got rid of the condom in her wastebasket and laid back on her bed.

What was the protocol here? Did I stay over? Did I get dressed and leave? I was so out of my element. How did one-night stands even work?

I opened my eyes and saw her peering down at me, staring intently at my chest.

"Who's Astrid?" she asked.

"My ex," I sighed.

She cringed and got into the bed beside me. She curled into my side, and I put my arm around her. Her blue and black hair spread out on my shoulder, looking like the ocean at night.

She traced the lines of my ex-girlfriend's name marked on my skin. "You never get a girl's name tattooed on you."

I sighed again and grabbed her hands so she'd stop touching me, mostly because my cock was lifting in interest again. I had great stamina, but she already made me come twice tonight. I didn't think a third time was possible.

"I thought she was my forever," I admitted.

"I understand that."

"You do?"

She nodded into my chest. I lifted her chin up and found she looked defeated. I didn't know this woman, but I didn't like the sadness in her eyes.

"My ex left a week before our wedding," she explained. "He didn't even leave a note. He packed up all his things and left."

"Oh, I'm so sorry."

She shook her head. "Not your fault. No offense, but men are garbage, so I don't do relationships anymore."

Hmm. That explained why she invited me up for sex and nothing more. She just wanted a casual fuck. Maybe I should want that too, but that had never been who I was.

She removed herself from me and leaned over to grab a card off her bedside table. She pushed it into my hand. "Here. They can help you with a cover-up if you want it."

I glanced at the card. It read Golden Rose Tattoo on South Street. Wait...

"Do you know Eddie Mezzanetti?" I asked. Eddie was my tattoo artist here in Philly.

"Yeah! He's my brother-in-law."

"Nice! He did my phoenix."

She grinned and pointed to her leg. "Mine too. He's amazing."

I ran my hands down the tattoo on her thigh. The head of the bird started right below her hip bone and ran down to her mid-thigh, the red and gold feathers of the bird contouring her luscious body. Touching her again was doing something to me, and the way her whiskey-colored eyes bored into me, I knew our night wasn't over.

"You see something you like?" she asked huskily.

"Yeah, a very hot naked lady with beautiful tattoos that I want to lick and kiss."

She mewed a little as I kissed her neck, and my hands went to her perky tits. They fit in my hands like they were built to be cupped. I kissed down her chest again, spending some much-needed time licking and sucking on her tits until she moaned for me again. It surprised me when I slid my fingers down the juncture of her thighs and found her soaking wet again.

She pushed me off her and opened the drawer to her bedside table again. She pulled out a strip of condoms and threw them at my chest. But I was more interested in the oblong object in the purple cloth bag.

"Is that your vibrator?" I asked.

"Yeah..." she trailed off and gave me a funny look.

"I need some time to recover before I can go again. Can I use it on you?"

She looked at me like I had two heads. "What?"

I took the vibrator out of the bag, and her eyes went wide. The vibrator was purple with a long shaft and a section closer to the top that looked like two bunny ears. I tested the button, and it hummed to life. There were several settings, and her eyes widened more when I went through them all.

"Which setting do you like?" I asked.

"You can't be serious," she said with a shaky breath.

I grinned. "I love using sex toys. I'm gonna make you cry for my cock while I use it."

"Oh my God! Who are you?"

I flashed her a naughty smile. "Blaise Holmstrom, hockey player and a good lay."

"That's for fucking sure. Get over here!" she demanded.

"Which setting?"

She bit her lip. "I like two. Or three."

I switched the setting and pressed it against her clit. She immediately shuddered at the sensation. I grabbed the bottle of lube from her bedside table and slicked it down the toy's length. I looked her in the eyes while I slowly pushed the vibrator inside.

"Okay?" I asked.

She nodded and arched up while I pushed it further in, making sure those rabbit ears were rubbing on her clit. I kissed her neck and caressed one of her tits with one hand while the other used the toy on her.

"That feel good, sweets?" I whispered into her ear.

"Oh, fuck me..." she moaned, and she reached out to grip my arm.

I grinned while I continued to use the toy on her, loving the sound of her whimpering cries. So fucking hot.

"That's a good girl," I whispered, and then dipped my head down to tug her nipple into my mouth.

She writhed against the bed as I flicked to the next setting on her vibrator. I sucked on her tit and pleasured her with the toy, getting harder the more she cried out. She sank her teeth into her bottom lip as the waves of ecstasy washed over her.

"Come for me, Veronica," I urged. "Again."

She thrashed her head against her pillow as the orgasm took over. It was so hot to watch. It might not have been my cock doing it to her, but I was in control here. I was using the toy on her to get her to this wild orgasm, and that turned me on.

"Please, Blaise," she cried out.

I caressed my thumb across her cheek gently. "What, sweets?"

"I want your cock again. Please?"

"You'll have me. After you be a good girl and come for me again," I purred and put more pressure on the vibrator.

"Oh my God!" she cried out.

I leaned over and kissed her. "How's that feel?"

"So good."

She was crying, like actually whimpering, because the pleasure was too much. It was awesome.

"Fuck yes..." I breathed out while I watched her come again. She shuddered and squeezed my arm until she flopped back on the bed.

I pulled the toy out of her with a wicked grin. She looked so at peace and sated, but I was going to make her come all over my cock next.

She looked at me with a raised eyebrow. "Okay, you can say no about this, but how do you feel about your hands being tied against the headboard while I ride your cock?"

"I'll try anything once," I said with a grin.

She smirked at me. "Right answer, hockey boy!" she exclaimed, and then she pulled some rope out of her drawer.

FUCKKKK...this woman was going to rock my world again.

CHAPTER FOUR

VERONICA

There was a loud vibrating against my bedside table, and for a moment, I thought we had left my vibrator on before we passed out last night. No, that sounded like my phone.

I groaned and rolled over, only to hit a hard chest. I slid my eyes open in confusion. There was a man in my bed. A muscular man with a sleeve of tattoos on one of his arms and another woman's name on his chest. He groaned and pulled me into his arms. That's when I realized we were both still naked.

His eyes slid open sleepily. "What is that? Did we leave the vibrator on?"

I wanted to laugh at that being his first response too. Nope, I definitely remembered him carefully cleaning my vibrator last night before we had sex again.

I pushed out of his arms to slap my phone off. It was only nine a.m. on a Saturday, but I had spent all night with this hot hockey player, having wild sex until well into the morning. Holy fuck, he got off on using my vibrator on me, and then he agreed to being tied to the headboard while I rode him. Men usually hated that. This dude, oh boy, I was pretty sure last night had been the best sex of my entire life.

I didn't like to let men stay over, but it had been super late by the time he said he was down for the count. I let him stay against my better judgment, but now I needed him to get out.

He pulled me back against his chest and wrapped his tattooed arm around my waist. He nuzzled his face into my neck and kissed me softly, like a gentle lover.

I sighed when my phone buzzed again, and I saw my brother's name on the screen. I answered with a growl, "What?"

"Hello to you too, baby sis," my brother chuckled on the other line.

"What do you want?" I snapped. I was so not a morning person, and Alex knew that.

"Can you come into the shop?"

"Are you serious?"

He sighed. "Andy called out sick again. I need you."

I grumbled. "You know it's my day off, and I'm running on a few hours of sleep."

"Why?"

"Do you really want to know that your sister was up all night having marathon sex with a hot guy she brought home?" I asked. I ran a hand down my face, trying to rub the sleep from my eyes.

Blaise chuckled into his hand next to me.

"Ew!" Alex exclaimed. "But please, can you come in?"

"Give me a few hours. I need to shower, and it'll take me at least another hour to get into the city."

Alex grumbled on the other line. "Why do you still live in the 'burbs?"

"I like my small town! And my rent's cheap. I'm not moving in with you and your husband. I already see you two enough."

I hung up on him without another word and ran a hand through my messy hair. I wanted nothing more than to ride Blaise's cock again, but I had to shower and get my ass to work. Fucking Andy. I told Alex and Eddie hiring that kid was a mistake.

I swung my legs out of the bed and groaned again. I was so sore. This hunk of a man rode me to completion last night. I couldn't remember the last time a hookup left my entire body aching.

"Everything okay?" Blaise asked.

I shook my head and stretched. I saw his cock sticking up, especially as his gaze traveled down my naked body. His eyes looked hungry, and I had to bite my lip at his ridiculous body. I was so sore, but my pussy didn't care; it wanted that cock inside it again.

"I need to get a shower and head back into the city," I explained.

He sat up on the bed. "I can drive you. I need to get home, anyway."

I shook my head. "No, that's okay. You probably need to get going, right?"

"Nope. It's the off-season. I've got nowhere to be."

"Oh...well I still need to get a shower."

He gave me a cocky grin. "You want some company?"

"What?" I asked, and then my lips parted in a gasp as he looked me dead in the eyes and stroked his cock right there in my bed.

Who was this guy?

He was a dirty, dirty man. I loved it. Too bad he lived in Toronto, or I could see a fuck buddy's situation between the two of us.

"I see you staring at my cock like you can't decide if you want to ride it or put it in your mouth again."

"Uh huh," I mumbled, mesmerized by this beautiful man in my bed stroking himself as he looked at my naked body.

"You want me to join you, sweets?"

"Yes," I whispered. He gave me that cheeky grin again, like the one he gave me when he ate me out last night.

He got out of bed and followed me into my small bathroom. I turned on the showerhead and stepped inside, with him right behind. The water had barely hit me when his strong arms lifted me, and he pressed me against the wall. I wrapped my legs around his powerful hips as he buried his sheathed cock inside me. He must have grabbed a condom from my drawer before following me inside. Damn, this man knew how to make a woman silly. I clutched onto his shoulders while he held me up and pumped into me with the water sliding down our bodies. I didn't know hockey players were this built, but this man was strong. We didn't last long, and I dug my nails into his muscular back as we came together beneath the water.

He stepped out to get rid of the condom while I washed my hair. We helped each other clean up, and I giggled as he made my breasts super clean. The water had gone cold by the time I washed the conditioner out of my hair.

Ever the gentleman, he handed me a towel when we got out, and I dried myself off. I dressed quickly and ran the blow dryer through my hair. I braided it so it was out of my face, not caring if it was still damp.

Blaise stood in my hallway, looking down my steps,

when I came out of my room, dressed and ready to leave. "What?" I asked.

"You need a railing. Is that even code?"

I shrugged. "It's fine. Let's go."

He walked down the steps behind me, and I locked up my apartment. The ride to South Street wasn't as awkward as I thought it would be. Blaise was nursing some sort of heartbreak, so maybe a no-strings night of animalistic fucking was just what he needed.

"So how many siblings do you have?" I asked, trying to keep the conversation light to pass the time.

"Six."

"Six of you?" I exclaimed. "All boys?"

He laughed. "My parents were only children. I have one sister, Maja. Her and Michael are twins."

"That's wild. I have one older brother. I think."

"You think?"

I frowned. "My mom ran off when I was a baby. Who knows? I might have other siblings."

"I'm sorry to hear that. My mom's gone too, but it was cancer."

That one I already knew. Hal was a total silver fox, and ladies certainly took notice of him. I've sat at his bar many times and watched him flirt with women until they propositioned him. I thought he had a rule about not dating customers. When I asked him why he never took up their offers, he pointed to his wedding ring and said he was still in love with his dead wife.

Blaise's knuckles were white as he gripped the steering wheel. He was tense, and I got the feeling talking about his mom was hard.

"I'm sorry," I offered.

He unclenched his fists and gave me a weak smile. "It was a long time ago."

"Your dad still wears his wedding ring."

He made a grumpy noise in his throat.

"What?"

"My mom's death broke him. I don't want to be like him."

Before I could ask him what he meant, he turned down onto South Street and miraculously found a parking spot in front of the shop. That never happened.

"Thanks for driving me to work."

His hand clasped my thigh tightly. "Thanks for the good time last night and this morning."

He had that cocky grin on his face again. Blaise Holmstrom would be a hookup for the books. "It was a good time. Thanks for the ride!"

His smirk grew. "See you around, sweets."

"Bye, hockey boy!"

I got out of his car before I did something foolish like kiss him goodbye. I walked into the shop and one look at our receptionist, Olivia Yang, did me in.

"You look like hell," my bestie quipped.

"Just got my world rocked all night long."

She laughed and I went into the office to drop my purse and look at the schedule. I was working a lot for Andy, but I needed the money, so it was okay.

Olivia came into the office, waving a Wawa coffee and a bag that was definitely a greasy breakfast burrito. That was why this girl was my best friend. She arched a black eyebrow at me, and it looked flawless against her olive-toned complexion.

"Girl, eat before you work," she ordered. She slumped

into the seat in front of me with a grin. "And tell me all about your night. Date that good, huh?"

I shook my head. "Nah, it was a bust."

"Really?" she asked but narrowed her eyes at a spot on my neck. "So why do you look like you were ravished last night? Also, you have a bite mark on your neck."

"Ravished? You gotta stop reading so many historical romances. I got laid, just not with my date," I explained.

Olivia shook her head at me but grinned in amusement. "What am I gonna do with you?"

My face flushed at her words because they were pretty damn close to what Blaise had said to me last night before he held me across his thick thighs and spanked me like the bad girl we both knew I was. It had been nice to be with a man who took control and let me feel free. Sleeping with Blaise Holmstrom had been a Grade A good idea.

Olivia threw some napkins at me and I sipped on the 'black like my soul' coffee she brought me.

"Spill," she ordered.

I smirked. "I don't kiss and tell."

"Bullshit, you love giving me play-by-plays of your recent conquests."

I waggled my eyebrows at her and shoved more of my burrito into my face. I loved that Olivia never slut-shamed me for the past year while I discovered the hookup game. It was nice she didn't think only men were allowed to do that shit. Because that was utter bullshit. The good news about my promiscuous side? I wasn't bad at sex like Seth told me. The bad news? He definitely was.

"Hockey player," I answered.

"From the Bulldogs?"

I shook my head. "He's from here, but he plays for

Toronto. He was sweet at first. He said he didn't do one-night stands."

"Aw," she cooed. "Did you believe him?"

I nodded. "He was going through a breakup, and I think it had been a while for him. But he seemed to know what I wanted. And..."

Olivia's dark brown eyes lit up. "And what?"

"He used a sex toy on me and let me tie him up later," I gushed.

Her eyes got wide.

Olivia was into what I would call 'vanilla sex.' Not to her face, but when we got drunk after my break up, and I revealed I liked to get my ass slapped during sex, I thought her head would explode. It was okay to enjoy vanilla sex, but it was okay to like what I liked too. What wasn't okay was to judge people about their desires.

"Wow, are you going to see him again?" she asked.

I gave her a sour look. "One, he lives in Canada. Two, I only do casual."

She frowned. For the past year, Olivia had been trying to get me to see that I could find love again. I had a good guy, and then he walked away. So what was the point?

"Was he hot?" she asked instead of pressing the issue I knew she really wanted to talk about.

"So hot, like muscles on his muscles, big ass I wanted to take a bite out of and thick muscular thighs. Mmm...he was delicious."

She laughed. "Oh, my God! Well, anyway, eat quickly because Andy left us hanging."

I sighed, but she pulled out a piece of paper and started reading off it. "I also had someone call specifically asking for you. An Aaron Riley? Ring any bells? Rox Desjardins referred him."

I chewed thoughtfully and sipped on the last of my coffee. The name didn't ring any bells, but Rox did. I did a big piece on her thigh last winter. It was a collection of different-sized blue snowflakes running from the top of her hip to mid-thigh. If she was bringing me more clients, I might do her touch-ups for free. Okay, not really because I needed the money, but it was cool she was referring people to me.

I held my hand out, and Olivia handed me the schedule book so I could look over my clients for the day. "Can you call him and tell him I have an opening today?"

She nodded. "You got it, boss. But hurry up. You have an appointment in ten."

I groaned but threw my garbage in the trash can. I took a quick trip to the bathroom. There *was* a bite mark on my neck, and that made me smile. Blaise Holmstrom was an interesting man. I was glad to help with rebound sex to get over his ex, especially after he melted my brain with unending orgasms. I hoped he came into the shop soon to get that tattoo on his chest covered up. Maybe it would help him get over her for good.

I fingered the lotus petal on the inside of my wrist, where it covered my ex's name. There was a reason I refused to tattoo lover's names on client's skin and also why cover-ups had become my thing. I didn't want anyone to end up like me.

CHAPTER FIVE

BLAISE

"Are you just getting home?"

My youngest brother Michael fixed me with a raised eyebrow when I walked into the door of our dad's row house in South Philly.

Being one of six meant you were never alone. It had been nice growing up when Dad was so distant with everyone after Mom's death, but now that I was a grown-ass man and living with Dad again, it was irritating.

"Yeah, why?" I asked dryly.

I was tired and irritable after a night of no sleep. Not that I regretted spending it with Veronica. She was hot, and that lady rocked my world. The mental image of using her vibrator on her was locked away in my spank bank for the future. Holy hell, was that hot.

Michael sat on the couch with his laptop in front of him, and I knew that meant he was working on his book. Michael was an amazing hockey player, but he had no aspirations to play professionally. Which was surprising when you looked at our family. Nope, what career aspirations did my brother have? To be a romance writer! Which had been so weird to me. He swore me to secrecy and then chastised me when I thought only women wrote those kinds of books. Oh, my baby brother gave me a lesson on that for sure.

"Dad was looking for you," Michael said.

I sighed and slumped down on the couch next to him. "Did he say what he wanted?"

"To train with you."

I groaned again and closed my eyes. I was exhausted, and the last thing I wanted to do was train like a dog with Dad. He could be more hardcore than any of my trainers.

Michael tried to hide his laughter as he typed away at his computer. "You look like shit."

I gave him the finger. "I had a late night."

"Hmm."

I slanted open an eye. "What?"

"Nothing."

I kicked his foot. "Bro, what?"

Michael stopped his incessant typing and pinned me with a serious look. "Do you know you have a hickey on your neck?"

"Fuck..." I muttered and rubbed my neck. Veronica was a hellcat in bed, and I was all about it, but I didn't realize she'd left her mark on me. I'd never hear the end of it from my asshole brothers.

He laughed again. "Good for you, man. I was worried about you."

"What does that mean?"

"I don't want you to end up like Dad. He let losing Mom consume him. You remember how much it sucked."

"You and Maja had it worse than the rest of us," I argued.

Maja and Michael barely remembered Mom. They were two when she died, so I didn't blame them. It was hard to relate to the twins when they didn't understand the rest of our pain. Hard to explain that my heart felt like someone put it in a blender when they had no memory of her.

"Not the point," Michael argued back. "Eli had to be Dad to all of us at thirteen because Dad couldn't deal without her. I don't want that to happen to you."

"Hey, have you ever had a girl tie you up?" I asked, changing the subject. I laughed at my brother's wide eyes.

"No...I'm usually the one doing the restraining," he admitted. He clearly said it without thinking because his cheeks reddened. "Don't tell Mei I said that."

"Too bad," I said and ran a hand along the stubble on my jaw. "I didn't hate it."

"Are you going to see this woman again?"

"Nah, V made it clear she wanted something casual." The frozen look on his face made me pause. I kicked his foot again. "Dude, what?"

"Please don't tell me you took home one of the bar regulars," he explained with a shake of his head.

"What's wrong with Veronica?" I asked.

Michael couldn't answer because the clomping of footsteps alerted us of Dad's presence. He had his headphones on and was in exercise clothes, clearly coming back in from a run. That man was a machine, I swear.

"Oh, Blaise, good you're home. Did Veronica get home okay?" he asked.

"Yeah."

And then she sucked my cock and fucked me within an inch of my life. I wasn't gonna tell him that last part, though.

"Good. I worry about that girl," Dad admitted, and then he walked off.

Michael and I shared a 'what the fuck' look with each other. I ran a hand through my hair and realized I had left my beanie at Veronica's. I guess I was never getting that back. At least we made it a night and morning to remember.

I pulled out my phone and stared at the black screen, jabbing my finger on the home button until I realized it was dead.

"Dude!" Michael exclaimed from next to me on the couch. "Did you see this shit?"

"What?" I asked.

"Call your agent right now."

"Why?"

"Dude, do it."

I held up my dead phone.

He kicked me. "Go plug it into the charger and call your agent!"

I grumbled and stomped upstairs to my childhood bedroom. I plugged my phone in and waited for it to load up. My notifications blew up across the screen. I swiped them away and called my agent, not bothering to see all the calls or texts.

"Dude, where have you been?" Doug huffed out.

"Sorry, late night, and my phone died. What's going on?" I asked.

"Have you heard?"

"My little brother told me to call you. I have no idea what's going on."

He sighed on the other line. "Jesus, you're out of the loop. Open your email right now and look at what I sent you."

But I didn't have to open his email. I put him on speakerphone and looked at my phone, and the first thing I saw was a push notification that read, 'Toronto Wolves trade Blaise Holmstrom to–'

All the blood drained from my face as I read the word 'trade.'

The Wolves traded me. After a shitty season where I let my emotions get the better of me, they showed me the door.

"What the fuck?" I screeched out, raking a frustrated hand through my hair. This was not how I wanted this season to start.

"Relax, kid," Doug reassured me. "Open your damn email."

I looked down at my phone and clicked into the news story, allowing me to read the full headline.

'Toronto Wolves trade Blaise Holmstrom to the Philadelphia Bulldogs.'

Holy shit.

The Bulldogs wanted me. I had three years left on my five-year contract, and Toronto didn't want me anymore, but Philly did. My home team wanted me. The team my dad had played for and who I still rooted for when I wasn't playing against them. *My* team wanted me.

I opened Doug's email and scanned through the finer details about the trade.

"Is this real?" I asked.

I kept staring at my phone at the words on the screen. Getting traded sucked but to my dream team? To the team that was always at the top of my list if I wanted to go elsewhere? It was like a childhood dream come true. I had to pinch myself to make sure I was reading this right.

"Yeah, kid, it's real."

"Whoa," I breathed out.

"Congrats, you can move back home. I'm sure your dad'll be thrilled."

"Okay," I muttered.

I was still in shock, my mind racing to all the things I needed for the move. I didn't have a house in Toronto; I kept it simple with a condo in the city. My sister Maja lived with me, but she could stay until she was done with school.

"It's a good thing, Blaise. Toronto was taking a hit on their cap, but Philly had the room. Don't fuck up this season, okay?"

"Okay, okay. I got it. Thanks, man."

I hung up the phone and sat on my bed with unease.

I always dreamed of playing for Philly, of being a hometown guy, but getting traded felt like a failure. The dark part of me couldn't help but feel like Philly only wanted me because I was Halvard Holmstrom's son. Like it was a publicity move.

A knock sounded on my door, and I saw Dad standing in the doorway, rubbing his grey hair with a towel. "I just saw. That's good, no?"

I swallowed hard and nodded. "Yes and no. Toronto didn't want me anymore."

"Fuck them. You were born to play in Philly, Blaise. And raised in that barn, and don't forget that."

He disappeared from the doorway before I could say anything. I never understood that man. Sometimes I felt like he was proud of me, but other times I couldn't get a read on him. Was that some stoic European thing? I could never tell.

The only thing I knew for sure was that I couldn't let Astrid breaking my heart mess up the rest of my career. Next season would be a fresh start with Philly. I wouldn't mess it up. Not this time.

My phone vibrated against the bedside table, and a grin spread across my face at the slew of texts from my sister.

MAJA: !!!!!!!!!!!!!!

MAJA: HOLY FUCKING SHIT! Is this real?

MAJA: Bro! Tell me it's real!

MAJA: TELL ME!!!

MAJA: Also, am I homeless now??

I shook my head with a laugh and called her instead.

If there was anyone excited about this trade, it was definitely my Bulldogs-obsessed baby sister. I had to love her for that.

CHAPTER SIX

VERONICA

OCTOBER

"Okay, why the cherry blossoms?" I asked. I laid out my tattoo sketches on the counter and stared up at the hot six-foot-four giant.

Behind him, his curvy girlfriend smiled. "Because it's my favorite flower," Rox explained.

"Ugh! Love! It makes me sick!" I teased. "What do you think?"

Benny nodded. "Your artwork's amazing. Let's do it."

I put the sketches aside and grabbed the stencil I had already made up. "Come on, big guy. Take off your shirt."

He technically wasn't getting her name tattooed, but a dude getting his lady's favorite flower on his heart entered that territory. I almost said no to this client, but it was Rox, and she pleaded. I didn't have time to argue, and I needed the money anyway.

The shop was swamped. Back in July, when we were

having issues with Andy, it only got worse. He up and quit last month, and we had been down staff for a while. We wanted to hire two more artists, but the artists coming in weren't that good. Since I had been right about Andy, my brother and his husband had been leaning on me a lot. Served them right, but it meant I was scrambling to make all my appointments.

"That's what all the women say," Benny teased.

Rox glared at him. "They better not." She looked so mad at the thought of other women macking on her man.

He smiled and pulled her by the waist to him. He kissed her quickly, and I swear she melted into a puddle on the floor.

"Do I need to spray water on you?" I teased.

The two lovebirds pulled apart reluctantly, and I walked them over to my station. Benny shed his leather jacket and took his black t-shirt off. Holy fuck, he was big. I had him lie down on his back in my tattoo chair while I pulled on my gloves and put the stencil on his chest.

"This isn't your first tattoo, right?" I asked.

He pointed to his arm, where he had a cool Calavera tattoo. I leaned over to study it, and the artwork looked vaguely familiar to me. "Did my brother do this?"

"Is your brother a light-skinned Mexican guy?" he asked and squinted at me.

I knew what people thought when I said Alex was my brother. We called him Alex, but his first name was Alejandro, after his mom's dad. People got confused because I was pale as a ghost, and my brother had light brown skin.

"We have different moms," I explained. I peeled back the paper on the stencil and held up a mirror so he could check the placement. "Are you good with this?"

He nodded. "Looks good. Rox trusts you, so do what you gotta do."

I put down the mirror at my side table and got out my machine, turning it on and dipping it in ink. "Ready?"

"Not really, but go for it," he said with a smile.

My smile was hidden as my machine blared to life, and I started inking his skin.

He reached out to Rox and gripped her hand in his. "Oh, love, it's not that bad," Rox assured him.

"Angel, hold my hand and stop teasing me." He cringed at the pain.

"I thought you were supposed to be a big tough guy. Don't you play hockey?" I teased while I did my work. But it was cute to see this big guy ask his girl to hold his hand. These two were perfect for each other.

He glared at me, and I laughed. "No wonder you like her," he said to his girlfriend. He looked like he was sweating from the pain. Poor guy.

I tried to distract him by getting him to talk more. "What position do you play?"

"Left-wing."

"I don't know what that means. Does that mean you play offense or defense?"

"Offense. I'm a forward, but I work mostly on the outer playing area."

"Yeah, I don't know what that means," I admitted. "I hooked up with a hockey player over the summer, but I don't know what position he played."

"Really?" Rox asked, her interest peaked. "Who?"

"Not on our team, but he's from here," I explained. "How are the Bulldogs doing? I don't pay attention to sports."

Rox beamed. "Sales are good. We got a new

defenseman on the team, so everyone's trying to figure out the new arrangements. Coach has been experimenting with the lines, trying to figure out special teams."

I had zero idea what she was talking about, but I nodded as if I did.

Benny laughed. "Rox, she doesn't care about hockey."

The curvy woman smiled. "Sorry! Now that I'm playing again, it's like I eat, sleep, and breathe the sport."

"I've actually been trying to send the new guy your way," he said to me.

"Why?" I asked. I wiped at Benny's skin and checked my work before starting back in on the line work.

"He has his ex-girlfriend's name tattooed on him," Rox explained. "You're good at cover-ups, right?"

Alarm bells rang in my head, but I didn't know why. "Yeah, they've become my specialty. I made that mistake before, so now I want to fix it for everyone else."

"We'll get him to come in. I think he's a procrastinator," Benny explained.

I laughed and continued with my work, knowing when to change the conversation to distract Benny from the pain. Once we got to the shading, he relaxed. Rox was a champ at getting inked, so it was hilarious to me to see her big hulk of a man pretending it didn't hurt. When I was almost done, my brother came over to inspect my work.

He and Benny shook hands. "Nice to see you again, man. My sis take care of you?"Alex asked.

Benny nodded. "She's good at distracting you when she's stabbing you."

Alex laughed. "Yeah, she is."

I wiped at Benny's skin, admiring my work. This piece was awesome. I loved doing flowers so much, it had become my brand. I held up the mirror for him to see again. "What do you think?"

"Damn, V, it's awesome!" Benny said.

Rox smiled. "Told you she's great."

I grinned back and covered his tattoo up. I took my gloves off and discarded them into the trash. "Rox knows the drill about taking care of your new ink, so listen to her."

He smiled at Rox and kissed the back of her hand. A pink tinge crawled up the pale woman's skin. "I always do," he said.

"Oh my God! Please get out of here with all your love and shit," I teased.

The couple grinned at me, and I wished them goodbye, watching them walk out the door.

I noticed Alex was standing around waiting for me to finish. That was odd since we had customers waiting. "What?" I asked.

He frowned. "I need to tell you something, and I'm really sorry to do this to you, but I have no choice."

"Alejandro, what?" I seethed, using his full name, but my big brother flopped his mouth open and closed.

The bell on the shop door rang, and his worried gaze darted in its direction. I turned and clamped my mouth shut because I knew what he was about to say, but I had a lot of questions.

Standing in the doorway, his six-foot frame filling it, was my ex-fiancé, Seth. He wore a leather jacket, hiding the sleeve tattoos that went up both of his arms. The tattoo that used to depict my name peeked out of his v-neck t-shirt. But it wasn't a red heart with a scroll anymore. Now it was an atrocious wolf's head. For some reason, that pissed me off even more. Even though I covered up his name as soon as he left.

I cut my gaze across at my brother. "What the fuck?"

Alex cringed, and Eddie looked up from the work he was doing on a client to mutter a swear. I wondered if they'd fought about this decision and when to tell me.

"V, I'm sorry. It's temporary until we get another full-time artist. He's doing us a favor," my brother tried to explain.

I give him my middle finger in response. My ex was in the shop to help us out while we were busy, and I wanted to spit fire at him.

I never got an explanation from Seth. He straight-up ghosted me after he left. I'd heard from a friend at a shop in Kensington that he was working there now and was already shacking up with a pretty petite blonde. She didn't say, but I was pretty sure I knew the woman was prettier than me. I would still be in debt from all the wedding cancellations had I not gotten an apology letter from his older sister with a check for his portion of the bill. I felt guilty cashing it because I knew it came from her and not him, but I needed the money.

Seth walked over to us and had a grimace on his face. Good, I'm glad this was as awkward for him as it was for me.

"You're dead to me," I hissed at my brother.

"V, I'm sorry. I had no choice," he tried to argue.

"Hi, Roni," Seth greeted, but I only stared hard at him.

"No!" I shouted and put a finger into his bony chest. "First of all, go fuck yourself gently with a chainsaw, and second of all, I'm not Roni. Not to you. Not anymore. You do your work, and I'll do mine, but stay away from me."

"V..." My brother pleaded for me to be civilized. But fuck that motherfucking shit.

"I deserved that," Seth admitted, and then he went to say something else, but Olivia was at my side.

"V, your next appointment's here," she said with a grin.

What?

I was open right now and was about to go on my lunch break. I cast a glance at the front desk and saw a tall blonde man standing there. We locked eyes, and the smirk across his pale face made me remember a night of marathon sex last summer.

Blaise Holmstrom was standing there, grinning at me. Blaise Holmstrom was in my shop. My hockey hookup who had ruined my pussy for all other men.

The two men next to me must have seen the wideness of my eyes. "Isn't that—"

"My boyfriend!" I exclaimed.

What the fuck?

Suddenly, a plan formed in my head. A really stupid plan, but if I had to deal with my ex being in the shop with me, I wanted him to see all the shit he was missing. That I was perfectly fine without him and didn't need him. To prove he hadn't shattered my heart into a thousand pieces when he left. I just hoped Blaise was okay with this because I was about to startle the poor man.

"BABY!" I called out to Blaise. His brows knitted together, but he didn't have time to think about it because I jumped into his arms, wrapping my arms around his neck and my legs around his trim waist. "Please, go with it. I'll explain later," I whispered in his ear.

His eyes showed his understanding, and his hands gripped my ass tightly while he slanted his mouth against mine like I really was his girlfriend and he was happy to see me. There was definitely a part of him that was happy to see me.

He pulled away after a long kiss, his eyes sparkling with a look that said, 'woman, you have some explaining to do.'

"You missed me, sweets?" he asked, but it was all for show. I owed this man a beer. Maybe a whole six-pack because I felt eyes staring at the scene we were making.

I slipped off him and turned to Olivia, who was wide-eyed with confusion. "You could have told me it was just Blaise here to take me to lunch, Liv."

"Um..." she stammered.

"We'll be back," I told her. I dragged Blaise out of the shop onto the busy sidewalk of South Street.

What was I doing?

CHAPTER SEVEN

BLAISE

I stared at Veronica with amusement. I had no idea what was going on, but if I got to kiss this hellcat again, I was down for that. I studied her while she stood on the sidewalk, trying to catch her breath.

She looked as good as I remembered. She wore a long-sleeved black sweater that made her tits look great, a red plaid skirt, and Docs. Like a woman who could fuck you up, and you'd like it. Her hair was different. Instead of blue at the tips, it was now red, almost matching the Bulldogs colors.

She hadn't explained what was going on, but I cast a glance at the shop window, and the two men she had been talking with were still staring at us. I stepped forward, cupped her face in both my hands and kissed her again. I slid open one eyelid after the kiss had gone on too long to find the men had walked away. I gave her a hard look when I pulled away.

She squinted up at me. "Blaise, I'm sorry."

"You want to tell me what that was about?"

She sighed but walked off down the street, forcing me to jog to catch up to her. "Yes, but first, I need to get something to eat. It's my only break of the day, and I have a ton of clients."

"Pat's or Geno's?" I joked.

She scoffed at me. "Do I look like a tourist? No. I want a big-ass slice of pizza from Lorenzo's."

I barked out a laugh. "How's that anymore less touristy than Pat's or Geno's?"

"Shut it, Holmstrom. Sometimes a girl just wants a big-ass slice of pizza."

I laughed.

I liked her logic, and I mentally calculated how much cardio I'd have to do this afternoon to make up for it. When I came down to South Street, it was to see Eddie Mezzanetti and get my tattoo covered up. The boys kept ragging on me about having my ex's name on my chest. Imagine my surprise when I saw my hookup from last summer looking like she needed to be rescued. So I told the receptionist to tell Veronica I was here for my appointment, which confused her because it wasn't in her system, but she seemed to go with it.

I didn't imagine Veronica would yell 'BABY!' at me and jump into my arms. I really wanted to know what was going on. Also, I was interested in watching this woman go HAM on a slice of Lorenzo and Sons pizza. They *did* have massive slices.

"So...you want to tell me what's going on?" I asked as we continued our walk down the street.

She sighed. "My brother hired my ex to help at the shop."

"Which one was the ex?"

"The white guy."

"Your ex who left you high and dry?"

She nodded. "I saw you, and...I don't know. I thought maybe if I had a new boyfriend, he would get jealous, and then when he tried crawling back, I could go, 'hahahaha, go fuck yourself.' Is that bitter and petty?"

I laughed. "Little bit, sweets."

She groaned. "I'm sorry I dragged you into this. I think I owe you a beer."

Our conversation stopped as we got to the counter for the pizza shop, and we ordered slices, which I totally didn't let her pay for. We stood on the sidewalk eating our slices, as one did on South Street.

Damn, I had missed Philly.

"Okay, so...you thought we could fake date each other to make your ex jealous?" I asked.

She shrugged as she chewed a huge bite. I wiped the grease from her mouth with a napkin, and my lizard brain thought about wiping it off with my tongue. Good god, this woman was hotter than I remembered.

"Come on, V. Do you want me to be your fake boyfriend?" I teased.

"God, what was I thinking? What are you doing here, anyway?"

I pulled down my t-shirt and pointed at the lettering above my heart. "I was trying to see if I could finally get this covered up."

"I can do it; it's my specialty," she said but frowned. "But you don't have to help me out with the fake dating thing. I'll tell them we broke up in a couple of weeks."

"Actually...this might work in my favor, too."

"How?" she asked.

I sighed and threw out our trash as we walked back to

the tattoo parlor. "My family's very concerned about me since my break up. And...well..."

"Well, what?"

"I haven't been with anyone since you. My horny brothers think there's something wrong with me because I don't want to plow everything in sight. Not like I haven't gotten offers. The guy hitting on me at the bar last night was pretty hot, but I don't know..." I ran my hand through my hair.

She squinted at me and cocked her head at my admission.

I blew out a breath when I realized I had to come out to her. I hated that shit. "I'm bi."

"Oh!"

"Is that a problem for you?" I snapped.

She looked taken aback by the harshness in my voice, but then shook her head. " Why would I have a problem with who you're attracted to?"

I sighed. "Sorry. I got a lot of heat when I came out. Hockey's not exactly LGBT friendly, despite what everyone says. And then there's the whole fact I've never been with a guy, so people who accept it want me to show them a report card of my sexual experiences."

She wrinkled her nose. "Fuck that! You know you're attracted to more than one gender, right?"

I nodded. "Yeah. I've known since I was thirteen."

"Then you're bisexual, and you don't need to prove yourself to anyone."

I blinked back at her.

She shrugged. "I have a lot of bi and pan friends. I've heard the shit that gets tossed their way." She chewed on her lip. "So you want to fake date me to get your family off your back?"

I laughed. "Yeah, I guess."

She pursed her lips. "Okay...but how's that gonna work when you live in Toronto?"

"Oh, sweets, you really don't pay attention to hockey, do you?"

She shook her head from side to side, the tips of her hair swinging back and forth, mesmerizing me.

"V, I got traded to the Bulldogs."

Her eyebrow arched in confusion.

"I moved back to Philly."

Her mouth formed a little 'O' in understanding, and it was taking everything in me to not think of it doing something else.

Shit. I was horny. Maybe this was a bad idea.

"Wait, I thought your dad said I was off-limits?" she asked.

"He'll get over it. He likes you, but he'll definitely give me shit for you being too good for me."

"Me?" she asked, her voice hitching up in surprise. "Not his hot, successful pro-athlete, son? I'm the mess of the lady that gets too drunk at his bar."

I grimaced. "I doubt my dad thinks I'm hot, V."

She laughed. "Why not? You look just like him."

I frowned at her. "What?"

She shrugged. "What? Your dad's a total silver fox. Sorry, I'm not sorry."

"Ew, gross!"

She stared intently at my chest. "Do you want to come inside and see what we can do about the cover-up?"

I nodded. "Please, help me."

She laughed. "Come on, hockey boy. Let's discuss it, and I'll think of some ideas."

That's how I ended up in her chair, but not with her

machine turned on. Instead, she asked me questions and sketched while we talked about ideas for the cover-up. Every once in a while, her ex would glance over at us, and I'd give him a small wave, and she'd glare at him. I may have done the 'fake boyfriend' thing of grabbing her hand and rubbing my thumb over the back of her palm to comfort her. It calmed her down, especially if I kissed the back of it.

"Do you like any of these ideas?" she asked, exasperated because I couldn't make up my mind.

"Sorry, I'm indecisive today," I offered, sincerely this time.

"What about something hockey related?" she suggested.

I pointed at the hockey sticks on the inside of my wrist. "I think I have that covered."

She sighed. "What about a maple leaf? That would be meaningful, right? Because your mom was Canadian?"

I frowned at her. "How did you know that?"

"Hal told me," she explained and went back to sketching.

"He talked about my mom?"

He never talked about Mom. Never ever. Not since she died, and her death broke him apart, leaving the rest of us fending for ourselves.

She nodded and hummed to herself while she worked. "It was during my mental breakdown after that asshole left. I think he wanted to tell me he understood loss and sorrow." She checked her watch. "Blaise, I have another client soon, but how about you think about what you want, and we'll set up a time to do the piece, okay?"

I nodded and put my t-shirt back on. Her ex was staring again, so I bent down and kissed her goodbye, rubbing my thumb against her cheek. "Call me later?" I whispered.

"I don't have your number," she whispered back.

I slid a piece of paper into her hand. "Call me, okay?"

She nodded as if in a trance. I walked out of the tattoo parlor, not sure what I was doing. By the time I got back to my car, my phone buzzed with a text message.

UNKNOWN NUMBER: If you're serious about being my fake boyfriend, can we meet tonight to iron out the details? I want to set some ground rules.

I grinned at her message and immediately added her to my contacts.

ME: Ground rules? Baby, you're killing me.

VERONICA: Not funny, Blaise. I'm serious.

ME: Bossy, I like it. Okay...I'm free tonight, but you can't keep me up too late. I have morning skate tomorrow.

VERONICA: Fine. I'll call you when I'm done with work, and we can talk. Maybe get dinner or something.

ME: This sounds like a date.

VERONICA: A fake one!

ME: Okay, I'm all in for being your fake boyfriend so you can be petty to your ex, who, by the way, seems like a douche, and I'm hotter.

VERONICA: That much we can agree on.

VERONICA: Also, BTW, you're like 1000X better in bed.

ME: Oh yeah?

VERONICA: Yeah! What other man would get off using a toy on me and then let me tie them to my bed?

ME: Hah. That was a good night. Want a repeat?

VERONICA: I'll call you later.

Okay, maybe I had ulterior motives for agreeing to this fake dating thing. Maybe I was thinking about if that meant I got to get her underneath me again.

I put my phone in the cupholder and drove off to the gym where I was supposed to meet TJ for a workout. As a hockey player, when I wasn't at practice, going to team meetings, having a morning skate, traveling with the team, and oh yeah, playing a game, I was hitting the gym as much as possible.

TJ was on the bench press, being spotted by one of my defensive partners, Logan Cullen.

"Come on, T, one more," Logan urged.

"Fuck you, rookie!" TJ huffed out as he finished the set.

I shook my head at TJ's antics and began my stretches.

Being a professional athlete, you had to be in peak physical condition. I had no aversion to working my body hard, but I had to prove myself this season. To prove to the Bulldogs they didn't just sign me because of who my dad was. That I deserved my spot on the team, and I was a good defenseman who knew how to check a guy into the boards and cover the slot.

TJ wiped down the bench. "Hey, man, you made it. Wasn't sure you were going to show. You get that shit covered up yet?"

"Not yet."

"Why do you look so happy, though?" TJ asked.

"I think I have a date tonight."

"What do you mean, you think?" Logan asked.

TJ kicked my foot. "Date? Explain!"

"Well..." Shit, we needed a good cover story. How would people believe this? "I've been hooking up with this girl, but it's been casual since she lives here and I was in Toronto. But now that I'm back...we're gonna try."

"Really?" TJ asked, and he had a twinkle in his eye.

"Good luck, man. Where you gonna take her?" Logan asked.

I shrugged. "Not sure yet. I have to think about it."

"Wait, what does that have to do with going to get your tattoo fixed?" TJ asked.

I rubbed the back of my neck. "Oh. She's a tattoo artist."

"Hot?" TJ asked.

I nodded. "Definitely. It's kind of complicated, though."

Logan cocked his head. "How so?"

"Well, she's one of the regulars at my dad's bar, and according to my brothers, she's off-limits. But I don't know, my dad's soft on her, so we'll see," I explained.

"Wait...are you telling me you hooked up with Veronica O'Malley?" TJ asked.

I didn't even know V's last name. For a fake boyfriend, I was bad at this.

"Isn't that Rox's tattoo artist?" Logan asked.

"And Dinah's brother's married to V's brother," TJ explained.

Dinah was one of my other new teammates' fiancée. I forgot she was Eddie Mezzanetti's little sister.

This got way more complicated than I realized. This team was too much of a small world at times. When Benny said that this team was like six degrees of who fucked who, I thought he was joking. What did I get myself into?

CHAPTER EIGHT

VERONICA

"Hey, can we talk?" Eddie asked.

"Busy," I said, trying to push him off. I was finishing up with my last client of the night, and then I wanted to get out of there.

I wiped at my client's skin, a biker who had become a regular. "How ya doing, Rocky?" I asked.

A grumble came from the large man.

I examined my work, wiping at Rocky's skin, and felt satisfied with it. I turned off my machine and threw out my gloves. Eddie was still standing there, running his pale hand through his dark hair.

"V..."

I cut him off with a glare and took a picture of Rocky's back for our social accounts. Then I patched him up and helped him to the register. The big man gave me a hug afterward, which surprised me, but despite how he looked, he was a teddy bear on the inside.

"That's it for the day, right?" I asked Olivia.

She smirked at me. "Yes, but now you have to tell me what the hell that was earlier."

I sighed. "Later, okay? I gotta meet Blaise for dinner."

"He's really your boyfriend?" she asked, her eyes raising up high in shock. A dark shadow of hurt crossed her face, and I felt awful that she thought I had kept this from her. I should have canceled with Blaise and told him we should call the whole thing off.

"I'll explain it later," I told her and gave her hand a little squeeze. "Promise."

When I returned to my station, Eddie still stood there chewing on a nail. He looked apologetic, but I didn't care.

"Save it," I snapped at him.

"If it makes you feel any better, I told him not to do this. And I'm making him sleep on the couch," my brother-in-law revealed.

I shoved my hands through my hair and brought it up into a ponytail. I didn't want my issues to cause my brother and his husband to have marital problems. "Don't do that on my account."

"It's not right," Eddie argued.

"He's a good artist. I get why he did it. I would've liked a warning."

Eddie gave me a small smile that crooked into a wicked grin. "But, you and Blaise Holmstrom, huh? I thought you didn't do relationships anymore?"

"He's different," I admitted.

Which wasn't exactly a lie. Blaise was the hottest man I'd ever slept with, and that night with him last summer was the best sex I'd ever had. So good I hadn't been interested in fucking anyone else since. Which was annoying.

Eddie gave me a calculating look. "He's a smoke show. Good for you."

I laughed. "Eds, I love you, but don't hit on my boyfriend."

He held up his hands. "Hey, you know your brother's my one and only."

"Don't make him sleep on the couch, okay? I'll deal."

Eddie gave me a sad smile, and he went to open his mouth to say something else, but his face turned into a scowl at something behind me. I turned around and glared when I saw Seth standing in front of me.

"What do you want?" I seethed.

He wrung his hands. "Look, Lily thought this was inappropriate, but since you moved on and look happy, I wanted to give you this."

Who is Lily?

I narrowed my eyes further when I watched him take something out of the pocket of his jeans and stretch his hand toward me. Against my better judgment, I took his offered card-stock postcard.

You are cordially invited to the wedding of Seth O'Connell and Lily Mathews on Friday, November 6th

I stared at the piece of paper in my hands and then back at my ex-fiancé. He had to be joking. I didn't know who this Lily person was, but she was right to say it was inappropriate to invite your ex-fiancée to your new wedding. Which was in a couple of weeks.

What the fuck!

"I understand if Blaise can't come, but..."

I stopped listening to him. Oh, now I got it. He was only inviting me because he wanted a hockey player at his wedding. I continued to stare at the piece of shit I thought I loved and didn't know how to respond. For the sake of the shop, I couldn't punch him in the dick and walk out with my middle fingers in the air. No matter how much I wanted to do that.

"Sweets, you ready to go?" a deep voice asked, startling me.

I jerked my head up and saw Blaise standing in front of us. He stared into my eyes as if mentally asking me if I was okay. He must have seen the shocked look on my face because he plucked the invitation out of my hand and scanned it.

"I have to check my schedule," he said.

Then he pocketed the invitation and leaned down to kiss me, not caring who saw. He was good at this fake dating thing. A little too good.

When he pulled away, his eyes sparkled, but they were also dark with desire. If we were really doing this thing, I had to lay down the ground rules. We couldn't end up in bed again. It would make everything so much more complicated. But why did he have to be such a good kisser?

He pulled away and brushed a stray piece of hair from my face. "You good?" he asked.

I nodded and tried to catch my breath. "I need to wipe down my station first."

"V, I'll do it. Go be with your man," Eddie said.

I gave him a small smile while Blaise helped me into my leather jacket and untucked my hair from underneath the collar. It was nice but unexpected. He threaded his hand through mine, and we walked out the door. Blaise didn't let go of my hand when we walked past the shop, so I was the one to yank away.

"Hey, what was that for?" he asked.

"We don't need to put on the show anymore."

"Okay..." he trailed off.

I sighed. "I'm sorry. Maybe this was a bad idea. Also, where are we going?"

"To my car."

"To go where?"

"My place."

I stopped in my tracks. "Blaise."

"For privacy," he explained. "My family's all at the bar."

"What does your family have to do with it?"

"I live with my dad. Come on, I'll make you a cheesesteak."

I laughed. "You'll make me a cheesesteak?"

"Yeah, woman, let this Philly boy make you a legit cheesesteak. It's literally the only thing I can cook, so don't get too excited."

I laughed again. This man was entertaining at best. "Okay, lead the way."

I followed him to his car, and we drove the quick drive to the row house where he lived with his family. It surprised me Blaise didn't drive a fancier car. It was nice, but it wasn't flashy like any of the other hockey players I knew. Dinah's fiancé Noah had a fancy new SUV, but nothing too outlandish. Rox's brother, on the other hand, had a Maserati, which seemed dumb to me if you lived in the city, but I had been to their condo building. They lived in a nice place with a secure underground garage. Still seemed foolish to me.

Blaise led me into the house and walked me through the living room to the small kitchen. The house was modest when you thought about the fact his dad was a hockey legend. Blaise instructed me to sit at the table while he worked on dinner. He undid the buttons at his wrists and pushed up his sleeves. Holy forearms, I forgot how built this man was. Goddamnit, I don't think the no-sex rule was going to work with this man; I wanted to be underneath him again.

I pulled my sketchbook out of my bag to distract myself and tried to think of an idea to cover up Blaise's tattoo. He didn't love the maple leaf idea, but he didn't give me anything else to work with. I rolled up one of my sleeves to inspect the new tattoo I let Eddie do on my blank arm. It was this cool design of a compass with swirls of watercolor around it. Eddie had been experimenting with the style, and I let him practice on me.

"Is that new?" Blaise asked and nodded at my arm.

I held up my arm for him to see. "Fresh ink. Just healed last week."

He came over to me and ran a finger across my skin while he studied it. "Pretty. I like your colorful tattoos."

"So do I."

"Brat," he teased.

I stuck my tongue out at him. "Go back to making me dinner."

He gave me a little sarcastic salute and went back to the stove. My mouth watered at the smell of the meat cooking.

"So, are you going to lay these ground rules on me yet?" he asked.

I sighed. "Honestly, I was gonna tell you we shouldn't go through with this. But then he gave me that wedding invitation."

He scrolled through his phone. "I actually can go to that. We don't have a game."

"Of course you don't."

"What do you mean by that?"

"Seth's a diehard Bulldogs fan. It's why we were at your dad's bar all the time. I think he only invited me because

I'm dating you. Of course, he'd want a hockey star at his wedding."

Blaise scowled. "If you want to drop this...thing we have, that's fine with me. You don't have to go."

I groaned. "I don't want to go, but I also do."

He busied himself at the stove but held up his end of the conversation. "Why?"

"Before, I wanted to be a petty asshole, but now, I want to show him I'm fine without him. That I moved on, and my life's better off without him in it," I tried to explain.

Except it was complete bullshit. I don't think I ever got over the abandonment. Not when my mom did it, and not when my fiancé did it. I wished my dad was still alive so I could ask his advice. He would have known what to do. He'd have told Alex not to hire Seth, and we wouldn't have been in this predicament. God, I missed that big teddy bear so much.

I must have zoned out because before I knew it, Blaise came over to the table with plates of awesome steak sandwiches on long hoagie rolls. The smell was amazing. "You want a beer?" he asked.

"Sure. What you got?"

He peered into the fridge. "Oh, look, 611 Ale!"

"Oh! That's a MacGregor Brothers beer," I said.

He grabbed us beers and popped off the tops. He handed me a bottle. "Yeah, I'm a fan. Can't get that in Canada."

I closed my sketchbook and put it back in my tote bag before taking a sip of my beer. "Oh, the brewery's in my town. I go there all the time."

"Nice. We should go sometime. I love craft beer from the source."

I nodded, but I wanted to remind him that just because

we were fake dating didn't mean we needed to actually go out.

Instead, I bit into my cheesesteak and moaned at how this Philly boy actually knew how to make a good one. I guess you could take the boy out of the city, but you couldn't take the Philly out of him.

"I'll go with you," he said after we had been eating in silence for a few minutes. "I'll help you prove to that asshole you're stronger and better without him."

"Why?" I asked. "You barely know me."

"True, but I know how you feel."

"Are you still not over her?"

He shook his head. "Nah. I'm good. Just tired of people asking me if I'm okay. I figured if we pretend to date for a little while, then my brothers will get off my back. Let me live my life the way I want."

"Okay, but remember, this is fake. We're not in a relationship."

He furrowed his brow and picked at his cheesesteak. "I know."

"Don't go falling in love with me, Blaise Holmstrom," I warned.

"I won't."

"We can't have sex," I blurted out.

His eyebrows shot up in alarm. "What?"

"It'll complicate everything. It's not a relationship. We're not a real thing—we're just pretending. Okay?"

"Is that what you meant by 'ground rules'?" he asked and did air quotes.

I nodded. "I don't want the lines to get blurred."

He cocked his head at me. "Doesn't have to get blurred if we're just having a good time."

"Are you asking me to be your fuck buddy while we pretend to date?"

He shrugged. "Puck's on your stick, sweets."

His sapphire eyes seared into me like he could see my naked body under my clothes. I had to clench my thighs together in anticipation. He was so hot, and it didn't have to be complicated if it was a purely sexual arrangement until my ex's wedding. If fake dating him had an expiration date, then maybe we could have some fun together with no strings attached.

"Um..."

He smiled at me and patted my hand. "No pressure. If you don't want to, I'll respect your wishes."

"I...let me think about it."

He scrolled through his phone. "Oh, what the fuck."

"What?" I asked.

"Nothing," he said a bit too quickly.

"What?" I demanded.

He handed me his phone. "They have one of those wedding sites."

"Okay, and?" I asked for clarification. Lots of people had those things.

"V, they have a baby together."

"What?" I screeched.

I looked at the page he had opened on his phone. I skimmed some bullshit story about how they met and the unplanned pregnancy they had last year. Last year. Last year, when I was supposed to marry Seth. When he left in the middle of the night.

Oh my God, no wonder his sister cut me a check for the wedding cancellation fees. She probably felt sorry for me. I was trying to match up the timelines, and it was clear Seth had been cheating on me.

Why were men such garbage? This was why I didn't do relationships. I pushed back the phone to Blaise.

"I'm sorry," he said.

"It's not your fault."

I pushed my plate away and stood up. "Let's go."

He furrowed his brow. "Go where?"

"Blaise, do you want to fuck me again or not?"

"V...I don't think that's a good idea."

"Why not?" I snapped at him. "You literally just asked me to be your fuck buddy!"

"Because you look upset, and I don't want you to do anything you'll regret."

I narrowed my eyes. "Do you want me to suck your cock or not?"

"Not with that attitude." He pushed me back down into my chair. "Finish your dinner. Then we'll talk."

Normally I would have fought him, but instead, I lifted my cheesesteak to my mouth and devoured the delicious sandwich this man had made me. It didn't mean the raging storm inside me had subsided, though.

CHAPTER NINE

BLAISE

It took every ounce of my willpower to push her back down into her chair instead of dragging her upstairs and fucking her brains out. I still wanted to do that, but only if she wanted. I felt bad that what she saw on the wedding website hurt her so deeply.

I was a dick for suggesting a friends-with-benefits situation with her, but I was horny as hell for this woman. I hadn't been with anyone since her. I liked that she didn't care about hockey or tried to impress me with her 'hockey knowledge.' Plus, she was hot with her colorful hair and tattoos, and she liked to be spanked in bed. I definitely wanted to do that again.

A LOT.

"If we're gonna fake date, we need to post pictures together on social media," I suggested.

"Oh, I'm not on social media."

"Really?" I asked incredulously. I didn't post all that

much on social media. I didn't even read the thirsty messages in my DMs anymore.

"I manage the accounts for the shop, of course, but I don't have a personal account."

That might be for the best. My sister and my sister-in-law dealt with their fair share of cyberbullying because of their relationships with hockey players. We were public figures, and puck bunnies were a thing, but it bothered me that the women in our lives got hate because we were with them.

"C'mere," I ordered.

"What?" she asked and furrowed her brow.

I patted my lap. "Come over here."

She hesitated, but then she stood up and walked over to me. I pulled her into my lap and wrapped my arms around her waist. "Why did you want me to do this?" she asked.

I took my phone out and hit the camera button. "So we can take a selfie together."

I kissed her temple and took the picture. I pulled back from her, but she didn't move off my lap, rather curled into my neck. I went into the app, selected my filters, adjusted the photo, and wrote a mindless caption. 'Glad to be playing in Philly, so I'm never missing my girl again.' I watched the heart notifications come in almost instantly, and I set my phone down on the table.

Veronica pulled back to look at me. "Should we talk about our story?"

I nodded. "I told my teammates we've been casually hooking up, and now we're giving it a go."

"Okay, good plan. I need to tell Olivia the truth. Is that okay?"

"Whose Olivia?" I asked.

"My best friend. The shop receptionist," she explained. "She seemed hurt today when she found out we were dating. I tell her everything."

"Okay...she won't say anything, right?"

She shook her head, the black and red strands bouncing against my jaw.

I pushed one of those strands behind her ear and rubbed my thumb across her cheek. God, this woman drove me wild, but I had to remember this was all pretend. I just got out of a ten-year relationship, and I wasn't trying to get into another one. But if she was into it, I would be okay with having a little fun. I never had a fuck buddy before, but there was always room to figure it out.

"Blaise..." she breathed.

"Tell me to stop," I said as I fisted her hair and slanted my mouth onto the side of her neck.

"Mmm..." she moaned and tipped her head back to give me more access.

"Tell me," I breathed in her ear. I shifted so she was straddling my thighs, and my other hand went to her ass.

"No..." she moaned.

"No what, V?" I asked.

"Don't stop," she begged.

My cock thickened against my leg, and she had to feel it pressed up against her spread thighs. She looked so hot in that plaid skirt; I wanted to bend her over and fuck her from behind in it. I gripped her hair harder, and she cried out at the sensation while I finally pressed my lips to hers.

She kissed me back roughly, biting my bottom lip and grinding herself against me. Our tongues battled each other, and she slid her hands around the back of my neck, one hand plunged into my short hair. At that moment, I missed having my long hockey flow. I loved getting my hair gripped hard in the throes of passion.

"I want to take you upstairs," I growled against her lips.

She nodded.

"V, do you want this? Are you okay with this?"

"I knew as soon as I said no sex, I'd cave. Why do you have to be so hot?"

I chuckled and stood up from the chair, holding her against me. She wrapped her legs around my waist, and I carried her upstairs to my bedroom. As soon as the door shut, I pressed her against it and kissed her hard. My cock strained to be inside her again while my hands slid underneath her skirt and cupped her pussy. I felt her arousal through the thin fabric of her underwear. I pushed it aside and slid my finger across her seam.

"Don't be a tease," she whined. She ground her hips against my hand, trying to get me to find her entrance and slam my finger inside.

"Hey, who's in charge here?" I growled and removed my hand.

She whimpered at the loss and tightened the grip of her legs around my waist.

"You be a good girl, and I'll give you what you want."

"I'm not a good girl," she insisted. "I'm a bad girl. I need someone to teach me a lesson."

I cocked an eyebrow at her. "Yeah? Do I need to spank you tonight?"

"It's the only way I'll learn," she said with a sly smile.

This fucking woman. So naughty, and I loved it.

I walked us further into the room and set her down on her feet. I sat on the edge of my bed and gestured to her clothes.

She slipped her black sweater over her head to reveal a black lacy push-up bra. Then she shimmied the skirt down her hips to reveal a matching lacy black thong.

"The rest," I ordered.

She unhooked her bra, turned around, and wiggled her ass at me as she slid the thong down off her hips.

"C'mere you," I ordered, my voice thick with my arousal. She knew exactly what she was doing to me.

She came over to me, and in a flash, I had her over my knees, my hands sliding down the smooth skin of her exposed cheeks. I gripped her hair in one hand while my other hand swung down to spank her cute little ass.

"You gonna be a good girl now?"

She shook her head.

I slapped her ass harder this time. "How about now?"

She nodded into the bed, and holy fuck, it was sexy to have her over my knee, letting me dominate her.

"Who's in charge?" I asked after another slap. Her ass cheeks were pink from my hand, and I rubbed my palm against her skin to soothe the injured spot.

"You are," she whimpered.

"That's right, sweets."

I flipped her onto her back, and her hair spread out like a cloud on my comforter. I hadn't expected this to happen tonight. I thought she was going to be firm about the no-sex thing.

I got up from the bed and unbuttoned my shirt, dragging it off my wide-set shoulders. I unbuttoned my jeans and did the slow undressing thing again.

"Blaise..." she whined from her place on the bed.

"My terms, remember?"

"Please, I want you now."

I went even slower at taking my boxers off. I kicked my clothes to the side and crawled into bed beside her. I lifted her off the comforter and pushed back the sheet so we were both underneath it. I realized I never turned the light on, which was a bummer because I couldn't see her in all her glory, but sex in the dark could be fun, too.

I leaned over and kissed her, my hand traveling down her gorgeous body and giving her tit a little squeeze.

"More," she begged.

"More what?" I asked.

"Blaise, please touch me. I'm so horny right now. I need you."

"You need me, huh?" I asked while I traveled down her body, stopping to lick and suck at her awesome tits.

She held me against her chest while I feasted on her. She moaned at the sensation of my tongue on her nipple, but I moved on quickly. I pressed tiny kisses down her stomach, getting closer to the sweet spot between her thighs.

"You don't have to," she said.

I put her legs over my shoulders and looked up at her with a grin. "Woman, don't tell me what to do. I want to make you come on my tongue before you do it again on my cock."

"Fuck..." she breathed as I bent my head and gave her that first lick.

I tried not to moan into her while I tasted her again. She tasted so sweet, and the way she moaned made me do figure-eights with my tongue. I sucked on her clit, and her thighs shook against my head. I licked her slowly and deliberately, smiling while she moaned and writhed against my mouth.

"Blaise, that feels so good," she moaned.

"Mmm, I missed this pussy."

"You did not!" she protested with a laugh.

I pumped two fingers into her entrance and gave her a wicked grin again. "Did so. Missed tasting you and making you come. You gonna come for me, sweets?"

She nodded.

I went back down to suck on her clit while my fingers thrusted in and out of her. She gripped my hair, and I felt her walls clench around my fingers. My dick got harder while I thought about how she'd squeeze around it soon. She gripped my hair harder while she came, moaning loudly.

I should have been concerned about the noise, but Michael was back at college, and Dad was still at the bar. Also, I didn't give a fuck, and I wanted to hear her scream my name.

I slid her legs off my shoulders and reached into my bedside drawer for a condom. Veronica's chest was still heaving from her orgasm, and her eyes were closed. I slid the condom on and spread lube onto my cock, fisting it a couple times to make sure I was still hard. Her eyes fluttered open, and she twisted around in the bed so she was on all fours.

Fuck yes. Veronica knew exactly what I wanted.

"Grab the headboard and hold on, sweets," I ordered.

She did as she was told, and I slid in behind her. We sighed in relief as I buried myself to the hilt. I fisted her hair as I pounded into her from behind, and she cried out.

I slapped her ass again and fucked her with wild abandon. Her soft cries egged me on to keep going faster and rougher than I normally would have. She made me feel like a wild animal.

"Yes, yes, right there," she moaned into my bedspread.

I gripped her hair tighter. "You want it hard and rough?"

"Mmm..." was her only reply.

"Talk to me, sweets. Tell me you love when I fuck you from behind."

"I love it. I want more. Rougher, faster. Break me in two."

I leaned over her and kissed her neck. She moaned at my lips on her skin, but then I pulled out of her.

"Why? I was so close!" she cried.

I laid on my back and pulled her over my thighs. I readjusted myself to find her entrance, and she slid down on my cock. "Ride me," I ordered.

She did as she was told, riding me like she was meant for it while I fingered her clit and made her shake above me.

"I'm gonna come," she moaned and put her hands on my chest to brace herself. Her eyes flashed as she touched my tattoo. "I hate seeing her name here."

I grinned at her. "Jealous, sweets?"

She covered Astrid's name with her hand as she rolled her hips against mine. "I don't like seeing another woman's name when I'm fucking you into oblivion."

I lifted my knees up behind her and arched my hips to meet her downward strokes. She cried out while she rode out her orgasm on top of me.

"I'm gonna come, baby," I moaned.

"Please," she begged. I gripped her ass tighter, pushing her down onto my cock while I moaned and moved beneath her. I clenched my teeth together and made a guttural noise as my orgasm wrenched through my body.

When I opened my eyes, she lay across my chest, breathing hard and her hair sweaty from the exertion. I lifted her off my body and moved to get rid of the condom.

She curled onto the spare pillow on my bed. I threw the condom into my trash can beside the bed and got back into it, pulling the sheets over our naked bodies.

She smiled at me and kissed my shoulder. "Um... where's your bathroom?" she asked.

"Oh, middle door. Wait, I'll give you one of my shirts to put on."

I got up and went to my dresser drawer, and pulled out one of my Bulldogs Hockey t-shirts. She got out of bed, and I handed it to her. She quickly pulled it over her head and walked out of the room toward the bathroom. I slid my boxers back on and dug into my jeans on the floor for my phone and nearly shit a brick at all the notifications. Not just from my social media but text messages, too.

I scrolled through them with a scowl.

AYDEN: You're dating Veronica?!? For real?

AYDEN: Dad's gonna be pissed

ASTRID: Blaise, call me. I miss you.

The last one pissed me off because I knew she didn't miss me. She was just jealous I had moved on. In re-examining my relationship with Astrid, we were young and didn't know what we were doing. She had to always have control over me...but now I was free.

I stabbed at my phone.

ME: Too bad. I moved on. You should too.

ASTRID: Blaise, don't be that way.

ME: You broke up with me. I've got a good girl now. Have a good life, Astrid.

I put my phone on the bedside table and climbed back

into my bed. I lay back, relaxing, and put my hands behind my head. I hadn't expected the sex tonight with Veronica, but I wasn't complaining.

I could do casual. We could do this fake dating thing, and then after her ex's wedding, we'd go our separate ways. It would totally be fine.

CHAPTER TEN

VERONICA

I woke to lips on my neck and a hand on my bare ass. I opened my eyes, trying to remember where I was because I didn't recognize the darkness of the room. When I felt a cock poking into my back, I remembered I slept with Blaise Holmstrom again, and I had been sleeping in one of his t-shirts.

I had no intention of sleeping with him last night. Well, that wasn't true. My pussy had screamed 'Yes,' while my brain screamed 'No,' and my hormones won out. I didn't want to spend the night either, but it had been getting late, and when I started looking up what train I needed to get home, he asked me to stay over. His sparkling azure eyes had given me those sad puppy dog eyes, and I couldn't say no to him.

Of course, then he went down on me again, so I forgot what the argument was. This mountain of a man was trouble for me with a capital T.

He pulled me against his chest, his lips traveling down my neck. "God, you're sexy."

"I try," I joked.

He nuzzled my hair. "I love your hair like this."

"I told you I like to switch it up."

"It's Bulldogs colors."

"Not on purpose."

"Still, I love it."

My alarm blared on the bedside table. I turned it off and laid back on the bed with a sigh. Shit, I didn't have time to run home and change. Eddie and Alex bought the storefront on South Street because they lived above it. I kept clothes there if I stayed in the city and didn't have time to go back to Drakesville. My first client wasn't until noon, so I could take a shower there. It wasn't ideal, but I could manage.

I shouldn't have had sex with Blaise again, not that I regretted it, but it was going to make things more complicated. Which was even harder when he was so hot and knew exactly what I liked.

Blaise's hand stroked across my hip, and I mewled at his touch. His lips curled up into a cute smirk. He had to know he was trouble for me. But he didn't care, and neither did I when he gave me as many orgasms as I wanted. That's why I didn't protest when he cupped my face and pressed his lips against mine.

I sighed into the kiss, loving how he took charge by angling my head and kissing me deeper. I could get used to Blaise Holmstrom kissing me, especially if he took me rough like he had last night. I opened for him when his tongue slid across my lips.

"Blaise," I moaned when he broke the kiss so he could nose across my neck.

"What's the matter, sweets?"

"Morning breath."

He smiled on my skin as he traveled down my body. He gave me a cocky grin as he muscled his way between my thighs. He looked good right there.

"I don't care," he said. He pushed the t-shirt up my body, dipped his head down, and parted my pussy with his tongue. And then I was done for. Yet again.

I arched up and felt him laugh into me. With one firm hand, he held my stomach down on the bed as he licked me thoroughly. My phone vibrated on the bedside table, but I could give exactly two fucks while this hunk of a man was between my thighs, sucking on my clit and about to give me another orgasm. I hadn't even asked him to do that. He just immediately went to town, eating me like it was his last meal. Like he couldn't get enough of the taste of me on his tongue.

He pushed my legs further apart until I was spread eagle for him. He was splitting me apart with that mouth of his, and I was pliable for him. I'd let him do whatever he wanted if he kept licking me like that.

"Come for me, sweets," he purred.

I looked down at him and nodded vigorously. I was almost there. So close, I felt that tingle down my spine with my orgasm right on the edge.

But my phone kept ringing. I shoved it off the bedside table.

Blaise laughed. "Do you need to get that?"

"DON'T CARE!" I panted out and bucked my hips back up to his mouth. "Finish eating my pussy, and then we can have morning sex."

"Fuuuuuck," he groaned but did as I asked.

He pressed me back against the mattress, and I arched

my hips up as he took me over the edge. I didn't think about clamping my hand over my mouth while I cried out his name.

He fumbled in the drawer beside me and frantically rolled a condom down his cock while I was still catching my breath post-orgasm. His boxers were around his ankles, and I was still wearing his shirt when he nestled himself between my thighs.

He pinned my hands above my head and linked our hands together to use as leverage as he thrust inside me. I cried out at the sensation of him filling me up but rocked back against him, needing the sweet friction of his body on mine. He stared into my eyes as he glided out and then back in like he wanted to savor our connection while we had slow morning sex.

"Come with me?" he pleaded.

I nodded.

I squeezed my legs tightly around him and met his every slow movement. He pressed my hands into the bed while he hit me deep, finding the secret spot that made me unravel into a pool of pleasure. I cried out at the same time he groaned his release into my ear.

I melted back into the bed at that male guttural noise of ecstasy. I'd never tire of the moans he made when we were joined together. At the way I made him growl and grunt while we were pressed so tight against each other.

He slid my hair behind my ear and gave me a gentle kiss as we caught our breath and came down from the high of our orgasms.

I found myself disappointed when he pulled away and pulled out of me. He tossed the condom in his trash can and then laid back on the bed with me. He gently traced the lines of my tattooed arm as he stared at me.

"I'm sorry," he said.

"For what?" I asked.

"For basically waking you up for sex. I didn't even take your shirt off."

I laughed. "I'm kinda surprised at that. Most men like to see my boobs when they're inside me."

His eyes bored a hole into my chest. "You could take it off, and we could do it again."

I chewed on my lip. I was definitely thinking about it. Thinking about ripping off the shirt and riding him until my thighs were on fire. Until he groaned out that beautiful male sound again.

But then my phone buzzed on the floor again.

Geez, who needed to get a hold of me that bad?

I rolled out of bed with a groan and fished for my phone. All the while, Blaise watched my naked ass from his bed. It was not lost on me that he was hard again when I returned to the bed.

"Dude!" I yelled at him and shook my head with a laugh.

Men!

He gave me a cute grin. "Can't help it, sweets."

I unlocked my phone, half paying attention to him, and nearly died at all the notifications.

DINAH: You could have warned me you were dating one of Noah's teammates!

ROX: So...is Blaise Holmstrom your summer hockey hookup?

ALEX: I'm sorry. Can you come to the shop earlier? We have an interview at nine.

"Shit," I swore and leaned up in bed. I ran a hand

through my hair in frustration. It was only seven, so I had enough time to get to the shop and shower at my brother's apartment before the interview.

"Sorry, no round two for me. I gotta jet," I told him with a frown.

"Hey, what's wrong?"

"I gotta get to the shop," I explained. I reluctantly got out of bed and searched for my discarded clothes on his floor. I sighed when I found my underwear.

Shit, I was going to have to commando until I got to the shop. There was no way I was putting on my cum-streaked thong. Damn Blaise for getting me all hot and bothered last night.

I slid Blaise's shirt off and paused when I heard noises downstairs. I glared at him. "Blaise."

"What?"

"Is your dad home?"

He shrugged. "Yeah, I guess."

"You guess?" I shrieked and shoved my hands into my hair. I hoped his dad hadn't heard me shouting out my orgasm a couple of minutes ago. I found my bra and put it on, pulling my sweater over my head and tugging on my skirt.

"What's wrong?" he asked.

I cringed. "What if he...heard us?"

Blaise shrugged. "I don't care."

"But I do!" I shrieked again. "I care what your dad thinks about me, and supposedly, I'm off-limits."

He made a face. "I think he only said that because Ayden's a hoe."

I laughed at that. "Okay, fair."

He gave me a grin. "Besides, my dad's European. He

doesn't have the same hangups about sex like Americans do."

I shook my head. "Well, I'm American, so it's weird."

I looked around for my jacket, but it wasn't in his room because I wasn't wearing a jacket when he carried me up to his bed last night.

"My jacket's still in the kitchen," I said.

"Okay, let me put on pants first."

I didn't want Hal to hate me. But if what Ayden said was true, he was going to be mad at Blaise.

Blaise got out of bed and went over to his drawer, pulling on a pair of jeans and a black t-shirt. I ran a hand through my hair and pulled it up into a ponytail using the hair tie I always wore on my wrist.

Blaise kissed my forehead. "It's gonna be fine, V. We're supposed to be dating, right?"

I nodded and followed him out of the room and down the steps. In the kitchen, we found Hal sitting at the table, drinking his coffee and reading the paper. Hal was old school like that.

"Hey, Dad," Blaise said with a sigh.

"Morning," Hal said. Then he glanced at me. "I thought I heard you, Veronica."

All the color drained from my face. Was Hal making a sex joke? I wanted to die. I wanted to melt into the floor and never face him ever again.

"Sweets, you okay?" Blaise asked me.

I nodded. "I gotta go."

"Will you come to the game tonight?"

I cocked my head at him. "You want me to come?"

He nodded. "I'll have a ticket at will call for you."

"Um..."

"You don't have to."

I thought it was important to him. Plus, if we were pretending to be dating, I knew I should probably show up and be the supportive hockey girlfriend. "Okay, yeah. I'll call Dinah and sit with her."

"You sure you don't want me to drive you to the shop?" he asked.

"I'm good."

"Sweets, let me drive you."

I shook my head and leaned up on my tip-toes to kiss him. He wrapped a hand around my waist and held me up to meet him. He was such a big man—I forgot about our height differences when we were horizontal.

I didn't let him get another word in and practically ran out the door. When I slept with Blaise last summer, I didn't know my life was going to get this complicated.

CHAPTER ELEVEN

BLAISE

I watched Veronica go with a hint of disappointment. She didn't even stay for coffee. I wondered if taking her to bed last night and asking her to stay over was a bad idea. Was I already in over my head?

"I need a coffee," I grumbled.

I went over to the coffee pot to pour myself a black coffee. I grabbed a yogurt from the fridge and begrudgingly sat down at the table across from my dad.

He arched an eyebrow at me, the type of look he gave me whenever he was disappointed in me. Which seemed to be all the time. I didn't know why I could never live up to my dad's expectations. Wasn't it bad enough that when Mom died, he mentally checked out on us all? Why did I even care what he thought about me?

"Blaise."

"What?" I snapped.

"Veronica..." he trailed off, giving me that same look of disapproval.

I gnashed my teeth to keep from saying something I'd really regret. "You think I'm not good enough for her."

"I never said that."

"Not like anything I ever do is good enough. I know I'm a disappointment to you."

"Blaise, that's not true," he said, sounding hurt.

"Then why do you act like my accomplishments are nothing? I know my season was shit last year, and I'm lucky the Bulldogs took me on."

"Because you're too much like me!" he snapped.

"What?"

He sighed. "I mentally checked out on you kids after your mom died, and it wasn't fair to any of you."

"What does that have to do with me?"

"Because I saw you do the same thing when that girl broke your heart. You wrecked a good thing with Toronto because you checked out on the career you worked for your entire life. I don't want you to make the same mistakes as me."

I pushed out of my chair, abandoning my breakfast. "You know what? Forget it. I'm not having this conversation with you. I don't know why the fuck I moved back in with you."

I stormed out of the house and sped off to the arena. I was pissed and in the wrong headspace, but hopefully I could get this shit out of my system once I got on the ice. And I was way too early for morning skate, so I turned back around, stopped at Wawa to grab another coffee and call my sister.

My sister and baby brother were twins, but Maja and I were closer than the two of them.

"Why are you calling me this early?" my sister moaned on the other line.

I laughed. "Shut up. I know you're up this early because you have practice before class."

"True. What's up?"

"I got into a blowout fight with Dad."

"What he say?"

I sighed. "That I'm too much like him, and I shut down after Astrid broke up with me, just like he did when Mom died. And then I got pissed and stormed out like I was sixteen years old again and I was the disappointing son. Like I always fucking am."

My sister was quiet on the other line for a few seconds, and it stretched out to minutes on my end.

"Maja?"

She cleared her throat. "Um...dude, I hate to break it to you, but Dad's right. You did exactly what he did after Mom died, only you didn't have six little kids depending on you. I love you, big bro, but you fucked yourself last year. I was really worried about you. We all were."

I banged my head on the steering wheel of my car. I didn't want to become like Dad. I didn't want to be a shell of a person or an old man who was scared to move on. This fake dating arrangement was a way to convince myself I could move on. Maybe Veronica could help me finally get over Astrid.

"I don't want to be him," I admitted.

"Then don't be."

"I'm moving on," I protested, even though it was a huge, fat lie. "I met a girl."

"I saw. Is Dad pissed because he told Ayden she's off-limits?"

I didn't know if that was for real or because Dad thought Ayden needed to stop sowing his wild oats. I didn't let Dad get another word in before I stormed out. Just like I did when I was a teenager. It was like moving back in with him sucked me into a time loop of being that angry teen who missed his mom.

"You really like this woman?" Maja asked.

"Yeah, I do," I admitted, and it wasn't a lie. It just wasn't the truth my sister was searching for.

Veronica O'Malley was still a mystery to me, but the parts I'd seen of her I liked. Not just the sex stuff, even though that was fantastic. I got why she was so anti-relationship. I felt awful that I discovered her ex had been cheating on her and got another woman pregnant. My heart broke for how upset it made her. But I also wanted to knock that asshat's teeth in.

"Well..." My sister trailed off. "I'm glad to see you moving on, but I have to ask you something."

"Okay?"

"Did you get your tattoo fixed?"

I had every intention of getting Astrid's name removed or covered up. I had seen Veronica's work, and it was gorgeous. I wanted her to do it, but I had no idea what I wanted to get done. Her suggestion for a maple leaf made sense, but I never felt tied to Mom's Canadian heritage.

"Not yet," I admitted.

"Uh-huh."

"Maja, what?"

She sighed. "I love you, bro. But if you were really over Astrid, you'd have gotten rid of that shit already."

"I'm going to. I don't know what to get."

"You've never been indecisive about a tattoo before."

"V suggested a maple leaf because of Mom."

"Mom liked hibiscuses."

Mom *had* like hibiscuses, and Veronica's forte was

colorful flowers. The idea of getting something for my mom, who I still missed every single day, appealed to me.

"Blaise, I have to go. I have class," Maja told me.

"Shit, sorry. I just needed to talk."

"I love you. You know you can call me to talk about this shit, right?"

"I know. Love you too, little sis. Give my love to Jules?"

"Of course."

I hung up with another long sigh.

Why hadn't I gotten Veronica to do my cover-up yet? Was my sister right? Was I still holding on to Astrid? I wanted to move on. I definitely didn't want to turn into my dad.

On that cheery note, I walked into the arena to prepare for morning skate.

I ran into TJ, but I steeled my features so he couldn't tell how upset I was. I was supposed to be happy. I was playing for the team my dad had played for, the one I had grown up rooting for. This was supposed to be a dream come true. I also just announced to the whole hockey world I was dating someone new. I should be happy, but it was all a lie. A carefully crafted lie to get my family off my back and for Veronica to get closure from her ex.

"Yo, dude!" TJ cheered.

"Hey, man," I greeted back and plastered on a fake smile.

His hazel eyes bored into me. "You okay, man?"

I nodded as we walked together into the locker room. I took my seat at the cubby in between Riley and Benny. Riley wasn't here yet, but Benny already had his practice jersey on and was lacing up his skates. He gave me a nod, and I started stripping off my street clothes.

I put my phone on the shelf, but I paused at the text message on the screen. My lips curled up at seeing Veronica's name.

VERONICA: Sorry about rushing out this morning. It was all very awk...and work's a mess right now.

VERONICA: I hope you're not mad at me.

ME: Not at you, sweets. I'll see you after the game?

VERONICA: Yup. D's excited to 'teach me how to hockey.'

I leveled a glance across the room at Dinah's fiancé, Noah. He was a quiet guy with long hair and a massive beard. Whereas Dinah was a tiny Italian girl with a loud mouth. She was my kind of people.

A stick jabbed into the back of my knee, forcing me to jerk forward, and I dropped my phone onto the shelf. I turned around to see Benny with a smirk on his face.

"Motherfucker, what?"

He and TJ snickered at me while I pulled on my compression shirt and started working on getting on my equipment.

"So, when Rox gave you the name of her tattoo artist to fix that shit," Benny began and motioned to my chest, "it wasn't so you could bang her."

"Was already banging her," I stated flatly and laced up my skates. When I looked up at Benny, he was slack-jawed, and TJ howled with laughter.

"Hmm," Noah muttered next to TJ.

"Bro, what?" I asked.

He ran a hand through his flow. "D said Veronica doesn't do relationships anymore. Period."

I narrowed my eyes. "What are you saying?"

"Be careful, man."

Shit, maybe convincing people Veronica and I were together was going to be tougher than I thought.

CHAPTER TWELVE

VERONICA

"I've got a last-minute walk-in. Can you take it?" Seth asked me while I was packing up, ready to take a bus over to the stadium.

I shot him a glare. "Are you kidding me?"

"Please, Roni?" he begged.

"No. I have to get to the game. Ask the other two."

Who did he think he was? Blaise asked me to come to the game tonight, and it was important if we were going for this illusion we were dating. I had to play the part of the good hockey girlfriend.

"I asked Olivia, and they're busy," he said.

"Figure it out yourself, asshole!" I screeched at him.

That caused my brother to look up from the client he was working on. I gave him a glare as I slid my leather jacket on my shoulders. I didn't have time for this. I was having a shit day already. The hot water was out upstairs, so I took a cold shower, and then the interview was a no-show, and I had back-to-back clients who were indecisive. I could use a drink or several, and as much as I didn't care about sports, I was excited to see Blaise on the ice and hang out with Dinah. That tiny brunette was a trip, and she'd explain all the hockey shit to me.

I passed Olivia on my way out. She gave me a sad smile and a big hug. "I needed that," I said.

She laughed. "I know. When can we hang out so you can fill me in on the details?"

I sighed. When I walked downstairs into the shop with my hair still wet this morning, she laughed at me and asked if I ever went home.

"I have off tomorrow. Maybe we could go shopping?"

Her dark eyes lit up. I hated shopping, like loathed it with a passion, but Olivia lived for that shit. Then she got suspicious. "Wait, why?"

I couldn't answer her because Seth was breathing down my neck again. "Roni?"

"What?"

"Are you at least gonna let me know if you're coming to my wedding? Lily needs to know for the seating chart."

I gritted my teeth and turned to my ex. "Yes, Blaise can come. We'll be there."

"Awesome!" he cheered.

That proved the only reason he wanted me there was because of Blaise.

He didn't want to let bygones be bygones; he just wanted my famous boyfriend to be there. My famous fake boyfriend, who was good at eating pussy and liked to spank me and call me a bad girl. It was too bad I didn't do relationships anymore because Blaise would have been perfect for me. But I would never again let someone break me down into a million tiny pieces like Seth had. No matter how much chemistry I had with them. Or how hot they were. It wasn't enough to put myself through that shit again.

"Ugh, goodbye!" I snarled and got out of there before he could drag me into taking one more client.

I felt bad leaving Olivia in a lurch with a furrowed brow on her face, but I'd explain everything to her tomorrow. I needed her help to find a dress for the wedding anyway, and I knew she loved that enough to forgive me.

I was still stewing by the time I got to the arena and found Dinah. Her green eyes grazed across me, and then she shoved her beer in my hand. "Here, you need this more than I do."

I hugged her tightly. "Oh my God, you have no idea!"

I took the beer she handed me while I watched the players on the ice coming out for warm-ups. I wasn't completely ignorant when it came to hockey, so I knew what warm-ups were. Dinah's smile got wider when her boy-toy tapped the glass with his stick.

I flinched at the sound of a puck hitting the glass in front of us. I turned and almost glared at the blonde giant standing in front of it with a cheeky grin. The same grin he wore last night before he went down on me. I clenched my thighs together just thinking about it. Blaise tapped two fingers against his heart, and then pointed at me.

I didn't know what that meant, but I repeated the motion back at Blaise. He smiled at me before he tore off down the ice.

"Um, that's adorable," Dinah said with a grin. "I'm so happy for you, V. You deserve to find happiness after that asshat."

"Guess who I have to see every day now?"

She frowned. "Eds told me. I'm sorry."

"Yeah, me too," I whispered.

I wanted to tell her I was pretty sure this Lily person was the other woman, and she got pregnant, so that's why Seth left. I don't know what would have hurt more, him leaving like he did or him telling me about it. Maybe he thought it would have hurt me less. Even though it cut my heart into tiny specks until there was nothing left. I was dead inside, a cold, feelingless person, but I was okay with that. Being cold-hearted was better than getting hurt again.

We settled into our seats as the game started. Blaise never told me what position he played, and it confused me when Dinah explained that he protected the blue line. Whatever that meant. I also gave her a strange look when she explained Blaise didn't put up a lot of numbers, but he was a good stay-at-home defenseman. I swear, I needed a dictionary to figure out what she was talking about.

"Oh my God, you really know nothing about this game?" Dinah asked with a laugh.

I shook my head, my black and red curls bouncing around my face.

I watched the players on the ice and saw one of the Bulldogs get possession of the puck. But I focused on what number 44 was doing. Blaise was such a big man, but there were a lot of big burly men on skates, hitting each other into the boards and speeding across the ice. Truth was, of all the sports, I liked hockey the most, but I never bothered to learn the rules.

Dinah groaned when the goalie made the save, and then I got distracted by a petite blonde woman coming over to us and taking a seat next to me.

"Hi, sorry," she said in a rush to Dinah.

"Hey, Max," Dinah greeted.

The newcomer pushed her hair behind her ear. "Still scoreless?" she asked, to which we nodded. Then she turned to me and put out her hand. "Hi, I'm Max, TJ's girlfriend. You're Blaise's girl, right?"

I shook her hand. "Right, Veronica."

"Okay, good. He asked me to get you a ticket last minute, so I'm glad it worked out," she said.

I eyed her carefully.

"She works for the team," Dinah interjected.

"Oh, cool."

"He's a good guy," Max said. "Even though he cheated off my math homework in high school."

"Oh, you went to high school together?"

She nodded and smiled. "I swear this team's all interconnected. It's not even funny."

I laughed and thumbed over at Dinah. "Yeah, you know our brothers are married?"

Max shook her head. "Nope! But I know you're Rox's tattoo artist."

Speaking of which, I spied Rox's man on the ice, taking the face-off. He was a big dude like Blaise, but I think he might have been slightly bigger. Man, where did they breed these mountain men at?

"Did Rox have a game?" Dinah asked Max.

Max nodded, but she wasn't paying attention to the question. Her hand was on her bottom lip, and she stared intently at the game in front of us. Man, was this the hockey WAG life? It seemed stressful. I was thankful I had an expiration date for this shit.

"What the hell was that?" Maxine suddenly yelled.

I searched the ice for what she was looking at, and one of the Bulldogs was getting pushed on the ice by one of the opposing players. It looked heated. I spied the name on the back of the jersey, Desjardins. That must have been Rox's twin brother TJ.

Dinah laughed at Max's outburst, and the other woman's cheeks tinged pink with embarrassment. "It's so cute when she swears," Dinah teased.

"Shut it, D!" Max teased back.

I watched the game with the girls, and they helped me when I didn't understand a penalty. Like offsides. Like how do you have an offside if it's on ice? They gave me an education on that one. There was apparently a lot of pressure on the team this year. They hadn't won the cup since the eighties, and the heat was on for them to succeed.

After two periods of play, the game was still scoreless. Which might explain why Dinah turned to me before the last period to grill me.

She raised an eyebrow. "So how long have you and Blaise been a thing?"

Max gave me a small smile in sympathy. I shouldn't have expected this to be easy. Especially with Dinah. Her family was nosy as fuck, so if it wasn't her being hounded, she was dishing it out.

"Not long. We were keeping it casual," I lied.

Dinah narrowed her emerald eyes at me. "You don't do relationships. You specifically told me if you ever got into a relationship again to slap you."

How did she remember that shit? Note to self: never tell a writer anything.

I shrugged. "He's bomb at eating pussy."

They laughed at that, and I hoped that would get me off the hook, but apparently not.

"But how did you meet?" Dinah asked.

"His dad."

"His dad? Hal?" Max asked.

"I'm a regular at Eileen's. Last summer, Hal insisted Blaise drive me home."

"But you live all the way out in the suburbs," Dinah protested.

I gave her a look. And then I paused. Why did Hal insist Blaise take me home that night? It was a far drive for Blaise. I knew Hal saw me as a surrogate daughter, and he was protective, but it was odd.

I shrugged. "I don't know."

Max laughed to herself.

"What?" I asked.

"He was setting you up," she explained.

I furrowed my brow. "I don't think so. He told Ayden I was off-limits."

"That's because Ayden goes through women like I go through tissues," Max explained.

I laughed because that was true. But people could also say the same about me. Why would Hal care about that?

"He didn't seem happy to see me this morning," I blurted.

Dinah poked me. "Explain."

I cringed. "I stayed at Blaise's last night."

"Okay..." Dinah said slowly, not piecing it together.

"He lives at home."

"Oh!" Maxine exclaimed. "Oh, that makes sense."

Dinah swiveled her head at Max and looked to me for an explanation.

Max sighed. "Blaise's mom died when he was a kid, and their dad kind of...lost himself. Pretty sure his brothers Eli and Brendan raised the twins more than their dad did."

"How do you know all of this?" I asked, which I probably shouldn't have.

Those names sounded familiar, but I felt like I needed a family tree to remember all of Blaise's siblings. If I was supposed to be Blaise's girl, I should have known this stuff about his family. I needed him to write this down for me. I needed a cheat sheet of all the Holmstrom siblings so it looked like I actually was his girlfriend.

Max shrugged. "We were friends in high school. Sometimes he'd talk about not feeling like he would ever live up to his dad's expectations."

"It's hard to stand out in a big family," Dinah said. Dinah was one of four, so she was uniquely qualified to understand.

"Why did you think his dad was mad?" Max asked curiously.

"Uh...that's a story for another time."

Dinah's eyes got wide, which meant now she was interested. "Okay, explain!"

"Um...his dad didn't know we were there last night."

"Okay..." Dinah conceded.

I cringed. "I wasn't exactly quiet."

Max's eyes widened and her cheeks went pink, but Dinah laughed her head off.

I wasn't sure how I was ever going to look Hal in the eyes again. It was a good guess he knew what Blaise and I had been doing upstairs. Especially after that comment about how he thought he heard me.

"Then what happened?" Max asked.

"I had to rush out for a job interview who didn't show. Blaise was in a bad mood, though."

Why did I care? He wasn't actually my boyfriend. I shouldn't care if he was upset. But I did. I cared so much. I didn't like seeing people hurt.

Dinah waved me off. "Eh, shit happens. Don't worry about it."

I nodded, but I wasn't sure I agreed with her.

CHAPTER THIRTEEN

BLAISE

I played my game close to an old-school style. I protected the net, blocked shots, and crushed assholes into the boards. I was a stay-at-home defenseman, and while some D-man might find that limiting, I loved being a traditional blueliner. It was also why my stats were mediocre and why I was pretty sure my career was over last summer when the Wolves traded me. I wasn't a big goal scorer, but I showed up in a big way on the penalty kill.

We had five minutes left in the game, and it was still scoreless. I was annoyed because I wanted to convince Veronica the sport I played for a living was fun and exciting. Then she came to the most boring game of hockey I'd ever played. Okay, maybe that wasn't true, but the scoreless game was getting annoying.

I shoved my mouthguard back into my mouth and chirped the New York defenseman while Noah took the face-off. I liked playing on the same shift as Noah and TJ. They were both fast and played smart hockey. Smart enough that I did an okay job helping them out with setting up a play or being that big body in front of our net. Right now, I needed to be that so we could kill this penalty and score a goddamn goal.

Noah got possession of the puck out from underneath one of New York's wingers, and he took it up the ice. TJ was neck-and-neck with him on the ice, and I labored behind them. Man, those two were fast. I needed to be faster if I was going to be successful in this city. If I was going to get this city to root for me and not just see the name on the back of my jersey and think of my dad.

In a flash, the red-lamp lit up behind the New York goalie, and the siren blared. Noah and TJ hugged it out in their typical celebration. Fuck yeah, that's how we do it.

I skated my ass off for the rest of the shift, and we all left the ice with our heads held high with a 1-0 win. I skated over to our goalie Metzy and gave him a little tap on his helmet. The kid stood on his head tonight.

We walked into the locker room with happy smiles and our victory song playing. I had no idea what it was because one of the rookies picked it, and I was more of a podcast person than a music person. I stripped off my jersey and started taking off my equipment.

"Victory drinks tonight!" TJ cheered.

Noah pulled him down by his jersey so he would calm down. The guy could get a little too excited. "Simmer down. We have to travel tomorrow," Noah reminded him.

"Okay, Dad!" Benny joked.

"Can it, lightweight!" TJ chirped.

I shook my head.

"Yo, Holmsy, bar tonight?" TJ asked.

I guess Holmsy was my nickname here. God forbid hockey players call each other by their real names.

"Sure. Gotta ask my girl, though," I said.

"Man, already whipped!" TJ teased.

Noah elbowed him. "Dude, shut it. Let the man be happy."

"We always end up at Eileen's," Riley said.

I groaned. "Can we go anywhere else?"

"Why?" TJ asked. "Isn't that your dad's bar?"

"Yes."

He gave me a questioning look, but I shook my head and headed for the showers.

After storming out like I was sixteen years old again, I didn't want to see my dad tonight. I dreaded going home, but at least we traveled tomorrow, so I had a couple of days to cool off. Might give me time to call my realtor and try to find a different place. Living with my dad again wasn't gonna work out if we were at each other's throats. I don't know why I thought it would be different now that I was older. No wonder Eli tried to talk me out of it.

I got out of the shower, and only a couple of the guys were still milling around. Benny was fixing his hair, and I changed back into my suit. He leveled me with a curious glance. "You okay, man?"

I nodded. "Yeah, just some family shit going on."

He nodded. "I understand."

I didn't question that but looked at my phone and smiled at a text from Veronica.

VERONICA: Are you meeting us at the bar?? I'm here and your brother keeps nagging me about dating you.

ME: He's jealous. On my way.

Benny scratched his chest. "Your girl does good work."

I slapped his hand. "Don't pick at it, or you'll have to reapply a saniderm."

He made a sour face. "You're worse than Rox."

"Did she come to the game tonight?"

He shook his head and checked his watch. "Nah, she had practice tonight. She'll meet us. Come on, let's get going."

We walked down the hallway toward the player's parking lot. "Rox plays too?" I asked.

"With The Liberty."

"My sister's definitely interested in playing for them, but the pay isn't as good as what we get."

"Rox resisted for the same reason, but she looked bored playing beer league."

We walked out of the building and parted ways when we got to the parking lot. I drove over to the bar, white-knuckling my steering wheel the whole time. I didn't want to see my dad tonight. I'd much rather bury myself inside Veronica instead of deal with my complicated relationship with my dad.

I parked my car and reluctantly went inside. I spotted Veronica at the bar, talking with Ayden. A hand gripped my arm before I could walk over to my fake girlfriend.

I spun around and scowled when I saw it was my dad. Dad was big, so at six-foot-three, I met his height, but sometimes he made me feel three feet tall.

"Can we talk?" he asked.

"No," I spat.

"Blaise—"

"I don't have anything to say to you."

He sighed and raked a hand through his greying hair. "Please, come into the office and talk to me?"

"Fine, whatever," I muttered and followed him into his office in the back.

Dad went behind the desk, took two beer bottles out of the mini-fridge behind him, and handed me one. I slumped into the chair in front of his desk and waited for the lecture.

"Blaise."

"What?"

He ran his hand down his face. "I'm sorry about this morning."

"Fine. Maybe I should find my own place. Kinda weird living with your dad at my age with my salary."

He nodded. "You don't have to move out, but if you want to, you can."

"Okay, thanks for the permission," I scoffed.

He glared at me. "Don't be like that."

"Like what? Shut you out? Shut down completely?"

"Be too emotional about shit. Fuck, you're just like me."

"Cool, great talk, Dad. Can I go now? My girlfriend's waiting for me."

"No. I need to talk to you about that," he said sternly.

I sighed and put the beer bottle down on his desk. "You know what? I'm a grown-ass adult, and so is she. This whole 'off-limits' thing is bullshit."

"Blaise..." Dad sighed.

I stood up and dusted myself off. "V's waiting for me. I don't have time for this."

"Kid, I need to talk to you."

I fixed him with a glare. "You had years to talk to me about serious things, but you became a shell of a person. I sure as shit don't want to be like you."

The hurt on my dad's face told me I'd hit a nerve, but I was so angry with him, I didn't care. It was like as soon as I came back here, all that resentment I felt from my younger days came bubbling up to the surface.

I walked out of the office without another word and made my way to Veronica. A tiny brunette sat next to her, and they looked in deep conversation. I wrapped an arm around Veronica's waist and pushed her hair to the side so I could nose across her neck. "I don't want to be here," I whispered in her ear.

I felt her tense, but then she relaxed once she saw it was me. She angled her head, giving me better access to her neck as I kissed her greedily. "Mmm, hey baby," she purred.

"Can we please leave?" I whispered. "I want to bury myself inside you and make you scream my name."

Her hazel eyes widened, but then she nodded. She turned back around to the other woman, who smiled at me. It took me a minute to realize she was Noah's fiancée, Dinah. "You two need to get a room," Dinah joked.

I winked at her. "That's the plan."

Dinah barked out a laugh. For a tiny woman, she had such a commanding presence.

Veronica put a hand on the other woman's arm. "It's gonna be fine. The wedding will be great, and you and Noah will live happily ever after, okay?"

She nodded. "I know. It's..."

"He's going overboard. It's only because he loves you, and he wants everything to be perfect," Veronica assured her. Her eyes slid over to me. "I better go. Someone wants my undivided attention."

Dinah laughed. "Have fun, you two."

Veronica went to pay her tab, but I threw some bills down instead. "You have a jacket?" I asked. She was only wearing that thin leather jacket she always wore, and it was a far walk to my car.

She shook her head. "Nah, I'm good."

I grumbled and took off my suit jacket, then helped her into it. I liked the way her head dipped down, and she thought I couldn't see her smile at the gesture. "Can we go to your place? I don't want to be home."

"It's far," she warned.

I rubbed my thumb across her cheek. "I don't care. I just want to be with you right now."

"Okay, sure. Let's go."

I spent the night doing exactly what I said I would, burying myself inside her. Making her scream while I gripped her hair and told her who was boss. I would have felt bad about using her to forget my issues if she hadn't made it clear she did the same thing.

A part of me wanted to tell her what was going on, to share the issues digging deep inside. But that teetered on the relationship line, and we couldn't cross it. We were only pretending and fucking until our expiration date. None of this shit was real. I had to remind myself of that.

CHAPTER FOURTEEN

VERONICA

When I woke the next morning to an empty bed, I wasn't surprised, but a part of me was disappointed. The fucking last night had been wild, animalistic sex, just the way I liked it, but Blaise was like a robot. He was pissed about something, but instead of asking him about it, I let him take me until I couldn't take it anymore. Until he had spent all his negative energy into me.

I didn't hear him leave this morning, but maybe it was better this way. If I got used to waking up beside him, it might make my heart think big foolish ideas. I shoved the feeling down inside and got up.

And immediately got annoyed by a text message from my ex.

SETH: Can you take my shift today?

ME: Eat a dick.

SETH: Come on, Roni. Don't be that way.

ME: FUCK NO!

I made breakfast and ignored his texts before meeting Olivia at the King of Prussia mall. Olivia was all smiles when I met her inside, and she gave me a big hug.

It surprised a lot of people when they found out Liv was my best friend. She had such a bubbly personality, whereas I was a cynical asshole. Liv truly believed there were good people in the world, and I loved her for that, but I knew better.

"Okay, so why are we shopping?" she asked as she dragged me into the nearest department store.

"For asshat's wedding," I said through gritted teeth.

Her big brown eyes went wide. "You're really gonna go?"

"Yeah, to be petty about it and show him I'm better off without him."

"You *are* better off without him," she agreed. She rifled through the racks looking for something that would work for me. "So spill. What's up with you and the hockey hunk?"

I bit my lip at that because Blaise Holmstrom totally was that and more. That man knew exactly what I wanted in the bedroom, and I loved this fuck buddy situation we had going on.

"We're not really dating," I explained. I took the navy blue dress she shoved at me, making a sour face that she was trying to get me to wear colors.

She handed me a few black dresses. "Can I put you in any happy colors?"

I shook my head. "Black's my happy color."

She groaned. "But it's so boring!"

"Classic," I argued.

She shoved a bright blue dress at me to spite me, then

she shooed me away to the dressing room. She was nipping at my heels, though, because of course I was going to try these on and show her. We'd probably take pictures too and decide what was best. I already knew it was going to be whatever black dress looked hot on me.

She shoved me into a dressing room, and I put on the bright blue dress to appease her.

"What do you mean you aren't dating?" she called through the closed door separating us.

"We're fake dating," I explained and tried to shove myself into the dress. I only got the zipper halfway up before I had to open the door and ask for her help. She zipped it all the way, and we inspected it in the three-way mirror.

"Not bad," she said. "Okay, what do you mean, fake dating?"

I took a picture of myself in the dress and sent it to Blaise.

ME: What do you think??

ME: For the wedding.

"We're pretending until the wedding," I explained.

"What does he get out of it?

"Sex." I shrugged and went back into the dressing room. I put on the navy blue dress and made a grossed-out face at my reflection in the mirror. It looked a little too mother of the bride.

I opened the door, and Liv wrinkled her nose. "Ew, no, not that one!"

I laughed and went back to try on one of the other black dresses. Ooh, I liked this one. It had thick straps up top but a sexy thigh-high slit in the leg. It was floor-length, but since it was a November wedding, it would work. I snapped another photo and sent it to Blaise.

When I walked out to show Liv, she looked appraisingly at it. "Hmm...that one's promising. But you need to back up on what you just said."

"I think this is the one."

"Go try on the others," she ordered.

"Fine," I grumbled but did as she asked.

The next one was an off-the-shoulder dress which was nice, but Liv didn't like it. I tried on the mid-length black dress with the sweetheart neckline. I liked it, but not as much as the first black one I tried on. I sent a photo of this one to Blaise too. Liv made me try on the one I liked the best again, and she circled around me, inspecting it.

My phone buzzed in my hand.

BLAISE: Um…on my floor, right?

ME: Maybe if you're a good boy!

BLAISE: Fuck…woman…

BLAISE: The black one. That's your color.

ME: Duh, but which one?? Help me! You're supposed to be my date!

BLAISE: The sexy one.

ME: BLAISE!!!

BLAISE: The one you already like, and you're just asking my opinion, so you can choose the opposite.

ME: You're so smart!

When I looked up from my phone, Liv had her hands

on her hips. "Okay, I haven't seen a smile on your face like that in a really long time. Are you sure this thing between you and Blaise is just for show?"

I nodded. "He's helping me go to this wedding and not murder everyone, and I'm helping his family see that he's over his ex and for them to stop babying him."

She arched a dark eyebrow at me. "So you had sex again?"

"I tried to say we shouldn't, but he proposed a friends-with-benefits situation. And, oh my God, Liv, he's like the hottest man I have ever been with. How could I say no?"

Her eyes widened."Jesus, V!"

"I can't help it. I forgot to tell you the most ridiculous part."

"What?"

"His dad didn't know we were there."

She gave me a confused look.

"He still lives at home."

"Really? On his salary?"

I nodded. "I don't think it's a money thing. I think Blaise worries about his dad, but he didn't want to tell me that."

I noticed Blaise walk into the bar last night, but before he walked over to me, I saw him in a heated conversation with Hal. They disappeared behind the employee's only door for a few minutes, but then Blaise snuck up behind me and got needy about wanting to leave. Something had been bothering him, but I wasn't his girlfriend, so it hadn't been my business to ask.

"Hmm. So what happened? Was Hal pissed?" Liv asked.

She knew about my mental breakdown at Eileen's Tavern because I called her to come get me. She'd met Hal at the bar before and knew he was protective of me.

"Nope. It's worse."

"What do you mean worse?"

"He made a joke about 'hearing' me."

Her mouth hung open. "No..."

"Yes."

"What did you do?"

"Nothing! I had to jet for that no-show interview. I wanted to melt into the floor, though. How will I ever look Hal in the eye?"

"Was Blaise embarrassed?"

"No. He didn't seem to care."

She shrugged and pointed to the dressing room door. "Go get the rejects. I think this is the one."

I went into the dressing room and changed back into my street clothes. It surprised me she didn't make me try on eighty-thousand more. The black dress was perfect, and I looked hot in it. I'd show up at Seth's wedding with my head held high to prove to him that my life was better without him. I wanted to prove to him that abandoning me didn't change me, even though it did. Even though he made me scared to open myself up to love again.

Liv helped me put the rejected dresses back where we found them, and she linked her arm with mine. "I'm glad we could do this today. You're working too hard lately."

"Hey, anyway, what are they doing without a shop manager today?" I asked.

It was a Saturday, and that was a busy day for the shop.

"Eds and Alex were fine when I told them what was up. They can manage without me for a day," she explained as we walked to the shoe department.

No, they couldn't. A good tattoo shop could be made or broken by a shop manager. Liv was amazing at keeping our shit together. That's why we stole her from my last shop.

Liv walked over to the display of a pair of black wedge heels. "These won't hurt as much as a stiletto."

I groaned. Why couldn't I wear my docs or chucks all the time instead?

"I hate wearing heels."

She sighed and brushed a strand of hair behind her ear. "I know, honey, but Blaise is huge. He'll tower over you when you're dancing."

"I don't—"

She gave me an annoyed look, and my protest died on my lips. "If you're taking that hunk with you to this wedding that you'd rather die than go to, make him dance with you. You should still try to have a good time."

She was such an optimist. Sometimes I wondered how we were friends.

"Liv, I..."

"What?"

"I think I know why Seth left," I blurted.

Her eyes were saucers. "Did he tell you?"

I shook my head and felt tears pricking my eyes.

No, go back in there. I don't have feelings!

"No, but when I talked with Blaise about how this would work, he looked at their wedding webpage."

"Yeah?" Liv asked. But she wasn't paying attention, having gotten distracted by a pair of sparkly pink heels.

I bit my lip and clenched my hands into fists. "They have a baby together."

"What?" she screeched. "Show me!"

I pulled up the webpage. I read through it a million times while I ate breakfast this morning. I shoved my phone at my friend, and I had to smile at how her face turned from confusion to anger. Liv was such a good friend.

"What the fuck!" she exclaimed. "Oh, V, I'm so sorry."

"I guess it's good he left," I muttered.

She raised an eyebrow and fixed me with a concerned look. "Are you sure about that?"

I shrugged.

She sighed and ran a hand down her face. "V..."

"It's fine."

"Do you think she knows?"

"Who?"

"The woman he's marrying."

I swallowed and tried not to look at her. I looked down at the shoes in my hand, pretending I was going to buy these ridiculous heels. "I don't know. Maybe that's why she told him not to invite me. She said it was inappropriate."

"Hmm."

"What?" I demanded.

"If she doesn't know, if she's another woman that got played by him and the only reason he chose her was because she got pregnant, maybe she deserves to know what sort of man she's about to marry."

I shook my head and gave her a stern look. "No, Liv. I'm not getting involved."

"But—"

"No. End of story. That's not my business."

But on the drive home, it was all I could think about. Even when I spent my Saturday night alone working on a new painting. I couldn't focus on how to mix the colors right for this landscape because all I thought about was if this poor woman was also getting played.

Did Seth do the right thing with her because she got pregnant? Or would he do to her what he did to me?

I shouldn't have, but I went down the rabbit hole of stalking her social media, and what I found made me feel worse. She looked sweet, and all her captions talking about how she'd finally found a good man broke my heart.

She didn't know about me when they started dating. There was no way. Seth had obviously lied to her. It would have been easier if she were a homewrecker who destroyed my relationship.

Rage crawled up from deep in my stomach. I didn't want to work in the same shop as that asshole. I was so pissed at my brother for doing this to me. Maybe it was time to cut my city ties for good. I could find a shop closer to home—hell, there was an all-women-run one in town that I'd been to a few times. I didn't think they were hiring, but I could talk to the owner. Maybe I should cut myself off from everyone and start fresh. That way, I'd finally get over what Seth did.

CHAPTER FIFTEEN

BLAISE

"Is your girl gonna come to the game tonight?" TJ asked me from across the table.

We were back home tonight and having our pre-game meal in the players' lounge. We'd lost two games on the road, and things were looking business as usual for the team. I had been a fan of this team for a long time, so I had that Philly pessimism about me. Not good when you played on the team.

I shrugged. "Not sure. I don't know if she's working today."

I hadn't talked to Veronica in a couple of days. She texted me some photos of dress options for the wedding, but since then, she'd been radio silent. We might be sleeping together and pretending we were dating, but she made it clear that was all it was. I wasn't about to get clingy over it.

"What does that have to do with anything?" TJ asked with a furrowed brow.

Noah nudged him. "Veronica lives out in the suburbs."

"So?" Benny asked. "Lots of guys live out on the Main Line, and their girls always make the trek out."

I shook my head.

I hadn't been on the team all that long, but I already felt like I slotted in with these guys. Knowing TJ's girl helped. Or the fact I was a Holmstrom. I didn't let it show, but it was annoying when guys asked what it was like to have such a legend for a dad. The only thing I remembered from my dad's playing days was when he left it all behind because Mom got sick.

I turned around at the tap on my shoulder and was a little surprised to see our head coach, Claude LaVoie, standing behind me. "Blaise, can I have a word before you head out for your pre-game nap?"

I was thankful for the interruption, as it distracted the boys from their interrogation. "Sure. I'm just about done."

I threw my trash away and followed him into his office. He took the seat behind his desk and steepled his hands.

I uncomfortably took a seat on the other side of the desk, but I felt like I had been sent to the Principal's office. That was a familiar feeling; I was there a lot as a kid.

"Blaise, I want to level with you. You're a good defenseman, but I don't think you're working to your potential."

"Okay..."

"You're great at being a stay-at-home defenseman, and you and Cully are working well together, but with your defensive style and Riley's ability to put up numbers, you need to be back on the line together."

I nodded. Riley and I were a good pair, but Logan and I worked well together, too. LaVoie was the head coach, so he was the person in charge of making the lines. I wasn't sure why he was telling me this.

"Okay, sure."

"Kid, are you okay?"

I nodded. "Yeah, I'm fine."

He squinted at me. "You seemed distracted in the last couple of games. I know adjusting to a new system, new team, new locker room hierarchy, and all that bullshit can be tough, but I thought you were slotting your place here."

I ran a hand through my hair. "It's family shit. I'll sort it."

He nodded in understanding. "Okay, get out of here. I want you well-rested for the game tonight. Your girl gonna come?"

I shook my head. "Ah...she does not give a fuck about hockey."

He laughed. "Honest! I like her already."

I laughed. "Yeah, me too."

"It's nice to have the support, though, you know? Sometimes it helps us knowing they're cheering us on and that if it goes to shit, they'll pick up the pieces."

I nodded.

I assumed it was nice, but I never knew. I could count on my hand the number of times Astrid came to support me. I didn't think it was fair to ask Veronica to always cheer me on when Astrid never did.

Coach dismissed me, and I headed home for my pregame nap. I was thankful Dad wasn't home. We'd barely said two words to each other since I stormed out of his bar. I shouldn't have moved home. I should have found my own place, but there was a small part of me that worried about the old man. He'd been a distant shell of a person since Mom died, and Michael was worried about him being lonely now that we were almost all out of the house.

That was probably why sleep didn't come. My brain replayed how I acted like a child. I still had all this animosity toward Dad for shutting down when we were kids and forcing us to fend for ourselves. The worst part? He was right. I was exactly like him, and I hated that.

I stared into the dark of my bedroom and noticed there was a pair of women's underwear on my floor. I got out of bed and threw it in my hamper. Veronica hadn't done that on purpose, she had been in a rush when she left the house that morning, but it didn't stop my horny brain from thinking about all the fun we had gotten up to. Or how the last time I saw her, she let me take her as hard and rough as I wanted, letting me take my frustrations with my dad out on her body.

That was the best thing about this casual arrangement with her. She didn't ask for anything. I didn't have to get attached to her. We'd fuck our way through the month, and then after her douchebag ex's wedding, we'd go our separate ways. I didn't need her to come to my games.

So why was my hand hovering over the text message thread with her, trying to see if I should even bother?

ME: Will you come to the game tonight?

VERONICA: You need your fake girlfriend to make an appearance?

ME: Something like that.

VERONICA: Sure.

I re-taped my stick for the fifth time and bounced my knee in anticipation. Riley put his hand on my leg. "Dude, stop obsessively stick-taping. That's my thing," he joked.

The big blonde man looked like he could be another

one of my brothers, only he was tanned, and I was so pale, I was translucent. I ran my hand through my hair and put my helmet on. I didn't know why I was nervous tonight. Maybe because Veronica was coming to another game. Or because Riley and I were paired again, and I was worried about my performance on the ice.

Girard, our captain, was doing a pep talk and getting us amped to go out for warm-ups. He was an excellent captain, a little serious, but a good leader. He reminded me of my oldest brother, Eli, which was funny because we were playing Montreal tonight.

No wonder I was nervous.

"Fuck," I swore.

"What?" Riley asked.

Shit, I didn't mean to say that out loud.

I shook my head and got up to walk down the tunnel. TJ stood at the front, chanting everyone's nicknames to pump us up.

"Holmsy!" he cheered, and I couldn't help the smile from sliding across my face. TJ might laugh at his own jokes, and sometimes he was a little loud, but he was fun to play with.

I headed out onto the ice, taking my first lap around the freshly zambonied surface. I stopped in front of the glass where the girls usually sat. Veronica was sitting beside Dinah, her hair in a ponytail, the fire-engine red ends peeking out behind her.

The thing that stopped me on my skates and made me stare at her? She was wearing my jersey. My fake girlfriend came to my game when I asked, and she was wearing my jersey. My ex-girlfriend of ten years never did that. Ever. I had to tamp down my heart beating loud in my chest as I stared at her.

She must have felt my gaze because she turned away from Dinah, and we locked eyes. Her smile seemed genuine, and then she tapped her fingers against her heart and pointed to me. I wanted to laugh at that. I repeated the gesture back to her. I don't know why I did that when she came to my first game. Before I could process my feelings and why that gesture made me feel warmth across my chest, a big body checked me into the boards.

Eli.

"Hey!" I yelled, and he nudged me with his shoulder. Big brothers were the worst.

"That your girl?" he asked and pointed to V.

I nodded.

"Hmm."

"What, asshole?" I seethed.

"Kinda Astrid's polar opposite, no? From the sunshine girl to the edgy goth girl."

I glared at him.

Ayden had made the same snarky remark about Veronica, and it pissed me off. Before I could shove Eli to the ice, the press photographers started snapping photos of us together. The league loved to run stories about hockey families. I got it, but sometimes I wished my achievements didn't always come with the asterisk of being Halvard Holmstrom's son or Eli Holmstrom's little brother.

Maybe I wouldn't have felt this pressure if any of my other brothers were in the league. My brother Brendan would have been an amazing goalie, but he knew being openly gay in a league full of toxic masculinity wouldn't have been a good experience. Brendan told me not to come out as bisexual, but he was why I did it. Because fuck that shit. Brendan was a brick wall, and he would have won the Vezina multiple years in a row; I hated that he held back having a career because of the issues in the league. But maybe one day, none of that would matter. That's why I came out. So queer kids could see themselves in me and know there was a place for them in hockey.

"I get to meet her later, right?" Eli asked and nodded at Veronica while we posed for more photos.

I jabbed him with my stick. "Be nice to her."

"I'm nice! Are you and Dad still not on speaking terms?" he asked, jabbing me back.

If grunts and hmmm were speaking, then sure, we were speaking again. I already talked with Eli about this and told him to stay out of it. But he didn't know when to mind his business. Eli picked up the pieces of our family when Dad was lost, but sometimes it was like having a second micro-managing dad, who you wanted to punch in the face.

"Stay on your side of the ice!" I told him with a grin. Then I skated off to shoot pucks into the Bulldogs net. It was going to be fun beating him and rubbing it in his face.

CHAPTER SIXTEEN

VERONICA

"You and Blaise are so cute," Rox sighed dreamily next to me during the TV time-out.

"Why are you sighing like you don't get fucked as much as you want?" Dinah asked her.

I almost spilled my beer at that. The petite girl gave me an innocent smile. Dinah was so blunt, but I loved her for it.

Rox smirked. "But D, they're so cute together. That whole heart-tapping thing they do! So cute!"

I felt a blush creep up my neck. That was all for show, but the smile Blaise had when he saw me tonight made it worth it.

"Do you think they can win tonight?" I asked.

There were ten minutes left in the last period, and it was 2-1 Philly, but the two women had informed me that anything could happen within ten minutes of play on the ice. I was learning so much about hockey just sitting and watching the game with them.

"Blaise has been good on the PK tonight," Rox said.

"And Metzy's been on fire," Dinah agreed.

"What do you mean by PK?" I asked.

Rox groaned. "Oh my God, girl, I need to teach you hockey."

"You're Canadian. Isn't it like the law to know this sport? I don't even like sportsball," I argued.

"Girl!" Dinah yelled at me.

"She means the penalty kill," Rox explained. "When the other team has the power play—the man advantage because our guys took a penalty—our guys want to kill off the penalty and keep them from scoring."

All this sportsball talk was so foreign to me. All I knew was that the Bulldogs could win tonight if they hung on. Blaise sat on the bench, but he looked focused and ready to go if his coach told him to get back on the ice.

I sipped my beer and watched the captain of the Bulldogs take the puck up into Montreal's zone. Everyone around us was yelling 'shoot,' but Dinah explained he was trying to set up a play. He faked a shot and then passed it to another player. His teammate went for the shot, but the goaltender covered it.

Rox rubbed at her maple leaf tattoo on her wrist and muttered something beside me.

"Dude! Stop! You're going to rub it off if you keep doing that, and then you're going to have to pay me to fix it," I joked.

She made a face. "Not true."

I laughed, but she looked frantic.

I spied Blaise tearing down the ice, chasing after a Montreal player. He looked beautiful on the ice. Like he belonged there, and he knew it. He was this big scary dude when he checked another player into the boards, but there was this part of his playing style that I found mesmerizing.

There was a beauty in how his big body carved across the ice.

I caught myself holding my breath while Benny got the puck down near Montreal's goal. He batted the puck on his stick, trying to find one of his teammates, and then he passed it to Blaise. In a blink, the red lamp behind the opposing goaltender lit up, and the horn sounded.

"That's my man! Getting that apple!" Rox cheered.

Whatever that meant. I felt like I needed to study hockey to understand what these women were talking about half the time.

Blaise skated by where we sat behind the glass, and we locked eyes again. He kissed his gloved fingers and pointed at me. That was all for show, but it didn't help that fluttering feeling swelling up in my chest. I tried to push it down. I cut the feelings out of my heart a long time ago, and they weren't coming back for a hot hockey player.

In the end, the Bulldogs won, 3-1, and the girls informed me it was a win the team desperately needed.

"Bar?" Rox asked, looking at me expectantly.

I checked the time on my phone and thought about it. The shop didn't open until noon tomorrow, so I was down for a few drinks before I had to navigate which train I had to get home. Sometimes it was annoying that I lived far away, but sometimes it was nice because then I had an excuse to go home and paint without interruptions.

"Okay, let's go," I told her.

I hitched a ride with Rox to Eileen's. As soon as I plunked down at the bar, Hal put a lager in front of me and gave me a sly smile. "Oh, you know me so well!"

"You're wearing his jersey," he told me matter-of-factly.

I pointed to Dinah, who sat next to me, drinking her own beer. "She told me I was supposed to."

"I'm glad you two figured this out," Hal said.

"Wait..." Dinah began. "Did you try to set them up?"

The older man gave her a wink.

"Hal! No, you didn't!" I squealed.

He shrugged. "You're good for each other, but..."

"But what?" I asked.

"Blaise wears his heart on his sleeve. He's too much like me. So be good to him, yeah?"

Dinah and I shared a confused look. "What are you saying?" I asked.

"I don't want to see either of you hurt again."

Guilt stabbed at my heart at his words. Were we complete assholes for fooling everyone with our fake relationship? We were tricking everyone because I wanted to be petty to my ex, and Blaise wanted his family to get off his dick after his breakup. But his dad wanted us to be happy and thought we could do that together.

"I—"

"Dad, will you give it a rest?" A deep voice grumbled from behind me. "Leave my girl alone."

"Blaise..." Hal warned.

But Blaise wasn't paying attention to him. Instead, he bent down and kissed me. I melted into his touch. We hadn't seen each other in about a week, and I forgot he was such a good kisser.

"Oh, my God. Get a room," another deep voice sighed exasperatedly behind us.

I pulled away and felt heat rise on my cheeks. Blaise gave me a wicked grin before turning around and gesturing to the man behind us. "Veronica, this is my asshole brother, Eli. Eli, this is my girlfriend, Veronica."

Eli was a few inches shorter than Blaise, and he didn't

seem as muscular, but he had the same blonde hair and blue eyes as the rest of the Holmstroms.

I side-eyed their dad. "Hal, tell the truth. Did you clone yourself?"

Hal laughed but walked to the other end of the bar to serve more customers.

Eli punched Blaise in the arm. "I'm not an asshole."

"I thought that was Ayden," I joked.

"Dude, I'm right here," the third brother said from behind the bar. I gave him a cheeky grin while he got drinks for his older brothers.

"Is this asshole still not talking to Dad?" Eli asked Ayden.

"What's going on?" I asked.

"Nothing," Blaise snapped, but in a way that told me it was definitely something. I wasn't really his girlfriend, so it wasn't my place to ask him.

Blaise and his brothers talked shop, AKA hockey, which was like listening to a foreign language. I drank my beer silently, enjoying Blaise's hand absent-mindedly rubbing the back of my neck. I wasn't sure he knew he had been doing it until I closed my eyes for a minute.

"You tired, sweets?" he asked.

I nodded.

"Did you drive tonight?"

"Took the train."

"Let me take you home."

I waved him off. "Nah. Walk me to the train." I cashed out with Ayden, and Blaise helped me into my jacket. He was so considerate; he'd make someone happy one day. "Hey, did you decide on a tattoo?"

Eli's eyebrows raised. "Another tattoo?"

I shook my head and pointed to Blaise's chest. "Nah, I want to cover this one up."

"Oh?" Eli asked.

I pushed up my sleeve so he saw my floral tattoos peeking out. "I'm a tattoo artist. I want to fix it for him so he doesn't have her name there anymore."

"What are you going to get?" Eli asked Blaise.

"I suggested a maple leaf...for your mom."

Eli nodded and looked at the flowers on my arm. "Mom liked hibiscuses."

"That's what Maja suggested," Blaise said and fixed his coat over his nicely tailored black suit.

I fingered the lapel. "You look great in this. This would be good with the dress I'm wearing for the wedding."

"What wedding?" Eli asked.

I cringed. "My ex's."

"Wait..." Ayden started from behind the bar. "That douchebag who left you a week before you were supposed to marry him? He invited you to his wedding?"

"It gets worse," Blaise muttered.

"How?" Ayden asked. He looked visibly angry, and that shocked me. Ayden and I had a playful banter with each other, so I didn't expect him to be so angry for me.

I couldn't look at any of the Holmstrom men right now. I felt their pitying looks burning into me.

Blaise didn't sense my discomfort. "He has a baby."

"He has a...oh shit! V, I'm so sorry," Ayden said.

"Baby?" I asked Blaise in a quiet voice. "Can we go? I don't want to talk about this."

His face fell when he looked at me, but I caught his dad's look instead. He narrowed his eyes at us, staring back and forth between us like he had sussed out what we were playing at. I tore my gaze away from him, shame crashing over me at what Blaise and I were doing.

"Sorry, sweets. Let's go," Blaise said.

I walked out of the bar and down the street, not caring if Blaise kept up with me or not. I wasn't angry at him for bringing it up; I just didn't want to talk about my ex or the fact he left me because he got another woman pregnant. I willed the tears to stay inside. I was supposed to be dead instead and not have feelings.

Blaise enveloped me in his big body, pulling me to his chest and banding his arms around my waist.

"I'm sorry," he said. God, such a simple touch from this man made me feel instantly better. He pulled back and wiped my face with his rough, calloused hands. "I didn't mean to upset you."

"Blaise?"

"Yeah?"

"Make me feel better?"

He smirked. "Always, sweets."

I tipped up my head and kissed him. He met me halfway and kissed me back. He broke the kiss, but only so he could nose across my neck. "You're wearing my jersey."

I nodded. "You want it on my floor?"

"No," he growled as he nipped at my neck.

"No?"

"I want to fuck you in it."

"Your place or mine?"

"Mine's closer."

I didn't even argue. I was horned up for this man, and I went with him to his place without a second thought.

We barely made it out of his car as we stumbled up the steps and into the row house. He lifted me up into his arms, carrying me up the steps while I kissed his neck and tried to get his tie off. I laughed when he kicked the door to his bedroom shut and dropped me on the bed.

"You like me in your jersey?" I asked.

He nodded as he shed his suit jacket, his ocean-blue eyes burning with his desire for me. "You came to my game and are wearing my jersey," he breathed out huskily. He made quick work of his suit, shedding it until he stood there naked in all his glory. God, his body was like a work of art, and I wanted to worship it.

I licked my lips and crooked my finger at him. "C'mere, big guy."

I reached for the hem of the jersey, but his hand reached out to stop me. "No. I said I want to fuck you in it."

He got to work unbuttoning my jeans and peeling my thong off. This must have been a weird hockey player kink because I thought he'd want to see my tits at least. I lifted the jersey up and spread my legs so he could see how wet I was for him already.

"Want you now," I begged.

I moaned when his finger grazed across my clit. "Want to make sure you're ready, sweets."

"I am. Get a condom on and fuck me."

He grinned and reached into the bedside table, sliding a condom on and slicking it with lube. I yelped in surprise when he turned me over. Then I moaned when he slid into me from behind, thrusting suddenly and without warning. God, this man knew just what I wanted.

"God, you're so sexy," he growled into my neck.

"Blaise..." I moaned. I pressed back into him, wanting to feel all of him as he slammed into me over and over again.

"What, sweets?" he groaned and continued his motions, which made my eyes roll into the back of my head.

"I'm gonna come," I moaned. "You make me come so fast."

"You love it." He punctuated each word with a hard thrust, hitting me deep where I needed it.

I gripped the headboard, so I didn't fall to the bed face-first, although I think he would have liked that view. "I do."

"You want it rough?"

"Always, please, break me apart."

He rode me harder and played with my clit, making me lose myself in the sensation of him.

Like the gentleman he was, he waited for me to spiral out of control. Then he hammered into me as hard as he could and roared out his release. He sounded like a wild animal when he came, and I loved it.

He kissed my shoulder and pulled out while I fell face-first onto the mattress. I was a melted pool of satisfaction, my body like jelly from the orgasm he gave me. He tossed the condom in his trash can and climbed back into bed with me. I crawled into his arms, and he enveloped me with his big body while my hair splayed across his naked chest. He played with my hair while I traced the tattoo on his chest.

"Let me fix this for you," I said.

"You will. I'm just...I don't know."

I traced across his pale white skin. Man, I thought Dinah was ghostly, but this big blonde man beat her at that. "I could do a grouping starting here and blend it into your phoenix. Then it could bleed into your sleeve."

"Wait, you like the hibiscus idea, don't you?"

I pointed to the same flower inked across my skin. "Yeah. I could do a red one."

"Why?"

"Some people say it symbolizes love."

He kissed the top of my head. "I wonder if my mom would appreciate me getting inked in memory of her."

"She'd probably like it better than having the name of the girl who broke your heart on your chest."

I laid my head back on his chest and nearly purred when he continued to stroke my hair. I barely remembered what he said when I drifted off to sleep. All I knew was that laying in bed with this giant of a man made me feel safe. I was glad sleep took me before I could think too hard about what that meant.

CHAPTER SEVENTEEN

BLAISE

Waking up with a woman in your arms who was only pretending to be your girlfriend was confusing. I only had a couple more weeks left with this hellcat, and I wanted to savor it all. Especially when she lay naked in my bed with her head on my chest. It was a sight to wake up to, but I had to keep telling my heart not to get any ideas.

I ran my hand through her black and red curls. The red was fading to orange, but it still looked amazing on her. I loved her hair. I loved that she had colorful tattoos, and she wanted to fix mine for me.

I smiled when I felt Veronica shift around. Her fingers danced across my chest. "Let me fix it, please?" she begged.

God, when this woman begged, it made me come undone. It was going to be a bummer when our expiration date came. I loved how much we got tangled up in the sheets together, and fucking her in my jersey last night had been hot. Like she was mine, and mine alone. Even if I knew that was the farthest thing from the truth.

She lifted her head, and she had a sleepy look on her face, but in the quiet early morning, she had never looked more beautiful. I couldn't think stuff like that about her. She didn't do relationships, and whatever we had was pure lust. Besides, I wasn't sure I was ready to open my heart to someone else again. Not after Astrid broke it into a million pieces.

"Please, Blaise?" she asked again, her voice cutting through my broody thoughts.

I kissed the top of her head. "Okay, sweets."

"Really?" she asked, a smile spreading across her face. When she smiled at me like that, my heart screamed at me to let her in.

I tipped her chin up and kissed her.

I stroked her cheek when I pulled away, brushing her hair out of her face, but before she could respond, my bedroom door slammed open, hitting the wall with a loud bang. My little brother Michael stood in the doorway, startling both of us. I pulled the comforter over Veronica and held her against my chest so he didn't see her naked body.

"Yo, dude..." Michael began, but then he trailed off, and his eyes got wide when he saw I wasn't alone.

"Dude, learn to knock!" I yelled.

"I'm sorry!" he yelled back and then slammed the door shut behind him.

Veronica shook against my chest, and when I looked down at her, I realized she was laughing her ass off. "There's really no privacy in your family, is there?"

I shook my head. "Nope. I don't know why he's not at school."

She slid out of bed, and my cock stood at attention

almost immediately. Well, not that it had far to go. I was getting hard as soon as I woke up to her naked form pressed up against mine.

"Hey, you left your underwear here last time," I blurted out.

She smirked at me. "Sorry, they were too cum-stained to wear. You ruin me, Blaise Holmstrom."

I squeezed my eyes shut. "Damn, woman. I'm already so hard it hurts."

She laughed. "Too bad your brother walked in, otherwise..."

"C'mere!"

"No. I have to get dressed."

She got dressed but folded up the jersey and didn't put it on over her black t-shirt. "Why did it matter so much that I was wearing your jersey?"

"It was a nice gesture. You're not actually my girlfriend, but you've supported me more than my ex ever did."

She got quiet then, and I figured I'd said the wrong thing.

"I know we're not—"

"We're just having fun, Blaise. It's fine." She sat on the bed and tugged on her Docs. "When can you come in so I can start on that piece for you?"

"How many sessions do you think we need?"

"Two, maybe three. I want to go lighter on the first session and see how it heals."

"It's so sexy when you talk about your work."

She shook her head at me. "I want it to look good for you. Your tattoo isn't that big, but I'll make the flowers a bigger piece and do some shading so you won't be able to see her name anymore."

I checked my phone. "I have practice today, but what about later this afternoon?"

"I have an opening at four."

"Does that give you time to do the stencil?"

She pulled out her sketchbook and opened it to a page where she already had three hibiscus flowers sketched out in pencil. I loved her style, and it felt like the right decision to have her cover up my heartache by remembering my mom instead.

She held up the book against my chest and squinted at me. "Yeah, this will work, and then the greenery can bleed into your arm."

"You're so talented."

She blushed. "You've only seen my sketches."

I shook my head. "Nah. I follow the shop on social media, and I looked at your work. It's good. How did both you and your brother get into it?"

She put her sketchbook into her tote bag, and I got out of bed to put on clothes.

"Family business. Dad had his own shop in the Northeast. I grew up in tattoo shops surrounded by art. I never thought of doing anything else."

Hmm. That sounded familiar.

"He must be proud of both of you."

Her face was a neutral mask. "He was." Then she opened my bedroom door and walked into the hallway.

I quickly caught up behind her. "Stay for breakfast?" I asked.

"Okay."

We walked into the kitchen together, where my dad and Michael sat drinking their coffee in silence. Dad smiled up at Veronica. "Hey, Veronica."

She gave him a side hug and sat in the seat beside him.

I walked over to the coffee pot and poured coffee into two mugs for us. "Black, right, sweets?" I asked.

My brother stared at me like I had three heads while I grabbed coffee and brought it over to her. I handed her a yogurt I grabbed from the fridge, and she gave me a small smile in thanks.

"Um..." Michael started.

Veronica squinted at him. "Michael, right?"

He nodded.

"Oh, I got it right. I think I haven't met Brendan and Maja. Right?" she asked, turning to me for confirmation.

I nodded, but Michael still looked confused. "Oh, this is my girlfriend, Veronica."

"I like your hair," he told her.

"Thanks," she beamed. She checked her watch and finished her yogurt. "I better go. I have to do the books before the shop opens. I'll see you later?"

She kissed me goodbye, and before I could say anything, she had already taken off.

Dad glared at me as soon as she left.

"What?" I growled.

"You better not hurt that girl. She deserves better," he said icily.

Is that what his problem was? Was that why he wanted to talk to me at his bar about me dating her? Because he didn't want me to hurt her? Like I ever would.

"I know, Dad. God, I'm not an asshole. You can't say a woman's off-limits. She's her own person."

"Dad's soft on her," Michael cut in.

"Her ex fucked her up," Dad seethed.

"Yeah? Well, so did mine."

Dad conceded, but he didn't seem convinced.

I nudged my brother. "What are you doing home? Except being a total cock block?"

Michael cringed. "Sorry. Mei was freaking out about a paper, so I came down to help her. Figured I'd check in on you until I had to book it to Ohio for a game tomorrow."

"How's the team doing?" I asked.

He shrugged.

Michael might not want to enter the league, but it didn't stop him from playing for PSU. He still loved playing hockey, but not professionally.

"I didn't realize you were gonna have a naked chick in your bed this morning," he said and made a face.

I shrugged.

He eyed me and pointed to my chest. "When are you going to get that shit fixed?"

"V's gonna do it today."

"What did you land on?"

"She's going to do a grouping of red hibiscuses and make it blend into my sleeve."

"Your mother liked hibiscuses," Dad mused.

"Yeah, Dad, that's the point."

"She would have been proud of you. I am," he whispered.

"You have a real funny way of showing it," I muttered and crossed my arms over my chest.

Dad's brow wrinkled. "What does that mean?"

"Anything I do isn't good enough for you. I'm not smart enough like Michael or good enough at hockey like Eli and Maja. I definitely don't have business sense like Ayden or Brendan. I'm the fuckup Holmstrom kid you always have to rein in. I'm your son, and you don't even think I'm good enough for Veronica!" I seethed at him, anger boiling up inside me.

I was so tired of my dad being harder on me than the rest of my siblings, acting like my accomplishments didn't matter. Anything I did disappointed him.

Michael put a hand on my arm to stop me from getting even more riled up.

Dad frowned at me. "Son, none of that's true. I'm so proud of all your achievements. All of you. It took guts when you came out."

"Then why are you constantly on my ass?"

He narrowed his eyes at me. "I saw you break apart last season, just like I did when your mother died. I left Eli at thirteen to pick up the pieces when I should have been the parent. I don't want you to end up like me—a sad and lonely shell of a man."

"Dad," Michael breathed.

When I glanced at my dad, really looked at him, I saw the longing in him. Saw the struggle etched across his face. Dad was lonely. And he was right. I *was* exactly like him. I let my emotions cloud my judgment, and it almost cost me my career.

"Why did you tell Ayden that Veronica was off-limits?" Michael asked for me.

Dad rolled his eyes. "That boy needs to settle down, and I knew which son she was meant for."

His gaze settled on me, and the way he studied me, I wondered if he could tell what Veronica and I were up to. That none of it was real because his gaze pierced me like he was searching for something. I shifted in my chair uncomfortably.

Michael looked giddy. "Wait...did you 'meet cute' them?"

Dad gave him a confused look. "Did I what?"

Michael laughed. "Holy shit! You totally did. You told

Blaise to drive her home last summer because you were trying to push them together, right?"

Dad shrugged, and a sly smile came across his features.

My baby brother howled with laughter. "Damn, Dad, you're quite the wingman."

"Dad?" I asked.

"Hmm?"

"Mom would've wanted you to be happy. She'd have wanted you to move on."

He twisted his wedding band on his finger. "I'm not sure I can. Your mother was the love of my life. Nobody can compare to her."

"You don't have to be lonely for the rest of your life," I insisted.

"Blaise, why did you move back home?" he asked, trying to change the subject off him.

"Because I got traded."

He pierced me with the 'dad look.' "You're old enough to have your own place. You didn't have to move back in here."

I rubbed the back of my neck. "Because we're all worried about you being alone. Okay? That's the real reason I moved back in."

Michael nodded in agreement. He slid his phone over to Dad. "Here, I'm making you a dating profile."

Dad groaned. "I'm not doing that."

"Yes, you are, old man," I teased him.

He glared at me. "Get out of my house!"

Micheal and I shook our heads. "No way, old man. Mom wouldn't have wanted you to live like this. We should have done this a long time ago."

He crossed his arms over his chest and glared at us, but he appeased us when we called a family meeting over video chat, and the rest of my siblings razzed him until he gave in. Even Maja's boyfriend Julien got in on the action. Dad shook his head, but the smile on his face might have been the first one I had seen in a long time.

Dad and I clashed. We were too similar, but laying it all on the table this morning had been good for us. I just hoped I didn't disappoint him when he realized what Veronica and I had wasn't real.

CHAPTER EIGHTEEN

VERONICA

"My appointment didn't show. You wanna get a coffee?" my brother asked while I was finishing up working on the stencil for Blaise.

"Busy," I muttered. I still wasn't on speaking terms with him. Us Irish girls knew how to hold a grudge.

"How about I get us a coffee, and then we can talk?" he suggested.

"Hard pass," I said and checked my phone. I smiled at a text from Blaise.

BLAISE: OMW

BLAISE: Are you excited to stab me with things?

"Veronica, I'm trying to apologize here," Alex sighed.

My eyes snapped up to him. "Then maybe you shouldn't have opened a shop with only three reliable artists. Or you should have listened to me when I said Andy was too green and needed to apprentice first."

"I'm sorry."

I sighed. "I know, but...Seth broke my world apart. Do you understand what it's like walking in here and having to see him working at one of the other stations? Do you understand what it's like to wake up one day and have your entire world turned upside down?"

"Everything okay here?" Blaise asked from behind Alex.

I nodded. "Yes." To my brother, I said, "Shoo. I have work to do."

Alex sighed but did as I asked. Blaise shed his jacket, but then he bent down to kiss me. I had no doubt doing it because Seth was watching us, but I leaned into the kiss. His lips against mine made me relax, calming the raging storm inside me.

He pressed his forehead against mine. "You okay?"

I nodded and stole one last kiss. "You ready?"

He nodded and pulled away. I had to bite my lip when he shed his long-sleeved henley. This man was ripped. Blaise lay down in my tattoo chair, and I paused when I noticed he had already shaved the area and his entire chest.

"I know the drill," he explained at my surprised look.

"One-second. I need to wash my hands."

I washed my hands, and when I came back to my chair, I donned my gloves. I laid the stencil down on Blaise's chest and carefully peeled it off to get the transfer onto his skin. I held up a mirror for him to see. "Okay with the placement?"

He nodded. "You're the boss."

"But it's your tattoo."

He smirked. "It's good, sweets. Do your thing."

I grabbed my machine and dipped it into the ink. "You

know I'm gonna need you in my chair for a couple of sessions, right?"

"I know."

"Ready?"

"Hit me."

I laughed but got to work. I had to admit Blaise took it like a champ, but I saw him gritting his teeth. "Breathe," I reminded him as I went over my line work carefully.

He sighed. "Sorry."

I wiped away at the area and then went back in. "Liv?" I called out.

"Yeah?"

"Can you get Blaise water?"

"Sure," she said cheerfully and grabbed a bottle for him.

He sipped on his water while trying not to move as I tattooed his chest. Olivia took her phone out and snapped pictures. Alex had her doing the admin and social media stuff now since he wanted me to focus on my artwork as much as I could. I still did the books, but he was looking for someone to take over soon.

"For our social pages. You don't mind?" she asked him.

Blaise shook his head. "Nah. I'll post something too when we're done."

"Practice good?" I asked, trying to distract Blaise from the pain while I worked.

"Yeah, especially after our win last night. Did you see I got a goal?"

"I did. We were too busy last night. I forgot to congratulate you."

"Aw, look at you, becoming the good little hockey girlfriend."

I stuck out my tongue and focused on my work. "You're in a good mood."

"Yeah, hashed some things out with my dad today."

"That's good."

"My siblings and I had to twist his arm to set up a dating profile. He's still in love with my mom."

"My dad was like that, too," I admitted.

"Oh?"

"My mom ran off when I was two months old."

"Three months," my brother's voice said behind me. "And it broke dad. He was already broken from my mom's death, but it made it worse."

"How's your dad now?" Blaise asked.

Without thinking, Alex shrugged and said, "He's gone now."

Blaise frowned."Oh, sweets. You didn't tell me."

I didn't answer, just continued with my work. "Was there something you needed?" I asked my brother.

"Nah, just checking your work."

I wiped at Blaise's tattoo and started working on the greenery. "I don't need help."

"It looks good. You can't see the script anymore," he praised me. "Don't you grow flowers like this?"

"Yeah. They're my favorite flower."

"Really?" Blaise asked.

"I thought that was why you were getting this?" my brother asked and knitted his eyebrows together as he surveyed my work.

"No...they were my mom's favorite, too," Blaise said.

Thank God I had to focus on my work and not his eyes, which I knew were boring into me. I bent my head and added in more color, laser-focusing on my task at hand and not the conversation.

"Well, in any case, it's looking good."

"K. Bye!" I dismissed Alex and continued working.

"Sweets," Blaise said softly. "You need a minute with your brother?"

I shook my head. His voice was soft and kind, and it was so damn nice of him to think of my needs right now. But I was here to do a job, not deal with my brother.

Eventually, Alex walked away. He hovered a little too long for my tastes, but once he left, Blaise and I lapsed back into conversation.

"You're doing so good," I told him.

"Hockey player. We're used to pain."

I laughed. "Umm...I had Benny in this chair, and I think he almost squeezed Rox's hand off."

"Ah, she can take him."

I laughed. "They're an interesting couple."

"They used to hate each other, which is baffling to me."

"Oh, she told me the story," I said. "I did an enormous piece on her thigh. We had a lot of time to talk."

I wiped at his skin and smiled to myself, as this was looking perfect already. I still probably needed to do a touch-up after it healed, but so far, it was doing the job. We talked while I shaded his tattoo. I gave him a break after a little while, and then we were back at it.

I was almost done when I felt his eyes on me again. "Stop staring at me. I'm trying to focus here."

"You're sexy when you work."

I stopped and lifted up my head to look at him. "Is that so?"

He nodded. "Yeah. You're so talented. It's a turn-on for me to see someone good at their job. I'm glad it's you doing this for me."

I beamed at his compliment and returned to my task at hand. "It's kind of like when I watch you play hockey. You're like...I don't know...graceful, elegant even on the ice."

"What? I block shots with my body and check dudes into the boards. I'm a rough and tumble guy."

"I know, but there's a beauty in it," I explained. I wiped at his skin and assessed my work. "I think we might be good."

"Let me see," he demanded.

I handed him a mirror so he could see the three groupings of flowers on his chest that went up into his shoulder and blended into the phoenix on his upper arm. I was proud of this work and glad I couldn't see that woman's name anymore. Once it healed, we'd see if we needed another session, but I wasn't sure it was needed. Maybe only one more to get the colors deeper.

"Thoughts?" I asked.

Blaise's features softened when he looked at me, and he opened his mouth, but words didn't come out.

"What? Is it okay?" I asked. I was never nervous about my work, but his silence sent anxiety through me.

"Baby..." he breathed out in awe. Relief spread through me that he liked it. I don't think I ever had a client speechless before.

"Oh wow," Liv's voice said behind me.

She held up her phone to take another photo for the shop's social media. Blaise pulled me toward him, hugging me to his side, and we smiled for the camera. Fake plastic smiles for our fake relationship that was on a ticking clock to expiration.

"Can you take one on my phone?" Blaise asked and handed Olivia his phone.

He kissed my cheek in this one, and I knew a blush was creeping up my pale face. Liv smiled at that, an expression suggesting we'd talk about that later. I'd rather not.

I patched Blaise up and went through the after-care

stuff, even though he knew the drill. I always tried to make sure my clients understood how to keep their tattoos looking fresh.

"Am I your last client for the day?" he asked.

I nodded.

"You wanna get dinner?"

I should say no. We couldn't go on dates. It was bad enough we were fucking while pretending we had a serious relationship. Plus, I had concept art I needed to work on.

"Can't. I have some work I still need to do."

"Go be with your man," Alex yelled after me. He stood at the front desk talking to Liv, and they both grinned at me.

"Yeah, the team travels again tomorrow," Seth cut in.

I didn't know that. How did assface know that before I did? I wanted to say something, but the bell ringing on the front door and a petite blonde walking in with a baby in a stroller distracted me. Seth smiled and went to greet them. That's when I recognized her.

I watched with anger bubbling up inside as Seth kissed his soon-to-be wife and picked up his child. What an asshole. He just came waltzing back into my life and had to shove it into my face how he'd betrayed me. I didn't know about this woman, but I wanted to give her the benefit of the doubt. I wanted to think she didn't know about me during their affair. It was possible since Seth and I weren't active on social media.

Blaise squeezed my hand and put his lips to my ear. "You okay?"

I nodded, but I was pretty far from okay. Especially when Seth and his cute little family walked over to us. The blonde looked nervous, and I didn't blame her.

"Hi, I'm Lily," she introduced herself.

I stared at her.

She shot a look at Seth. "Um...look, I told Seth it wasn't a good idea to invite you because I know you guys ended on bad terms."

"Bad terms?" I parroted. Behind her, Seth gave me a pained look, like he wanted me to drop the subject.

"He said you had a bad break-up. We met shortly after that, and then we had our surprise child."

She didn't know.

She had no idea.

She started dating this asshole when I was still dating him. When I was going to marry him, and then he left me in the lurch when she got pregnant.

I felt Blaise's hand squeeze mine again, and then he held it out to Lily. "I'm Blaise, Veronica's boyfriend."

She smiled. "Oh, I know you. You're both still welcome to come, of course. I just didn't want any hard feelings."

"Hard feelings?" I repeated.

"We'll still come," Blaise answered for me.

This was so messed up. Did I tell Lily her baby daddy was a piece of shit? That he had been playing both of us? I looked at Blaise, and he grimaced at me. "Well, it was nice meeting you, but V and I have dinner to get to. We'll see you at the wedding in a couple of weeks."

And then he whisked me away for the night, taking me back to my place and helping me forget in the best way he knew how.

Blaise had to wake up early to catch the charter jet to Carolina tomorrow. They had a Sunday afternoon game against the Carolina Thrashers and then a game on Tuesday against the Florida Hurricanes. He was supposed to get back Wednesday sometime, and I didn't know why I was so invested in his schedule when he wasn't even my boyfriend.

He had passed out in exhaustion after we fucked all over my bedroom, but I couldn't sleep. I studied his profile as he slept. He looked peaceful, and a smile came to my face at how he tried to make me feel better tonight.

After we left the shop, we went back to Drakesville and went to dinner at the local brewery. I realized how small of a town I lived in when a bunch of people recognized him, but he took it all in stride. The surly brewmaster had to tell people to leave us alone, so we could eat in peace, but Blaise just flashed his bright smile. We ate and drank good beer until I drug him back to my apartment to have my way with him.

It was going to be a bummer when this was all over because Blaise was a great fuck buddy. Not too clingy, and he knew what I liked. But I was starting to like him too much. I had to remember where the lines were. Relationships only hurt you in the end, and I couldn't let my heart make the decisions.

When he turned in his sleep, I made my escape and slid out of bed. I couldn't stop thinking about what Seth's fiancée said. They started dating after we broke up, but I didn't think that was true. Especially since Seth kept on calling me. Maybe he had tried to do the right thing, to be the parent to his child, but that didn't make it hurt any less. I never wanted a man to break me like that again.

The only place I let my feelings come out was on the canvas. I let my emotions pour out of me as I painted them in broad, angry strokes.

I gasped at hands sliding around my waist and a pair of lips pressing against my neck. Blaise chuckled behind me, the loud sound vibrating against my back. "Sorry," he laughed. "What are you doing awake?"

"Couldn't sleep," I sighed and moaned when he peppered my neck with kisses.

"Come back to bed."

"I—" I cut myself off and put my paintbrush down. "Painting helps when I can't sleep."

Blaise came around beside me and studied the canvas. Maybe I went too Georgia O'Keeffe with this painting, but I loved floral patterns. I loved doing flower tattoos and doing that tattoo for him today.

"You're so talented, Veronica."

"Thank you."

"Why don't you tell me what's wrong?"

I shook my head. "It's nothing."

I stood up and cleaned my paintbrushes and palette off in the sink. Blaise stood in my kitchen studying my painting. He was so kind and fun to be around. If I wasn't so afraid of getting hurt again, maybe I would have given him a real shot.

"I don't think she knows," I admitted.

"Oh."

"What do I even do?" I asked and turned back around to face him.

He shrugged. "Honestly, V? I don't know. Are you sure she doesn't know?"

"It sounded like it, but what if he's doing it to her, too? I get that he chose her and their child. That doesn't mean it hurts any less, but I get it."

Blaise walked over to me and folded me in his arms. "You didn't deserve that. But I don't know what to tell you. I'll still go with you to the wedding if you want."

I nodded into his chest. "That was the deal. We pretend until the wedding, then we can tell everyone we broke up."

He was quiet for a minute.

"We should talk about our breakup story," I told him. I looked up at him, and he was staring at the wall, his face neutral.

"Right. Can we talk about it later? I'm really tired."

I nodded and pulled away from him. "Sure. Why don't you go back to bed? I need a minute to clean up."

"I got worried when you weren't there," he admitted with a sheepish look.

"I'm a big girl, Blaise. Not like I would have left you in my apartment alone."

"Come back to bed?" he asked again.

I dried my hands on the dish towel and let him take me by the hand back into my bedroom. I still couldn't sleep, but it was nice to have this big man holding me. Nice to feel wanted, even if it was pretend.

CHAPTER NINETEEN

BLAISE

I stared up at the ceiling of Veronica's bedroom while my alarm blared next to my head. I had to get up so I could drive back into the city to catch the charter with the team, but I also didn't want to move from this spot. Veronica was curled in my arms with her head on my chest, and my arm was numb from the weight of her. I didn't care because this was a nice way to wake up.

And dammit...I had feelings for her. Maybe she'd want me if she hadn't been so dicked around by her ex. I don't know when it happened. Maybe it was when she showed up at my game wearing my jersey, but my heart was getting big ideas.

"Mmm..." she moaned into my chest all sleepily. I loved that sound coming out of her mouth. I shifted a bit to turn off my alarm and ran a hand through her hair. She snuggled down into me further.

"I gotta go, baby," I whispered and kissed the top of her head.

I had to knock it off with the 'baby' shit, or she was going to figure out I had caught feelings. But she hadn't minded when I called her that last night. Or when I called her 'sweets' which at first had been teasingly, but now I was skating on thin ice every time I used it.

"No," she whispered into my chest.

"No?" I asked.

"Don't go," she begged.

I looked down and saw her eyes were still closed. I wondered if she even knew she was talking to me since she was still half-asleep.

"I gotta go, baby," I told her again and shifted her onto her back.

"Everyone abandons me," she muttered.

How could I leave her when she said something like that?

I sat up and hovered over her, my hand going to her face. "Veronica?"

"Hmm?"

"I gotta go travel with the team, okay? I'll see you in a few days. I promise."

Her eyes shot open, and her brow furrowed when she looked up at me. "Blaise?" she asked, confused. "Oh, right. Sure. I'll see you later."

"You okay?"

She nodded. "Yeah. I'll see you when you get back, or whenever. Text me when you need another appearance from your fake girlfriend."

I wanted to scream. I didn't want her to be my fake girlfriend anymore. How did I let this happen?

I kissed her forehead. "Go back to sleep. I'll text you later."

She closed her eyes, and I reluctantly got out of bed. I

went into the bathroom and did my normal morning routine. I peeled off the saniderm bandage on my chest and applied ointment to my new tattoo. I opened up the drawer in her bathroom and found a roll of more of it in there and applied the new bandage. Was it smart to get a tattoo during the season? Probably not, but slapping on a saniderm bandage usually did the trick to let it heal.

I was glad I finally let Veronica do the cover-up because I loved the work she did. The dark red of the petals buried Astrid's name, painting over a past I'd rather forget. Veronica had blended the vines into my sleeve, marking my skin as if Astrid had never been there. Like her handiwork healed my broken heart.

I walked back into her bedroom and started getting dressed. We had stopped at my place last night for my travel bag. Thank god she was smart enough to mention that. Especially since I needed to be suited up for travel. I cringed as her closet door creaked, and I pulled out the white dress shirt. I shrugged it on, buttoning it quickly, and pulled on my pants, tucking in the shirt neatly.

"Damn..." I heard Veronica whistle from the bed as I stretched the matching suit jacket across my wide-set shoulders and wrestled with my tie.

"Go back to sleep, sweets."

"Sorry, there's a hot hockey player in my bedroom wearing a sexy suit."

She slid out of bed and came over to me. She fixed the tie for me and smoothed down my jacket.

"Thanks, sweets."

She nodded. "Damn, get out of here before I rip your clothes off."

I groaned and adjusted myself in my pants. "Don't tempt me. I don't have time."

She smirked at me.

"Go back to sleep," I said and gave her a quick kiss. I pushed her back down into the bed, and she laughed.

"Have a good game," she told me, and she seemed sincere about it.

Starting this thing with Veronica made me realize something about my previous relationship—Astrid never supported my career. She didn't care about it, and even though Veronica said she didn't like 'sportsball,' she understood how important it was to me. Why did Astrid stay with me for so long if she didn't even care? Why had I?

I kissed Veronica goodbye, and she surprised me by not flinching at the gesture. That was kind of relationship-y, and we weren't actually in one. We weren't at my house where my dad or siblings were around and would think it was weird if I didn't kiss her goodbye, but she didn't pull away to remind me of that. It felt so natural waking up beside her and kissing her goodbye. Like it was something we always did. Like we really were together. I had to keep reminding myself we weren't. Despite the way my heart was screaming at me.

I tried to push down the intrusive thoughts as I drove to the jet. Once I got there, I greeted my teammates while we walked on board. I took my seat and put my headphones on, trying to drown out all my conflicting thoughts. They only let up when I fell asleep.

After we touched down and settled into our hotel for the night, I got dinner with the boys.

"You ready for this road trip?" TJ asked and sipped his beer like he was in a hurry.

"Sure, just need to be good on the PK," I told him.

Riley pointed at me. "True."

"I feel like we barely see you outside the locker room," TJ said and gave me a pointed look.

I grinned and shrugged while taking a drink of my beer. I had been spending a lot of time with Veronica. I wanted to savor every moment I could get with her since I knew we were going to expire soon. No wonder I had developed real feelings for her. All I did was play hockey and hang with her. Shit, I was getting clingy. That was exactly what she didn't want.

Noah nudged me with his elbow. "Bro, what's up?"

"Do any of your girls ever ask you not to go when you gotta travel?" I asked.

TJ nodded. "Yeah, Max has before, but I don't think she means it. I think she just doesn't want me to leave the bed."

"Fi's the only girl that understood what the hockey spouse life was gonna be like. She likes me to leave," Riley explained.

I raised an eyebrow. "She does?"

Noah nodded. "Yeah. D said she gets a lot of writing done when I'm gone. Doesn't mean we don't miss each other."

"The girls figure it out," Benny explained. "They have each other to lean on."

I nodded.

"What's up, man?" TJ asked.

"Veronica was weird this morning. She was half asleep, though. I think she has abandonment issues."

"Oh," Riley breathed. "Shit, I understand that one."

"You do?" I asked.

"Sure. Fi felt a little abandoned when I left for the league, and then we weren't as close when we got older. All that shit changed when her asshole ex left her at the altar and I married her instead."

I don't think I knew that about their relationship. That was interesting.

I pushed my food around on my plate. "V's ex left and took all his shit with no note or warning a week before their wedding."

"Fuck!" TJ exclaimed.

"Shit, man. What an asshole!" Noah agreed.

"It gets worse," I muttered.

"How?" Benny asked, and he had a scowl across his face.

"Pretty sure he was cheating on her and got another girl pregnant...we're going to their wedding in two weeks."

They all stared at me.

"Are you serious?" TJ asked.

"What?" I asked.

"You're going to the wedding of the dude who cheated on her?" Riley demanded.

"Dude, why?" Noah asked.

I shrugged. "She asked me to go with her, and I said I would. She wants to show him she's better off without him."

TJ stared at me, confused, but Benny glared at me, and I didn't understand his expression.

"Dude, what?" I asked.

He ran a hand down his face and then looked at Riley. "This sounds an awful lot like the plot to Fi's romance book."

Riley's eyes hardened at me. "Wait...Holmsy, are you not actually dating?"

FUCK.

"I don't know what you're talking about. Of course we're dating," I lied.

Benny still gave me the stink eye.

"The traveling's getting to her," I tried to backpedal.

"Her mom abandoned her as a baby, and then her fiancé did the same thing."

"Oh, shit, dude, I'm sorry," Noah said with a frown.

One of the things I liked about the Bulldogs over the Wolves was that it felt like a family. I could lean on my teammates both on and off the ice, but I hoped they hadn't figured out what Veronica and I were playing at. I needed to distract them from finding out by diverting the conversation elsewhere.

"Can we talk about something less depressing now?" I asked.

Benny crossed his arms over his chest, still studying me with a suspicious look, but Riley came to my rescue by spinning it back to strategy for tomorrow's game. He took a look around the table, giving us all his serious game-day face. "Let's talk about tomorrow. I know all you fuckers aren't watching game tape as much as you should be."

TJ groaned. "Come on, man. Why you always got a hard-on for video?"

"Because we need to be better," Riley argued.

Noah rubbed a hand across his beard. "Not wrong."

TJ shoved Noah's shoulder. "Like you need to say that. You've got a fire under you lately."

Noah's cheeks got pink. For a guy who earned his paycheck by how many points he put up, Noah was humble about it. On the ice, he was a beast that dominated in front of the net, but off the ice, he got embarrassed by the compliments.

"Need you two protecting the net," Benny chimed in, giving me and Riley a hard look.

"We got it!" I razzed him back.

"That's why I'm saying we gotta make sure we know our opponent for tomorrow," Riley chimed in again.

TJ dramatically groaned. "BRO! Come on, we do! We got this."

My lips curled up into a smile at how TJ fucked with Riley. Riley was always on our ass about being better; it was one of the things I loved about being paired with him.

I got distracted by my phone buzzing in my pocket. I was disappointed when I saw it was from my ex-girlfriend and not Veronica.

ASTRID: I miss you.

I clenched my jaw and ignored the current dinner conversation while I typed back.

ME: K.

ASTRID: B, don't be like that.

ME: You broke up with me.

ASTRID: You don't miss me?

ME: Not anymore.

ASTRID: Baby, come on.

I ground my teeth and shoved my phone back into my pocket. I didn't have time for her bullshit. I pressed a hand against my chest, where Veronica had marked me with her artwork. I was done with Astrid, and it took having someone jab me with a needle to figure that out.

"Dude, you okay?" TJ asked.

"Yeah. Nothing," I muttered, taking another sip of my beer. I hoped Astrid took the hint and stopped bothering me. She was the one who cut me out of her life. What right did she have to try to reel me back in again?

He eyed me cautiously. "That sounds fake but okay..."

I grumbled. "My ex is being a pest. It's nothing. I want to go upstairs and call V."

TJ smiled at me. "Yeah, man, we understand."

Benny typed away at his phone and nodded at me. "Seriously, dude, talk to your woman. Make sure she knows you're not abandoning her."

I threw some bills down on the table and chugged the rest of my beer to the guys' amusement.

Calling Veronica had been my excuse to get away from the prying eyes of my teammates. I had to be careful not to reveal too much, lest they figure out what we had wasn't real.

I finished my nighttime routine and laid on the hotel bed in my boxers, but I ended up staring at the photos I had on my phone of Veronica and me. I missed her, and that was bad. I wasn't supposed to miss my fuck buddy.

"Fuck it," I muttered to myself and sent her a video call request.

I was a little surprised when she answered. She had her hair pulled up in a ponytail, and there was paint on her cheek. I had to smile at that because it made her look so cute.

"Hi, stranger," she said to me. "Hang on, I need to reposition my phone."

She went off-screen for a bit, and I heard the water running, and then she was back in focus a few seconds later. She narrowed her eyes. "Did you put ointment on your tattoo yet?"

I rolled my eyes but smiled. "Yes, sweets. I did it this morning."

"And reapplied your bandage?"

I pointed to my chest. "All good while it heals."

"Okay, what's up? You never call me when you're on the road."

I clamped my mouth shut. She was right about that. We had only been doing this fake dating thing for a couple of weeks, and it was going to be over soon, but I never talked to her that much when I was traveling.

What was I doing?

I sighed. "Astrid keeps texting me."

"Why?"

"I think she wants me back now that I'm with someone else."

"Ha, suck it, bitch, you can't have him!"

I smiled at that. "Possessive much?"

She shrugged. "You play tomorrow, right? You got in okay?"

"Yup, just came up to my room after dinner with the boys. Astrid annoyed me, and I wanted to talk to you."

"Okay, about what?"

I shrugged.

"Blaise, are you okay?"

"Baby, I don't know," I sighed and ran my hand down my face.

"Okay...how can I help you?" she asked, her brow furrowing in concern. It was kind of cute, like she actually cared about how I felt. I tried not to think about my heart and brain yelling at me in equal measure.

"Fuck if I know," I admitted.

"Do you want to get back with Astrid?" she asked tactfully. I watched her nervously push a strand of hair behind her ear.

"Fuck no! She broke my heart. She just pissed me off."

She laughed. "Okay, big guy."

"Sorry. I guess..."

"What?"

"Just annoying that she's acting like nothing happened. And..." I trailed off.

I shook my head.

I wasn't about to tell my fake girlfriend I missed her. Or that I didn't care if Astrid wanted me back because the person I wanted was on the other side of the screen. I couldn't tell her I wished I was there to kiss her cute paint-splattered face. Just like I couldn't tell her I wanted to brush her hair behind her ear before kissing all her worries away. Or how much I wished I was holding her in my arms instead of this stiff hotel pillow.

This was supposed to be a no-strings arrangement until the wedding; I wasn't supposed to have these feelings.

"Nothing, sweets. Don't let me keep you up," I finally said.

"Blaise, it's okay. I know we're keeping it casual, and this will be over soon, but we can still be friends."

"Friends?" I asked and raised an eyebrow.

I liked this woman a lot, and I enjoyed spending time with her, but I wasn't sure if we could be friends after this. Was that even possible?

"Just because it's not serious between us doesn't mean we can't still talk," she explained.

"Why didn't you tell me hibiscuses were your favorite flower?"

She fingered the colorful tattoo on her arm and shrugged. "I don't know. They're pretty, though. Oh! I can show you my flower."

I laughed. "Um...is that a euphemism for something?"

She cackled, and I loved how her face scrunched up when she laughed. She carried her phone over to the windowsill in her kitchen to a potted plant with three brightly colored flowers on it. "See my flowers! They're hard to maintain, but they're pretty."

She put a hand over her mouth and yawned.

"Shit, it's getting late. I don't want to keep you."

She smiled at me again, and warmth spread across my chest at the way she made me feel when she smiled at me. Her hazel eyes got bright, and it felt like that smile was made just for me. But I knew it wasn't. It was just my heart playing games with me, making me see what I wanted to see.

"Okay. Good luck in your game tomorrow," she said, and she seemed sincere, like she really wanted me to do well. Again, I was reminded about how Astrid called it my 'little hockey career' and never took me or our relationship seriously.

"Night, sweets," I told Veronica.

I sighed when the call disconnected, and I flopped back down onto my pillow. When it came to Veronica O'Malley, I was so totally fucked.

CHAPTER TWENTY

VERONICA

I yawned while I finished working on the concept artwork for the client I had coming in. Blaise was due back today, but we hadn't made any plans to get together. He called me after the team lost to Carolina. I think he wanted to vent, but it was nice to video chat with him again and see his smiling face. Almost like he was smiling because of me, but I knew that wasn't it. He was a fun guy, but I had to remind myself that there were certain boundaries we didn't want to cross.

Then the team lost again to Florida, which I knew because I actually turned the game on to listen to while I worked on my painting. It was bad, and I let Blaise rant to me about how the special teams weren't working hard enough. I didn't know what special teams were, but I let him vent because he needed someone to listen.

Liv put a coffee down in front of me. I hugged her. "Oh my God, you're an angel."

She smirked at me, her dark eyes twinkling. "That's what all the boys tell me."

I laughed. "Sit with me while I finish this concept art? I feel like I've been an awful friend lately."

She nodded and sat in my tattoo chair. "Why are you so exhausted today?"

I took a sip of my coffee. "Nuh-uh. Tell me about your date last night."

She sighed. "It was the worst."

"Why?" I traced my pen around the lines of the stencil while I waited for her to respond.

"He ordered for me."

I pretended to gag. "Ugh. Why are men? Well, what did he order for you?"

"Wine and steak!" she cried.

I looked up from my work. "You hate both of those things."

"I know! I told him I was veggie and everything. Ugh. Any hot hockey players you want to hook me up with?"

I laughed. "Hmm...not sure. Blaise might have a single brother...actually no, that's Ayden, and I'm not subjecting you to that."

She laughed. "So things with Blaise are good?"

I glared at her. "You know what it's like."

"Hmmm...okay..." she trailed off, unconvinced, and smiled at me like she was up to something.

"What?" I demanded.

"Why are you so tired?" she asked.

"Because I was talking to Blaise last night." She got the giddy look on her face again. "NO!"

"But what if it's turning into something more?"

I shook my head. "It can't."

"It could."

"You read too many romance novels."

I finished with my artwork just in time because my client showed up a few minutes later, standing at the reception desk waiting for Liv. I nodded at her, and she got up to prepare him for his appointment.

As much as I enjoyed my time with Blaise, I knew we would part ways in a couple weeks after asshat's wedding, and that would be that. No muss, no fuss, just the way I preferred.

So why did my chest hurt whenever I thought about it?

"Logan, right?" I asked the lanky redhead standing in front of me and held my hand out toward him.

He smiled at me and shook my hand. "Right. Um... Blaise probably called me Cully, though?"

I nodded. "Yeah, it confused me when you made the appointment. I didn't realize you guys got back already."

Was I upset that Blaise hadn't told me he got back to town?

No.

I wasn't right?

"Oh, we had practice right after we got off the jet. Blaise and Riley were still in the weight room when I took off, but I think they had plans to watch game tape with Cap for the rest of the day."

"Oh, right."

I had no idea what he was talking about.

"I saw the work you did on Benny and Blaise, so I'm excited," Logan said with a grin.

I showed him the stencil. "Okay, you said you wanted a more traditional black and grey piece. What do you think?"

"Yeah, let's do it."

"You sure?"

I loved doing flower tattoos, but when I got the call

Logan wanted to get a rose tattoo done, I had some questions. Not that it was weird for men to want flower tattoos, I did them all the time, but this was his first tattoo.

"It's for my sister," he explained.

"Oh?"

"She died."

"Oh, I'm so sorry."

He shrugged and took his shirt off. Geez, were all these hockey boys made of pure muscle? I could appreciate the male physique, but seeing him shirtless didn't affect me quite as much as when Blaise had his shirt off. Logan looked lanky, but underneath he was lean and athletic, different from Blaise, who had muscles as big as my head.

I put the stencil on his arm and made him look in the mirror to make sure the placement was good. "Remember to breathe, okay? And let me know if you need a break," I said as I turned on my tattoo machine and dipped it into the ink.

He nodded and gritted his teeth. I tried to distract him while I worked, and that seemed to help for a bit.

"Tell me about your sister," I said.

"Her name was Rose."

Ah, now the tattoo choice made sense.

"If you don't mind me asking..." I trailed off as I moved the machine across his skin, etching the flower on his pale white skin.

"It was a car crash," he hissed. I motioned for Liv, and she came over with a bottle of water for him and asked if he wanted to hold her hand.

"Am I that pathetic?" he asked with a laugh.

I shook my head. "You saw the cherry blossom I did on Benny's chest, right?"

He nodded and pretended the needle wasn't hurting. Tattoos hurt. Anyone who told you differently was a liar.

"Pretty sure he nearly broke Rox's hand. That chick takes tattoos like a champ."

That got a smile out of him, and Liv offered her hand again. "I think I'm good," he said.

She smiled at him, her dimples popping out. "Let me know if you need anything, and remember to breathe."

I wiped at his skin and went back in, working through the petals of the flower.

"Her husband was abusive," he admitted in a small voice I barely heard over the sound of the needle.

I felt my eyebrow rise but kept my head bent on my work."Oh, shit. You think he had something to do with it?"

"He was drunk. I guess the cycle repeats itself. I was trying to help her get out."

"Wow, I can't imagine that, man. That must have been hard."

"I have custody of my nephew now."

"Wow, Logan, that's... How do you manage with all the travel?"

He sighed. "My teammates have helped a lot. Nannies, too. Although, I'm desperate for a reliable one. You know anyone good?"

I shook my head. "Sorry, can't help you there. Is it hard being a single dad and playing hockey?"

"Yeah, it's hard, but I know I have to be the best for him."

"That's great, man. He probably needs a good male role model."

He nodded. "I want him to see that men aren't like his dad or my dad, that we can be decent people."

I didn't know what to say, but I thought what he said was admirable. He seemed like a decent guy. Blaise said he didn't know him that well. He was still a rookie, and Logan was worried about staying on the team.

I wiped at his skin and went back in to start the shading. "You doing okay?" I asked.

He nodded. "Good. Blaise said you're good at distracting customers."

"She is," my brother's voice said behind me. "That's looking good."

Logan grimaced. "Painful, though."

"We suffer for our art," I said.

Alex laughed. "Okay, goth girl."

I mentally gave him the finger and finished up. I explained the aftercare treatment to Logan and walked him back over to the front desk. Liv helped him check out and shamelessly flirted with him while I cleaned up my station.

"You got a minute?" Alex asked. He chewed on his bottom lip, the light above him reflecting off his lip ring.

I nodded but hoped this was work stuff and not personal stuff. I wasn't ready to forgive my brother. Not yet.

"You liked Kelly, right?"

Kelly was one of the artists we interviewed last week. She worked at the shop over in Kensington that one of my friends was at. She did a lot of cool pin-up style tattoos, and she would bring a unique style to the shop.

"Sure, I like her style," I said.

Alex nodded. "Yeah, me too. I want to offer her a chair here."

"Okay, cool."

"I think we also need another artist."

I raised an eyebrow. "Are we keeping asshat on?"

"For now."

"Okay. I have another client. I don't have time to chat."

"Veronica?"

"What?" I snapped.

"Don't come in tomorrow."

"But—"

"You need to take your days off," he insisted. "I don't need you burning yourself out."

"Fine," I grumbled.

I had back-to-back clients for the rest of the night until the shop closed at eight. The shop was hectic right now, but I'd rather be busy than hurting for money.

My feet were dragging by the time I walked to the subway and hopped on the regional rail at Suburban Station. Even worse, when I had to walk the four blocks uphill to my apartment. Maybe I should have moved back to the city, but the rent was my main issue. I was saving a lot, living here on my cheap rent. I had to calculate the cost of my commute and see if I was saving enough. I always had a room at Eddie and Alex's, but I didn't want to impose on them.

I was so burnt out, I nearly jumped when I walked up the steps to my porch and saw a man sitting on it in the dark. The light on the porch didn't work anymore. I think my neighbor had control over it, but I never bothered them about it.

"Sweets, it's me," Blaise's voice cut through the fog of my brain. Right as I was about to jab him in the face with my keys.

"Jesus! Blaise, you scared me half to death. A big guy like you can't lurk on a girl's porch."

He hung his head. "Shit, I'm sorry. I tried to call, but you wouldn't answer. I went to the shop, but your brother said you already went home. Guess I beat you here."

I looked at the phone in my hand. Dead.

"It's fine. I was just surprised."

He eyed me calculatingly. "Why are you out of breath?"

"Um...it's a four-block walk uphill from the station."

His gaze seared across mine, and even in the dark, I recognized that look. I had seen that look come across his face on the ice. When an opponent slashed one of his teammates' and got away with it or did something else that I didn't understand because I didn't understand the rules of the game. Blaise was pissed.

"You walked?" he bellowed.

"Calm your tits. I'm a big girl," I argued.

I caught my breath and untangled my keys from around my fingers to unlock the front door. We walked inside, and Blaise locked the deadbolt behind us before following me up the stairs. I dropped my bag on the kitchen floor and couldn't help the smile from spreading across my face when his enormous arms wrapped around my waist, and he nuzzled his face into the crook of my neck.

"Oh, someone missed me," I teased as I felt his hardness poking me in the back. Not like I was going to admit that I also missed it. His cock, not him. I definitely didn't miss my friend with benefits when he was off traveling for his job.

Nope. Not at all.

I didn't miss his scent on my pillows. Or the feel of his arms around me when I woke up the next morning. Or the wicked look in his eyes when he was about to go down on me.

I definitely didn't miss any of that stuff.

I couldn't.

He nosed across my skin, his hot breath teasing the shell of my ear. "Maybe."

I spun in his embrace, and he met me in a kiss I'd been hungry for since he left my bed three days ago. I leaned into that kiss and let my heart have feelings for once. But only when Blaise was taking me to my bed. In the morning light, I would shove those useless feelings back down inside where they belonged.

I woke up alarmed to a loud banging noise...no, a knock. Someone was knocking loudly on my door.

I groaned and turned in the bed, hoping to snuggle down into the warmth of Blaise's chest, but he wasn't there. The banging continued, and I looked at my phone to see it was only eight a.m.

Who was bothering me on my day off?

I groaned and got out of bed, only to walk out into the hallway to not find someone knocking at the door downstairs but to find a sweaty and shirtless blonde giant on the staircase installing a railing.

"Um...Blaise, what the actual fuck are you doing?" I seethed.

He looked up at me and smiled. "Hi, sweets. Sorry if I woke you. I got coffee and bagels from the coffee shop in town."

I glared but walked into the kitchen to retrieve the bribes. Why was he installing a railing on my stairwell?

I grumbled as I sat on my shitty futon in my tiny living room and bit into the French toast bagel. How did he know that was my favorite? And with the apple cinnamon cream cheese from the shop, too. I sipped on my black coffee but kept glaring when he walked into the living room with his shirt still off, looking so good. Fuck him for looking that way.

I waved the bag at him, but he shook his head. "Nah, too many carbs for me. I gotta be serious about training right now."

I glared again and watched him run his fingers through his hair.

"Dude, what the fuck!" I exclaimed

He bent over the couch and gave me a kiss on the cheek. "Eat your breakfast."

"I'm pissed at you," I said, pushing him away.

"Why?"

"Why did you install a railing in my stairwell? I could lose my deposit."

"Sweets, calm down. I can take it down when you move out," he explained and took a sip of his coffee.

I stared at him. That implied we would still be a thing past our expiration date, that he would still have time for me once this was all over.

"I didn't ask you to do that!"

I shoved the bagel into my mouth before I cursed him out anymore.

He knelt in front of me. "How can I make it better?" He bent his head to kiss my naked legs, his hand drifting toward my panties underneath the t-shirt I wore to bed. Or rather, his t-shirt. I wouldn't admit it, but I loved that he left it here so I could wear it every night and think of him. That was bad, very bad.

"Don't," I warned and put the bagel down on the coffee table.

His blonde head was still facing my legs, and his lips burned across my skin. "Let me apologize."

"That's not the point."

He lifted his head. "Baby, I'm sorry. Tell me what I did wrong. I was trying to help you. I worry about you."

"You shouldn't. You're not my boyfriend!"

His jaw ticked, and he stood up abruptly. "Right. Yeah.

Well, I'll call you when I need another appearance from my fake girlfriend."

"Blaise..." I sighed, realizing I had overreacted.

But he was already shrugging on his shirt and pulling on his jacket. He didn't even kiss me goodbye before he clomped down my steps and slammed my front door.

This was supposed to be what I wanted, but it felt like someone had twisted a knife in my chest.

CHAPTER TWENTY-ONE

BLAISE

TJ hit my shin with his stick while I was putting on my gear. I glared at him. "What?"

"What's up with you today?" he asked. He crossed his arms over his chest.

Riley looked up from taping his stick for the hundredth time. "Yeah, man, you were slow in morning skate today. What gives?"

I ground my teeth together. Being on a hockey team was like being in a big family. You spent so much time with this group of guys, you noticed all their quirks. Also nosy as fuck, just like my regular family. Only worse.

"Nothing," I lied while I tied my skates.

"You get into a fight with V?" TJ asked.

I rubbed a hand across my jaw and pulled my helmet on.

"Dude!" Riley exclaimed. "Don't bring that shit to the ice."

I sighed. "Can you guys get off my dick?"

They exchanged a look, and I walked out of the locker room and down the tunnel. Yeah, I was still pissed, but I had to get my head in the game. I didn't know why I was so mad. Maybe because Veronica was right. I wasn't her boyfriend at all. All of this was just so she could get back at her ex and I could get my family to stop worrying about me.

The problem? I cared about her. She was closed off, but those little slivers of herself she slipped through to me had me begging for more. I wanted to be her boyfriend for real, but she didn't want that. I wasn't like her; I couldn't do casual without letting my feelings get in the way.

The music started, and I skated out on the ice. I hit a couple pucks into the net and then got down onto the ice to do stretches next to TJ. He waved at his girl, who gave him a shy smile from behind the glass. I wasn't surprised when Veronica wasn't sitting with her or the other girls. A sour taste formed in my mouth, and my heart wrenched.

TJ nudged me. "Dude, how bad was the fight?"

"How do you know we got into a fight?"

"Because when Max and I fight and I have a home game, sometimes she doesn't show up."

"Really? You guys seem so solid."

He shook his head. "No. I was the last person I thought would work hard to maintain a relationship. I love her, but her PTSD and anxiety can be hard."

I stared at him. "Her what?"

"She has survivor's guilt, and she feels like she's a burden to me. When we first started dating, she tried to break up with me multiple times."

"I had no idea."

She and TJ looked so happy together, but I remembered after graduation, her parents died in a car accident. It was hard enough when I lost my mom; I couldn't imagine what it was like losing both of your parents at once.

"We're good, but we had to learn to talk with each other and work through our issues. We go to therapy and talk it out. Whatever you did, apologize and listen to what's bothering V."

I didn't think I would get pearls of wisdom from TJ of all the guys on the team. It didn't matter if I apologized; the problem was that I had blurred the line, and Veronica showed me where it was again. Maybe it was better this way. Now it wouldn't seem as bad when I told everyone we broke up.

"Don't let it affect your game," TJ warned.

I chewed on my mouthguard as I skated towards the bench. My line wasn't starting tonight. Coach paired Riley and me together with the second line of TJ-Benny-Noah. I watched with bated breath as the puck dropped, and our captain got possession quickly. It was still early in the season, but this team was thirsty for the cup again. Now that I was wearing the red and black, I wanted to bring them the cup again. To prove to the city they took on my contract for a reason. That I was worthy of the logo on my chest.

Tonight we were playing the Pittsburgh Miners, who I grew up hating, so it was going to be an intense game. It was always fun when it was The Battle of Pennsylvania.

G tried to break out of the neutral zone, but Logan and McCarthy weren't strong enough to defend. G passed to Hallsy, who broke out and skated up the ice to advance toward Pittsburgh's goal. A Miner forward stole the puck and got it out of his zone.

I cheered on my teammates from the bench until it was my turn to hop onto the ice. McCarthy was too slow getting to the bench, and since TJ had the puck in play, we got whistled for too many men on the ice. Riley tried to argue with the refs since he was an Alternate Captain, but they weren't having it and sent TJ to the box. The game was still scoreless, and now the Miners had the man advantage.

"Holmsy, let's kill this, yeah?" Riley tried to pump me up.

I grinned and nodded, watching the Miners' captain in particular. I was going to do everything in my power to be a nuisance to that guy and not let him score on Metzy. It was time to get to work.

We killed the penalty and then some, winning the game 3-2. I didn't even want to go to the bar, but TJ dragged me along.

"Woo hoo, another Bulldogs win!" TJ shouted.

His girlfriend pulled him to her, trying to get him to calm down. That guy could be a little much sometimes, but he was always a fun time. Max knew how to placate him, though, because now they were making out against the bar.

Next to me, Noah wrapped his arms around Dinah, resting his chin on top of her head. Dinah wrinkled her nose in TJ and Max's direction. "Gross."

"Lovey, you remember how we were when we first started?" Noah asked her. "Remember when T caught us making out against your front door?"

The tiny woman laughed. "Oh, yeah. I wanted to fuck you senseless, but you wanted to take me to dinner first."

I smiled at them.

Dinah looked up at me with a serious look in her eye. "Are you and Veronica okay?"

"Why?" I grumbled and took a sip of my beer to avoid the question.

She cast a glance toward her fiancé, who shrugged. "Because she didn't come to the game."

"So?" I tried to play coy. "She doesn't have to come to every game."

"Okay, but—"

"D, can you please drop it?" I snapped at her.

She looked taken aback at my snippy attitude, and Noah glared at me. Noah was a mild-mannered guy. Quiet and a little sensitive, but a good dude. Right now, he looked at me like he was ready to drop the gloves, and I felt like a dick. I saw Dinah squeeze his hand in warning.

"She wouldn't answer any of my calls. You know you can talk to us, okay?" Dinah reassured me.

"I know," I sighed and ran a hand down my face. "I'm sorry."

"Bro, what's up?" Noah asked.

"Nothing. It's fine," I lied.

"Blaise, what did you do?" Dinah demanded.

For a cute little thing, Dinah Lace could be scary.

"I was trying to be helpful," I grumbled.

I still didn't get why Veronica had been pissed at me. I hated that she didn't have a railing on her steps, but it was easy enough for me to fix it for her. All I had been doing was trying to help her out, but she lashed out at me.

"With what?" Dinah asked.

"You've been to her place, right?"

She nodded.

"I installed a railing in her stairwell."

Noah and Dinah shared a look.

I took a sip of my beer. "What?"

Noah rubbed his hand across his bushy beard. "Bro, that's like a husband move."

Dinah nodded. "I love Veronica, but her ex hurt her."

"Okay, but what does that have to do with me putting up a railing for her?"

"Because it scared her."

I picked at the label on my beer. "I don't understand."

"Bro, because it's the type of shit you do for your wife!" Noah argued.

Dinah nodded. "It might have seemed like a simple gesture to you, but to Veronica, that felt big."

"It wasn't that big of a deal," I muttered.

"To her, it was," Dinah went on. "Look, Veronica has walls upon walls up. She doesn't let people get close to her. She even keeps me at arm's length and our brothers are married. If someone gets too close, she pushes them away."

"This is because of that asshole, right?"

She nodded. "I hate that he made her afraid to open herself up to love again."

"So what do I do?"

"Give her some time," Noah offered.

"Let her cool off. Maybe some space will help," Dinah suggested.

I took another swing of my beer and mulled it over.

They were right, but not for the reason they thought. Veronica was not and would never be my girlfriend. That had been our arrangement, and I had to remind my heart where the line was so I'd stop crossing it. After the wedding, we'd go our separate ways; it didn't matter if she was pissed at me right now.

I had to keep reminding my heart none of this was real. To stop blurring the lines between what was fake and what was real. Veronica was supposed to help me get over Astrid; I wasn't supposed to fall in love with her in the process. Space would remind my heart of that.

CHAPTER TWENTY-TWO

VERONICA

I hadn't heard from Blaise in a week. The wedding was this Friday, so I should have been freaking out, but I wasn't because I had no one to blame but myself. I had to kick him out and show him the imaginary boundary between us. I couldn't have him thinking our arrangement could turn into something more.

So why did it feel like someone was jabbing a knife inside me?

"Hey," Olivia greeted.

I looked up from wiping down my tattoo chair. "What's up?" I asked.

"Are you okay?" she asked, giving me a concerned look. The same one she'd been giving me all week every time she caught me checking my phone and sighing in disappointment.

"Yeah, why?"

"You look like someone kicked your puppy."

"I'm fine."

The bell rang on the shop door. I didn't have another appointment for a while, so I wasn't that concerned about it. She looked over at the door and then turned back to me with a grin. "Ooh, I see."

Before I could ask what, a six-foot-three blonde giant stood in front of me, looking like I had kicked *his* puppy. My traitorous heart skipped a beat when I saw his apologetic face.

"Hi, sweets," Blaise said.

I gave him a tight smile, but inside, my heart was dancing around because I secretly loved that he called me that. And I missed him. I wasn't supposed to miss him. He was just my fuck buddy/fake boyfriend, who I was going to lose after this weekend. My heart wasn't supposed to flutter when he smiled and purred that pet name at me. I also wasn't supposed to be wearing the Bulldogs t-shirt he left behind because it smelled of him and made me miss him less. I wasn't supposed to get attached. That was never our deal.

"Hi," I said stiffly and wiped at my chair, even though it was already clean.

He held up a brown paper bag with grease at the bottom. "I come bearing gifts. Can we talk?"

"Take your break and talk with your man!" my brother called from his station across the room.

I glared at him, but he and Eddie both gave me cheeky grins.

"Jesus, make up already. She's been insufferable," Eddie chimed in.

I groaned but stood up. "We can talk in the office."

Blaise followed me down the hall into the office. He sat down in the chair in front of the desk, and I went behind it. I shuffled some papers off the desk, and Blaise handed over the cheesesteak. He really knew the way to this Philly girl's heart. I could appreciate the effort.

He took out a healthier grilled chicken wrap while I chowed down on my greasy sandwich.

"I'm sorry," he said.

"You didn't have to ghost me."

"I was trying to give you space."

I hadn't exactly reached out to him either, so that was fair.

He ran a hand through his hair. It was getting longer, and I had to admit I liked the look. I may have stalked his social media and saw his hair used to be longer, and I was into it. Dinah called it 'flow,' whatever that meant.

"I'm sorry. I shouldn't have freaked out on you. I understand if you don't want to come with me to the wedding," I said.

He set down his wrap on the desk. "Come here," he ordered.

I put my cheesesteak down and wiped my mouth. "What?"

He patted his lap, and I obeyed him. I got up from my chair and crossed over to him. He pulled me by the belt loops of my jeans down onto him, so I was straddling his tree trunk thighs.

His thumb caressed my cheek, and I tried not to melt into a puddle at the gentle gesture. "I don't go back on my word. Okay, sweets?"

"Okay..."

"Geez, kiss me already."

A laugh bubbled up inside me, but then he slanted his mouth on mine. I gave into the kiss, letting his tongue slide inside and his meaty hands run down my sides until he gripped my ass.

He kissed down my neck and sucked on my skin. I moaned and angled my head to give him better access.

"I missed you," he murmured against my skin. I should have pushed him away and reminded him what this was, but my heart was doing an Irish jig. I had missed him too, and I hated that we weren't talking.

I felt his cock pressed up against me, and it might have gone further had the office door not swung open, and my brother barged in. He glanced between the two of us, his face pale with shock, but then he laughed his ass off.

What a cock blocking dick.

"You should have gone up to the apartment if you were gonna do that," Alex teased.

I groaned and hid my face in Blaise's neck. It wasn't the first time my brother had walked in on something compromising. I felt Blaise's chest rumble beneath me from his laughter, but he didn't bother to take his hands off my ass. In fact, I think he squeezed it a little harder.

"Why do our siblings keep interrupting us?" Blaise grumbled into my neck.

I turned around to fix my brother with a glare. "What do you want? I'm in the middle of lunch."

"Is that what the kids are calling it these days?" Alex asked with a laugh.

"Eat a dick."

"Mmm, I probably will later, but we got a walk-in and could use your help."

I groaned. "Fine."

Alex was still laughing as he walked out the door. The last thing I wanted to do was get off Blaise's lap. His cock was pressed hard against me, and I was itching to have it inside me again. His cock was perfect, and I missed it.

Blaise shifted me off his lap and adjusted himself in his pants.

I got up and brushed myself off, trying to will my horny thoughts away. "Sorry, baby."

His ocean-blue eyes sparkled at the pet name I let slip. "S'okay, sweets. I have to travel tomorrow, anyway."

I tried not to look disappointed by that. "But you can still come on Friday, right?"

"Of course. I get in early on Friday morning. I can make it."

I ran a hand through my hair. "I'm going to get my tips re-dyed."

"Okay."

"I'm thinking of a different color."

He frowned for a second but then nodded. "What color? Maybe I can wear a matching tie."

I put a finger on my chin in thought. "Purple."

"Send me a photo when you get it done."

He stood up and bent down to kiss me. He smacked my ass lightly. "Get back to work."

I glared at him. "I only like that when I'm over your knee, and you're about to fuck my brains out."

"Fuuucckkk..." he drawled out. "Come over for dinner tonight, please?"

I smiled at him. "Maybe I should make you wait until the wedding."

"Sweets, please. I want to have you as much as possible until..." I knew why he trailed off. After the wedding, we were done. We would tell everyone we broke up and went our separate ways, but a part of me didn't want us to end.

I reached up on my tip-toes and kissed him. "Okay, I'll come over tonight."

I walked Blaise out and kissed him again at the door. "Oh my God, please go before I drag you upstairs."

When I walked back to the reception area, Olivia and a redheaded woman stood at the desk fanning themselves. "Whoa. That's quite the man you have there," the redhead remarked with a smile.

I smiled and put my hand out to her. "Yeah, he is. I'm Veronica. What are you looking to do today?"

I fell onto the bed face-first, panting. Blaise laughed from behind me. His big hand soothed down my back and slapped my ass as he pulled out and got rid of the condom. I laid my head on the pillow and smiled when he returned to the bed and pulled me into his chest.

I trailed a finger across his chest hair. "I was really wound up," I told him.

He kissed the top of my head. "You missed me."

I held my forefinger and thumb together. "Maybe just your cock."

"Liar."

I laughed into his chest, sighing at the feeling of being back in his arms. I had missed him so much. I really shouldn't have, but I did.

His phone buzzed on the bedside table, and his chest rumbled with a laugh.

"What?"

"Nothing," he said too quickly.

I peered up at him. "What?"

"My dad said and I quote, 'Tell your girlfriend to stop screaming so loud.'"

"Blaise! I didn't know Hal was home. You told me you wanted to hear me scream."

He shrugged. "Me neither. I thought he was at the bar tonight."

I laid on my back and put a hand over my face. "I can never look your dad in the eye ever again."

He shrugged. "I'm one of six. You think my older brothers didn't pull this shit before? I told you, my dad doesn't have those hangups."

I pulled my hand off my face. "But I do! I would have tried to be quiet if I knew he could hear me. I'm dead. I cannot come back from this."

He chuckled beside me.

"Maybe you should get your own place," I suggested.

As much as I loved having Blaise at my place, the commute was killer when he had to travel all the time. A lot of times, it was easier to come back to his dad's. Especially if I was already in the city.

He grunted.

I gave him a suspicious look. "Why do you still live at home?"

He rubbed a hand across his jaw. "I thought he needed me, and I didn't want him to be alone. Dad and I haven't always seen eye-to-eye. We clash so much because we're too much alike."

"How so?"

He grimaced. "You know why I got traded, right?"

I shook my head.

I barely understood the rules of hockey; I hoped he didn't ask me to understand the business side of it. My brain immediately shut off when Dinah and the girls talked contracts. Numbers and legalese? No, thank you.

"Because I let my breakup take hold of me. I let my

emotions cloud the game, so Toronto traded me. Dad threw it in my face that he did the same thing when Mom died."

"Maybe it was good you moved back home so you could hash those things out, then? Blaise, I miss my dad so much. Some days I want to call him up and ask for his advice, but I can't. You're lucky you still have time with Hal."

He leaned onto his side and cupped my cheek. "Oh, sweets, I'm sorry. Tell me about your dad."

I grinned as I told him about my dad. Paddy O'Malley was such a rough and tumble blue-collar guy, with tattoos all up and down his arms and legs. But my dad was a total softie. He never pressured Alex or me to join the family business. He actually wanted us to do something more stable, but when Alex and I followed in his footsteps, he couldn't have been more proud.

While I told Blaise all of this, he listened intently beside me and twirled my hair around his finger. And I knew he was actually listening and not pretending.

"How did your dad die?" he asked.

I scoffed. "Being a stubborn man! He didn't take care of himself. Heart attack. I had told him time and again to listen to his doctors. It was before Seth left. Seth had been there for me through that all, but now I wonder if he had been pretending then. Had he always been terrible? What is it about me that makes everyone leave?"

Blaise pressed a kiss to my forehead. "Oh, sweets, no. Your dad didn't leave you on purpose. And Seth? Fuck him. He doesn't know what he's missing. We'll show him, okay?"

I nodded and wiped the tears from my eyes. I barely talked about my dad these days, but it felt nice to talk to Blaise about it. Even though I really shouldn't have.

I snuggled into his chest, and he let me, holding me like we did this every single night. Like this was our life.

"I looked at houses last week," he admitted.

"So you *do* want to move out?"

"I'm not in a rush, but maybe I should find my own place. Dad's dating again..."

I looked up at him with interest. "Really?"

He grimaced. "Yeah...I might have heard some shit I didn't want to hear when he thought I was on the road last week."

I laughed into his chest. "Oh, sorry, baby."

He shrugged. "Guess that's what I get for being twenty-five and moving back in with my dad. But I want him to be happy. Mom would want him to be happy."

I squeezed his bicep. "You're a good son."

He shrugged. "Not always."

He stroked my phoenix tattoo on my hip and kissed my neck, and I knew what that not-so-subtle move meant. I glanced down and rolled my eyes at his cock, already standing at attention again. This man had a lot of stamina, and I didn't hate it. But I needed to pump the brakes.

"Baby, stop," I said.

"Why?"

"Because I don't know if I can go again."

He furrowed his brow and looked pained. "Sweets, did I hurt you tonight?"

"Well...I asked you to, but I'm sore."

He kissed down my chest, working his way down my body. "Can I help you with that?"

"Maybe..." I said cheekily and grinned as he continued to kiss down my torso.

I ran my hand through his blonde locks as he situated himself between my legs. He kissed my thighs, and I hitched in a breath as he got closer to my center. "Tell me to stop if you don't want me to."

I shoved his head down to my clit, and he chuckled into my pussy. I was sore but not sore enough that if he wanted to pleasure me, I was going to say no.

"Mmm...so good. I love tasting you, sweets," he moaned. He lifted up his head a bit to give me a cheeky grin, and then he went back to work.

I leaned back and gave into the pleasure, letting this man unravel my body and soul. Our time was quickly expiring, but I didn't care at this moment. Not when he feasted on me like it would be the very last time. Like he needed to draw out my pleasure for his own survival. I was sore and well-fucked, but it didn't stop me from arching my back and letting the pleasure take over.

"Fuuuck," I moaned and gripped his hair.

He lifted his head up slightly. "One last time for me, sweets. Come for me one more time."

All I did was nod, and then my orgasm exploded behind my eyes as he dipped his head back down and sucked on my clit.

I was done for. So done for. This man had broken me. And I didn't care. Not when his name was a scream on my lips. And not when the waves of pleasure washed over me. Future Veronica would deal with those pesky feelings later.

CHAPTER TWENTY-THREE

BLAISE

I moaned as the steak hit my tastebuds.

TJ kicked my foot under the table. "Dude, don't come in your pants over there."

I winked at him. "I might. We played a good game tonight."

"Fuck yeah, we did! Too bad, though," TJ mused.

"Why?" Benny asked.

"Because shutouts make me horny," TJ explained.

Benny shrugged. "That's what video chat sex is for."

Noah's face got bright red, and TJ gagged. Sometimes I thought Benny said shit like that to annoy TJ, but I roomed next door to Benny last night. I definitely heard some shit when I was trying to sleep that I didn't need to hear. He and Rox might be the horniest couple on the team. I wished I didn't know that.

"Dinah doesn't like that," Noah said, but he was still beet red.

Benny chewed thoughtfully. "Then get her a new vibrator. That worked with Rox."

TJ looked like he wanted to throw up.

I high-fived Benny. "Oh, co-sign, dude. I love using vibrators on women."

"Right?" Benny agreed. "It's so hot!"

"The hottest," I agreed.

"They beg for your cock," Benny laughed.

"It's the best," I agreed again.

TJ downed his scotch faster.

Noah's eyes were wide with shock. "I don't think D even has one of those."

I tipped back my head with a laugh. "Yeah, she does."

Noah shook his head. "No way, dude."

"How do you know?" I asked.

"I don't," he admitted and chewed his lip thoughtfully. "We're kinda vanilla."

"Nothing wrong with vanilla. You like what you like," I said.

"Check her top drawer when you get home," Benny said. "No way she doesn't have one when we're on the road all the time. I had to get Rox a new one because she broke her last one."

TJ gnashed his teeth. "How can one wash their brain out? I don't want to know that."

I took a swig of my scotch and felt my phone buzz in my pocket. I couldn't help the smile quirking up on my lips at the selfie from Veronica. Her black hair now had dark purple at the ends, and she was sitting on her bed wearing my Bulldogs t-shirt. I don't know what it was about women wearing my t-shirts or my hoodies, but this possessive streak in me always loved it. It would be even better if she was wearing my jersey again.

VERONICA: Does it look okay? I think she went too dark.

ME: Banging sweets!

VERONICA: You sure about going to this wedding tomorrow?

ME: Can't wait.

TJ kicked me again. "You and V make up?"

I ate more of my dinner. "Yeah, we did, for now."

"What do you mean?" TJ asked, his hazel eyes narrowing at me.

I sighed. "Me being away all the time's hard for her."

The three other guys nodded.

"Yeah, it's tough on them, but if she loves you, she'll make it through," Noah said.

Benny pointed his fork at me accusingly. "You've told her you love her, right?"

I shook my head. "Umm...we're still not there yet."

"Hmm. Didn't take me long with Rox," Benny said and raised his dark eyebrows at me.

TJ waved both him and Noah off. "Neither of you count. Noah sat there and pined for Dinah for years, and Benny, you eye fucked my sister for three years while you both pretended to hate each other."

Benny elbowed the smaller man. "Okay. It take you long with Max?"

"Well...not too long, but we took it slow. Max is shy," TJ explained.

That much I knew. Max had been painfully shy in high school, but I always thought that was because of her uber-religious upbringing.

"Holmsy, what gives?" Noah asked.

"Nothing, just thinking out loud. Besides, we have that wedding tomorrow."

"Wedding sex is the best!" TJ cheered.

My phone buzzing in my pocket distracted me from the conversation.

VERONICA: Call me before you go to bed?

ME: Give me a few minutes?

VERONICA: K!

When I looked up, TJ and Benny both gave me a grin.

"Get out of here and go call your girl," Benny teased.

"You guys are the worst," I teased back and threw some bills down on the table. I downed my scotch and took off upstairs. I got a quick shower and laid on the bed shirtless before hitting call on my video chat app.

Veronica's cute face appeared blurry at first, but then she came into focus. She smiled at me, and it made my chest hurt, but in a good way.

Damn, I missed her.

"Aw, sweets, your hair looks better on video."

She pushed her hair behind her ear and gave me a shy smile. "Thanks. What time does your flight get in tomorrow?"

I leaned back on the bed, putting an arm behind my head. "Early, don't worry, I won't miss it."

She nodded.

She was sitting on her bed with her legs crossed, and she was definitely not wearing panties as I got a quick view of her pussy. I wished she was here with me, lying in my arms and kissing me. Even if we weren't in a relationship, this traveling thing sucked. I don't know how I did it for so long with Astrid. Maybe that said something about our relationship because I never longed for Astrid the way I did for Veronica.

"Sorry, didn't mean to go all girlfriend on you," she said. "Just wanted to figure out some things. The wedding starts at four, so we should be good."

She looked nervous.

"Sweets, we don't have to go if you don't want to. You don't owe that asshole anything," I reassured her.

"I have to go. I have to show him he didn't break me when he left me," she insisted, her voice cracking a little.

I hated that this douche-canoe made her feel like she wasn't worthy of love. If I were home, I would have folded her into my arms until she felt better. But I wasn't. I was alone and horny in my hotel room.

"Do you still love him?"

She shook her head. "Absolutely not. It just proved to me love isn't real. Everyone leaves in the end. So what's the point?"

I frowned at that. I wished I could get her to accept my love, but she had been firm for so long that we had an expiration date. Nothing I did would convince her otherwise.

She wiped at her eyes, and that set my anger ablaze. She might say she didn't still love him, but what he did had affected her so much. I was angry for her, and I wasn't sure how I was going to attend this wedding without trying to drop the gloves with that asshat. How could he have done that to her? He took the coward's way out of not even telling her to her face, and that pissed me off even more.

"Sweets..."

"Please, Blaise, don't give me that pity. It's the truth."

"V..."

"I gotta go. I'll see you tomorrow," she told me quickly and then hung up.

I hated that I was in Buffalo, and I couldn't comfort her the way I wanted to. I wanted to hold her in my arms and dry her tears. She didn't want my pity, and she didn't want my love, and I wasn't sure what pissed me off more. Going to this wedding was a bad idea, but pretending we were dating was an even worse one. I wasn't sure how I was going to let her go after this.

CHAPTER TWENTY-FOUR

VERONICA

I twirled around in the living room of Alex and Eddie's apartment. "How does it look?" I asked them.

Alex and Eddie weren't much for fashion, but they were good at telling me if I looked like shit. Brothers were so great! Thank god for Olivia. She helped style my hair and did my makeup.

"I think he's gonna shit a brick when he sees you," Eddie said with a big grin.

"Who's the 'he' in this situation? Seth? Or Blaise?" Alex teased.

I rolled my eyes. "Blaise!"

My brother walked over to me and smoothed down the skirt of my black dress. "Look at you, little goth girl in black again."

I stuck out my tongue. "It was Olivia approved."

Olivia beamed from her perch on the couch. "She looks so sexy in that."

"She does!" Eddie agreed. "Blaise won't know what hit him."

My phone buzzed, and I pulled it out of my purse, smiling at the text from Blaise that he was outside waiting for me. I slid my feet into the black wedge heels Olivia forced me to wear. Blaise would still tower over me despite wearing them.

"Can you even walk in those?" Eddie asked.

I shrugged. "I'm gonna try."

"Take a jacket, will you?" Alex urged.

I shrugged on my signature leather jacket. "Okay, Dad!"

Alex put an arm around Eddie and smiled when Eddie kissed his temple. They were such a cute couple, and I loved that I got a second annoying brother out of that surprise marriage. Actually, three if I counted Eddie's brothers, Frankie and Tony, too.

"Don't do anything we wouldn't do," Eddie teased.

"What, like get drunk married in Vegas?" I teased back.

Alex shrugged and looked at Olivia and Eddie. "We like Blaise, yes?"

Olivia nodded. "They would have such cute babies."

"The cutest," Alex agreed.

"Aw, can you imagine Blaise putting their little ones on skates?" Eddie cooed.

"So cute," Alex agreed.

I gave them all the finger. "Okay, leaving now. Stop planning my non-existent wedding and babies."

I raced down the steps of the apartment, finding Blaise leaning up against his car with a sly grin on his face. He looked amazing in the nicely tailored black suit with the dark purple tie that matched my hair perfectly.

Blaise whistled at me, and his eyes walked up my body. "Damn, girl."

"You think it's okay?" I asked nervously.

"Okay?" he asked. "I'm trying to figure out how to get you out of that dress before we get there."

He opened the passenger door of his car, and I lifted the bottom of my dress so it didn't drag on the ground when I got inside. He waited for me to get situated before closing the door. He ran around to the driver's side, and we took off.

"Do you want me to drive back tonight so you can drink?" I asked.

The wedding was up in Chester County, so it was a bit of a drive, and I was pretty sure Blaise had a home game tomorrow.

"Nah, I got a hotel room," he explained.

"You did? You didn't have to do that."

"Hey, if this is it, I want to make it last tonight."

"Hope you brought the lube!" I joked.

He smirked as he got on the highway. "I did."

I laughed but ended up being quiet for most of the ride. There was a sour feeling in my stomach whenever I thought about this being my last night with him.

I didn't want to admit it, but I didn't want things to end between us. I hadn't felt this way about someone since Seth. I had been so concerned with showing Blaise the line that I ended up crossing it myself.

The timing was all wrong. Blaise just got out of a long-term relationship, and he wasn't looking for anything serious right now. After tonight, he was done with me, and even though I said we could still be friends, I didn't think we were going to see each other after this.

I frowned when I saw a text from the groom.

SETH: Are you really coming?

ME: You invited me.

SETH: I was just being polite.

ME: Don't worry, I'm not going to tell her she was the other woman.

He stopped texting after that.

"You okay, sweets?" Blaise asked but didn't take his eyes off the road.

"Fine," I muttered.

I was not fine, but I couldn't tell him what was wrong.

He didn't ask again, and I wondered if this was a good idea. Why did I come to my ex's wedding?

Before I knew it, we arrived at the venue. I barely took my seatbelt off before Blaise had my door open and offered me his hand. I took it with a smile, and he wrapped his arms around my waist.

"You look gorgeous," he said and then slanted his mouth on mine in a kiss that left me craving more. He nosed against my neck. "Can we skip the wedding and go bang in the hotel room?"

I slapped his chest playfully. "You can wait, you horndog."

He gave me a cheeky grin and threaded his hand in mine. We walked into the church together and took a seat in the back. Blaise unclasped his hand from mine, but only so he could lay it on my thigh. I loved that possessive move, like he was claiming me as his own.

We endured watching the ceremony, and it was a nice service. Lily's dress was gorgeous, and I even laughed when the baby cried during the 'if anyone has any reason these two shouldn't be wedded' part. The baby was really cute, and I wondered if Seth had changed. Maybe becoming a father had changed his priorities. That made the knife twist in my heart again because I thought we were going to have that together.

What was so wrong with me that everyone left?

Blaise threaded his hand through my smaller one again while I choked back my tears. It didn't matter if I really liked him; ending this after tonight was a good idea. It kept me from getting hurt again. I wanted a family and a happily ever after, but I didn't want it more than my desire to protect my fragile heart.

I let Blaise take me to the cocktail hour, where I downed two vodka cranberries in a row. People kept coming up to Blaise to ask him about being a hockey player and to tell him he needed to block the puck more. Like he didn't know he needed to do that. I barely understood hockey, and even I knew that. He wore a bright smile, but I could tell it was annoying him. His jaw ticked, and he gripped his beer, but he was charming with everyone who came up to him.

I was thankful when we got ushered to our tables for dinner. Somehow we got seated at a table with Seth's sister, Molly.

She hugged me. "I can't believe you actually came."

"I think I did it out of spite," I admitted bitterly.

Molly laughed, but others at the table gave me uneasy looks. I drank my third drink of the night. Blaise ran his hand over the back of my neck, massaging me lightly. He leaned over and pressed a kiss below my ear. "Behave," he whispered.

Molly smiled at me. "You look fantastic, Roni. Everything happens for a reason."

Blaise took my hand and kissed the back of it. He was great at this fake boyfriend shit. "That's true, sweets. We wouldn't have met if he hadn't left."

Maybe it was all the alcohol, but I practically melted at that.

Molly fanned herself. "Damn, girl. You leveled up."

I smiled at Blaise. "Yeah, I guess I did."

I felt eyes on me, so I finished my drink and made a trip to the bathroom. When I was washing my hands, I heard a baby crying. I turned and saw Lily sitting on one of the couches with the baby against her chest. The baby was crying her little heart out while her mama struggled to get her dress sleeve down.

I walked over to her. "Do you need help?"

"Please."

I sat beside her and pulled at the zipper on the back of her dress, and helped her pull down one of her sleeves. She put her baby on her exposed boob. "Come on, Rosie, just latch on, please," she begged the tiny thing in her arms who continued wailing.

"Why aren't your bridesmaids helping you?" I asked.

She sighed. "Because they are all a bunch of selfish B-I-T-C-H-E-S. Thanks. I figured you'd be the last person to help me."

"Are you okay?" I asked.

She shook her head. "No. This little stinker doesn't want to latch on. It makes me feel like I'm not a good mother. Like she knows I don't know what the F-U-C-K I am doing."

I laughed at her spelling out the curse words. The baby finally started to feed, and I stroked her little blonde head. "I don't think that's true. She's really cute."

Lily beamed. "And she knows it! Thanks, I appreciate it. Seth's zero help with the baby. I have to beg him to change diapers just so I can get a shower."

I bit my tongue. That wasn't a surprise, and the selfish

part of me felt like I had dodged a bullet. Then I felt like an asshole because this was supposed to be her happy day, and I was giddy I wasn't stuck with her husband.

A tug on my scalp pulled me out of my thoughts. "Ow!" I yelped.

"Rosie!" Lily scolded, and I found a tiny hand pulling on my long hair. Lily gestured to her short blonde hair. "Why I went for the 'mom-bob.' I love your hair. It's so cute that Blaise matched it with his tie. You two seem happy."

I nodded, afraid if I said anything, I'd tell her the truth.

"Honestly, I only think Seth asked you to come because of your hockey player boyfriend."

I laughed. "Yeah, I kind of figured. Blaise is a good sport."

I unclenched my hair from the baby's tight grip, and Lily pulled the baby off her boob. Lily burped the baby, and we laughed at how loud it was. I helped her pull her sleeve back up and zipped her up.

"Thanks, Veronica. I guess I found out who my real friends were when I got pregnant."

"You looked like you needed help."

"Can I ask you a favor?"

"Sure."

"Can you watch the baby for me for like ten minutes? I have to get pictures done, but I had to feed her first."

I took the baby out of her arms and held her to my chest. "It's Rosie, right?"

"Rose, but we call her Rosie."

"Hi, little Rosie," I cooed at the tiny baby in my arms, and she immediately pulled at my hair again. "Yup, knew that one was happening."

"You don't mind?" Lily asked. This poor woman. All her friends were useless, and she needed the help.

"I love babies," I said, and I tickled the baby's tiny belly. Rosie closed her eyes, and I held her tightly against my chest. "And she's so cute. Go get your pictures done, okay?"

Lily smiled and kissed the top of Rosie's head. "I owe you one."

CHAPTER TWENTY-FIVE

BLAISE

My eyes widened when I saw Veronica returning from the bathroom with a baby in her arms. What the fuck? Also, wow, she looked like a natural at it. Was it weird that it got me excited? Probably. I took the diaper bag from her and helped her back into her seat without jostling the baby. She was sleeping against Veronica's chest and looked so cute.

"Who gave you a baby?" I asked, amused.

"My sister-in-law," the brunette Molly, who had been sitting next to us, answered.

"You want her?" Veronica asked.

The other woman laughed. "Nah, if you got her to sleep, keep her. She hates me. She always cries when I try to hold her."

I stroked the baby's head. She was really cute. Veronica had this smile on her face that I'd never seen before.

"Do you want kids?" I blurted out and then wanted to kick myself for asking.

"I did," she muttered, and then her smile faded as she stared down at the little baby in her arms.

"You don't anymore?" I asked. I wanted kids and a family, but after Astrid broke up with me, I wasn't planning that anytime soon.

Veronica looked around at the strangers at the table cautiously. "I thought I was going to marry my high school sweetheart, but then a week before my wedding, he left. What do you think?"

The baby woke to Veronica's loud outburst and fussed. Veronica's face crumbled, and I knew she felt like an asshole for waking the baby. I held out my hands, and she passed her over.

"Hi, sweetheart," I cooed.

I was good with babies—being one of six helped with that. I bounced the little girl in my arms, and she seemed to settle down.

Veronica went back to sucking down her drink, and it struck me that all of this was a terrible idea. We shouldn't have come to this wedding. I could clearly see how it was affecting Veronica. She was not okay. We shouldn't have pretended to be together for all these weeks or decided on having casual sex when we knew it was going to end tonight. This was all a bad idea, and I went with it because she was hot. I thought I'd be okay with leaving her behind after this, but I wanted something real with her. I was an all-or-nothing guy, and she didn't want that.

"Aw, there's my little girl," Lily said from behind me.

The baby cooed in confusion at the sound of her mother's voice. "Okay, sweetheart, time to go back to Mommy," I said and handed her off.

Lily hefted the diaper bag over her shoulder. "Thanks, you two. I appreciate it."

I stood up from my seat and held my hand out to Veronica. "Come on, sweets, let's dance."

She smiled and took my hand. We danced for a while and had a good time. I was glad because her sour mood had improved when she got on the dance floor with me. I held her close during a slow song, and it was nice to be pressed up against her. In those heels, she was closer to my height, but I still had to bend my head to her lips when she tried to say something to me.

"Do you want to get out of here now?" she asked.

Hell yeah, I did. I twirled her off the dance floor and got our coats. "You only have your leather jacket?"

She nodded.

I shrugged off my coat and pulled it around her. She gave me a small, shy smile, and I tugged her hand along beside me. We checked into the hotel as quickly as possible, but as soon as we got into the elevator, my lips were on her neck. She moaned and melted into me. I was so glad our room was only on the fourth floor, any higher, and I might have done something illegal.

As soon as we got to the room, I shedded our coats and stripped off my suit jacket. She undid my tie, but I pressed her up against the door. Her fingers slid through my hair as we kissed like we were dying for each other's touch. My hands traveled down her body, caressing her perfect tits and groaning into her neck.

She pushed the skirt of her dress up and out of the way. My heart thudded in my chest because the vixen wasn't wearing underwear; she was bare from the waist down.

"Fuck..." I moaned and pressed a finger lightly against her clit. She arched her back, and I slid my finger down across her wetness. "I love how wet you get, sweets."

"Mmm...all for you."

"I'm so hungry for you."

"I want your cock inside me. Right now."

I pumped my fingers inside her. "You looking for a spanking tonight?"

"Mmmhmm," she moaned as she ground her hips against my hand.

"Naughty girl," I teased and dropped to my knees. I spread her legs and drawled my tongue across her pussy. Her hands gripped my hair as I explored her nice and slow. "Beg for me, you naughty girl."

She made an annoyed noise in her throat, and I continued my slow pace back to her clit. "Please," she pleaded. "I want you."

I pumped my fingers inside her while I licked slowly at that sweet nub. When I felt her walls contract around my fingers, I wrapped my lips around her clit. If this was my last night with her, I was going to make it count. I'd give her all the pleasure she could ever want.

She shook against the door, moaning my name as her orgasm flowed out of her while I sucked long and hard on her clit. I stood up, and she slowly opened her eyes. She gave me a devilish grin and pushed me further inside the room. I grinned as she guided me to the bed and pushed me to sit on it.

She reached behind her and unzipped her dress, letting it fall to the floor. I had to bite my fist. She hadn't been wearing a bra either, so now she was bearing herself to me, and if I hadn't been hard when I went down on her, I was now.

She smiled at me and threw my tie to the floor. I let her undress me, her delicate hands undoing all the buttons on my dress shirt. She peeled back the material from my chest, and I shrugged it off, letting it fall to the floor. Her manicured hand traced the lines of the hibiscus tattoos on my chest.

I grabbed her hand and kissed the back of it. "I love it. You fixed my broken heart."

"It's healed nicely, but I still want to do another session on it."

"Sweets," I groaned. "I don't want to talk about my tattoo right now."

She leaned over and kissed me hard. Her tongue darted into my mouth, distracting me while her hands deftly undid my belt and unzipped my pants. She gave me a grin when she pulled away and took my pants and boxers off.

She dropped to her knees and licked me from root to tip. She slid her lips down my cock, taking me as far back as she could.

"So good," I moaned and tipped my head back.

She pulled off to look up at me and gave me a sexy grin. "Mmm...love sucking your cock."

I reached my hand down and brushed my thumb across her bottom lip. Her lipstick was smeared, and she looked a wreck, but I loved that it was because of me. That I made her that sloppy mess, and she loved every minute of it.

She kissed my thigh, tickling me with the light caresses of her lips until her hand wrapped around the base of my cock, and she slid it back inside her perfect mouth.

"Fuck, yessss," I groaned.

She sucked on me, moaning while she took me further, and I felt myself hitting the back of her throat. I gripped her hair while she worked her magic.

"Veronica," I moaned when I couldn't take it anymore, and I came down her throat. "Sorry."

She freed her mouth and wiped it with the back of her

hand. She climbed on the bed on top of me. "Don't apologize; I like doing that."

"Why?"

"I like having you in my power. I can make you do anything when your cock's in my mouth."

I flipped her over onto her back, and I held her hands over her head. "Same goes for you, sweets. You would do anything I asked after I've eaten you out."

She grinned. "Well, duh."

I ran a hand down her tattooed arm, my lips repeating the path until I kissed down her leg on her massive phoenix tattoo. "So beautiful."

I got out of bed to retrieve the condoms and lube from my jacket pocket. She watched me hungrily as I rolled the condom on and spread some lube down it. She licked her lips while I pumped my cock.

"You hungry for my cock, huh?" I asked.

"Gimme."

I laughed and got back in bed, flipping her back around so she was up on all fours. I slapped her ass and entered her in a swift motion. "Gonna make you come."

"You already did."

"I'm gonna set a record," I told her, growling while I thrust slowly behind her. "We're going to fuck all night long. Until you can't come anymore."

"Do it," she dared. She ground back into me, making me groan at the sensation of her walls clenching tight around my cock.

I quickened my pace and gripped her hips as I pounded into her just the way she liked it. Until she was crying out and close to another orgasm. Then I pulled out and flipped her on her back again. She gave me a confused look until I re-entered her. I loved doggy-style, and so did she, but I also loved to see her come face.

I caressed her cheek with the back of my fingers. "I want to see your face when you come."

She wrung her hands around my neck and pulled me down for a kiss. "Blaise, you big softie!"

She wrapped her legs around my waist and met my every movement.

I slowed my pace, and she frowned. "Why are you going slow?"

I cupped her face and kissed her softly. "Want to savor you, sweets. That okay?"

She nodded and let me take the slow reins.

I loved sex when it was hard and rough, and she did too, but there was something different about slowly stroking your woman when you were making love to her. Tonight was where we would end, but I wanted to hang on to her. I poured my feelings into her body and gave everything I could to her. Trying to show her with my body what my heart felt, even though I couldn't voice it.

"I don't want to stop," I moaned into her ear and squeezed my eyes shut.

"Don't stop, baby," she moaned, her back arching up as she pressed herself closer to me. "Come with me, Blaise. Please."

I don't think she understood that I meant I didn't want to stop seeing her. That I had fallen in love with her, and I didn't want to end it here.

Pleasure coursed through me, and I was on the cusp, but I needed her to come first. I needed to hear her moan my name as I unraveled her.

I stroked slowly inside her, pressing her into the bed as I rolled my hips and found that spot deep inside that always set her off. In an instant, she came undone beneath me, her nails digging into my shoulders, as she came with my name a moan on her lips. Then I went off like a rocket. Ropes of cum spilled into the condom, and I groaned out my release, moaning her name like a plea for her to feel what I felt.

I laid my head on her chest, and she caressed my hair while I tried to catch my breath. If this was truly the last time I was going to see her, I'd give her my body until she told me to stop. I'd give her everything she wanted tonight.

"Blaise," she sighed.

I pulled out of her and got rid of the condom. "Yeah, sweets?"

"Thank you."

I laid back on the bed and pulled her into my arms, stroking my hand through her hair. "For what?"

She kissed my chest and looked up at me with a longing look I couldn't place. "For everything. For doing this for me...for being at my side."

I brought her hand up to my lips and kissed the flower tattoo on her wrist. I wanted this to be every night. For her to be in my arms all the time. Only I would fall in love with a closed-off woman who didn't allow herself love out of fear of getting hurt.

I gave her my body instead, even though I knew it wouldn't be enough.

CHAPTER TWENTY-SIX

VERONICA

I woke up to an empty bed, and even though I had been expecting it, it still hurt. The bed was cold, like my heart, and it was exactly what I deserved. I could barely move. I was sore from all the lovemaking Blaise and I did last night. He gave it to me roughly and dominated me like I loved, but when he shifted to missionary because he wanted to look me in the eyes, I knew I was done for.

It hadn't just been a casual sexual encounter last night. It had been something so much more. Something I craved but couldn't allow myself to have. I broke my own heart because of my foolish idea that I could keep my feelings out of it. He had stared deep into my eyes like he was staring into my soul as he made sweet love to me. But it had only been a goodbye.

It was good he was gone when I woke up; otherwise, my heart would have tried to convince me I needed him to stay. Ghosting me like this was perfect. Everyone did it this way, so having my fake boyfriend do it too was the perfect way to prove my point about why I didn't do relationships anymore.

I rolled over in bed and looked at my phone.

OLIVIA: You still want me to pick you up?

ME: Please.

OLIVIA: Good, because I'm here. Come downstairs.

I got dressed in last night's clothes, and I felt gross. But I left the room, collecting the few things I had, and walked out into the morning light to find Olivia waiting in her compact car. I slid into the passenger seat with a sigh.

She grinned at me. "You look like you got fucked six ways to Sunday."

And then I burst into tears.

"Oh, honey," Olivia comforted me. She pulled me into a quick hug and let me cry on her shoulder. When I pulled away, she leaned over into the glove box and handed me some tissues.

I nodded my thanks, and she drove off, seeming to get that I didn't want to talk about it.

Or so I thought.

"You fell in love with him, didn't you?" she asked when we were almost at my place in Drakesville.

"I don't understand. I'm not supposed to have feelings anymore."

That made her laugh her ass off. "Honey! You have feelings, but no one made you feel the way Seth did. I know you and Blaise started this as a casual thing, but I saw you together. Your eyes lit up whenever he texted. And when he came into the shop, I could see the love between you."

I wiped my eyes. "Liv, can you drop it? I want to go home, shower, and not think about this ever again."

She nodded and parked across the street from my apartment. "What did Blaise say when you left this morning?"

"He wasn't there."

"What?"

"He was already gone."

"Oh, honey."

"Let me wallow today, okay? I'm sorry, I've been a shitty friend."

She gave me a knowing smile. "Yeah, but I still love ya. Go upstairs and shower. I'm getting supplies. Then we're gonna sit on your uncomfortable futon and binge-watch terrible TV."

I hugged her. "You're such a good friend. I don't deserve you."

"Accurate, but I still love you."

I did what she asked, spending too long in the shower, mostly because I cried again in there. How could I have been so foolish? How could I have let my lust be confused for genuine feelings? I really liked Blaise, but we both knew the score. It wasn't real. None of it was real, and now it was over. I should be happy, but it felt like someone had cut my heart out of my chest and stomped on it in front of me. I hadn't felt this distraught since I woke up one day last year and my fiancé had disappeared.

I lay on my bed, with my hair still wet, staring at my phone. Blaise made me take a selfie of us last night with my phone, and we looked so good together. Like we were a real couple, but it had all been one big lie. I wasn't even sure what I was supposed to tell everyone. I had to ask him so we could get our stories straight.

I shot him a text that I hoped he'd ignore.

ME: What am I supposed to tell people?

BLAISE: My schedule was too much.

ME: K.

I watched the dots typing and typing, and then they stopped. It happened a couple more times and then stopped for good.

He was done with me. He'd made it clear he wasn't looking for anything serious, but my heart didn't listen. Why did I let Blaise into my heart? I didn't want to feel this way, this utter heartbreak and desperation. This was exactly why I didn't get too involved. It was why I didn't let men stay over, or cuddle me, or even call me by a pet name. I let Blaise do all of those things. I let him worm his way into my heart, and here I was in the exact situation I didn't want to be in. Heartbroken yet again.

I heard knocking on my front door, and I went down the steps to let Liv in.

"I come with junk food and good coffee," she cheered, holding up the Wawa bag.

"I love you," I told her.

"Hey, your landlord finally put that railing in," she noted as we walked up the steps.

I cringed, remembering how I shoved the boundary in Blaise's face. "Actually, Blaise did it. It's why we got into that fight."

"Aw, that's sweet. That's a total boyfriend move."

"Yeah, but I had to remind him he wasn't."

She gave me another hug and then shooed me into my tiny living room. I slumped onto my truly uncomfortable futon, a hand-me-down from Alex, and turned on my game console to open my streaming service.

Liv came back with a bowl of chips, a stuffed pretzel, and some chocolate. I clicked on the reality show she liked that I pretended to hate, and we melted our brains with it.

"Who's at the front desk today?" I asked.

"Oh, Alex and Eddie closed for the weekend since both you and Seth would be preoccupied."

"What? We're going to lose so much money not being open this weekend."

"We're okay," she reassured me. But I did the books; we were still a struggling new business trying to get our heads above water. Why would Alex and Eddie make that decision?

"No, we're not," I argued.

She kicked my foot. "Let's not talk about work, okay? Kelly starts on Monday, so hopefully that helps."

"I think we're going to keep Seth for a bit. Alex and I talked about it."

"Are you talking again?"

I sighed. "I'm still pissed at him, but I get why he did it. I wished he had warned me. Maybe I wouldn't have concocted the plan to fake date Blaise. Then I wouldn't be feeling like this today."

Olivia gave me a small smile. "Oh, V. You really fell for him, huh?"

"I didn't mean to. I wasn't supposed to. And now he's gone! Just like Seth."

I sipped my coffee and rolled my eyes when my phone buzzed. It hadn't taken long for everyone to start in on me about the breakup. I was a little surprised to hear from Dinah first.

DINAH: Are you okay? I heard about you and Blaise.

ME: Fine.

DINAH: V!

ME: Okay, I'm wallowing a bit.

DINAH: Look, I know them being away's hard, but if you love him, you'll push through.

I sighed and didn't answer her. I didn't want to think about this or have any of the other WAGs try to persuade me to get back together with Blaise. None of it had been real. I had to keep reminding my heart that we agreed to no feelings.

I noticed Liv staring at the work-in-progress painting I had leaning against the window. It wasn't my normal still-life or floral-type painting; it was a painting of Blaise looking strong and powerful on the ice. I wasn't even sure why I started it. Maybe because the man had dug his way into my heart. I hadn't shown it to him, and now I wasn't sure if I was going to finish it.

She gave me a sad look. "Oh, Veronica."

"I know."

"Don't you have that art show?"

"Yeah, but I think I'm gonna toss that."

My best friend squeezed my hand. "You should finish it."

I shook my head. "What's the point?"

She narrowed her dark eyes at me and put a finger in my face. "Veronica O'Malley, you never stop a project. As long as I have known you, you suffer over your art because it's the only thing that makes you happy. You never give up on something."

"Liv, can you drop it?"

She glared at me. "No! You finish that painting. And then when you have that art show, that needs to be what you display."

"Why?" I grumbled and shoved more food into my mouth.

"Because you put your heart and soul into it, and you can't leave it hanging."

I groaned because she was right. I had to finish the painting, and I had to hang it for the art show I was supposed to be a part of in a couple of weeks. Today I could wallow, but tomorrow I'd pick myself back up and get shit done.

"V?"

I wiped my eyes for the millionth time today. "Sorry, I'm a wreck."

Olivia gave me a sympathetic smile, and I felt the déjà vu of when I woke up and Seth had disappeared. Last night was it for Blaise and me, but when I woke up and he was gone, it was like all that pain from Seth came back to me. Everyone left me, so what was the point in even trying?

"Why didn't you tell him how you felt?" she asked.

I shook my head. "It was just sex. Our relationship wasn't real."

Olivia squeezed my hand. "Honey, I don't think that's true."

"No, we both knew the score. We're done. It's better this way."

She gave me a sympathetic smile because we both knew I was lying.

CHAPTER TWENTY-SEVEN

BLAISE

JANUARY

"AGAIN!" Coach LaVoie yelled on the other side of the ice, and we ran through skating lines again. My chest was heaving, and I felt like I was going to die. A side-glance to my defensive partner Riley told me it wasn't just me.

It had been a couple of months since I last saw Veronica, and I was playing like garbage. I knew it was because I let myself catch feelings. I didn't think one person could cause a whole hockey team to mess up their season, but guilt weighed me down. Hence why our practice was unusually long, and we were working our asses off trying not to piss off Coach.

We finished the set, and Coach dismissed us. "Holmstrom! A word after you hit the showers?" Coach called out to me.

I wiped the sweat off my eye-shield and nodded. Riley cringed. "Oh, what did you do?"

I sighed. "Not play good enough."

He nodded. "You've got things to work on, sure, but we'll figure it out together. We're a team."

"Appreciate it. Hey, how's Fi doing?" I asked. He beamed as we got off the ice and walked back into the locker room.

I stripped off my jersey and threw it in the bin, and started taking off all my pads.

Riley pulled out a piece of paper and handed it to me. I squinted at the grainy sonogram. A spike of jealousy ran through me, which was weird because I wasn't planning on having kids anytime soon.

"Dude, I'm so happy for you," I said to Riley, which was true. I was also sad for myself. The full-on Blaise Holmstrom emotional spectrum, everybody!

He took it back and left it up in the top of his cubby.

"You're not thinking of retiring, right?" I asked.

"Nah, dude. I'm an alternate captain while G's injured. Someone's gotta keep you fuckers in line!"

I laughed, then took off the rest of my equipment and hopped into the shower. I dressed quickly and knocked on Coach's office door. He looked up from his notes. "Holmstrom, shut the door."

That was never good.

I shut the door and took a seat in the chair across from him. "Am I getting traded?"

He laughed. "Fuck no! People like the hometown boy."

"So what's up?"

The older man leaned back and rubbed a hand on his jaw. "Look, I don't like to pry into my player's personal life, but you look like a robot out there."

"What?" I asked in disbelief.

I thought he was going to tell me I was sluggish on the ice and needed to work on blocking shots. Not that my playing looked apathetic.

"You look like you don't have passion for the game anymore. I'd like you to be more offensive, of course, but something else seems off."

I rubbed a hand across my jaw. "I've been busy moving out of my dad's house."

"You in the city?"

I nodded. "Rittenhouse Square."

He nodded.

After talking to a couple of the guys about where they lived, I decided I'd prefer to stay in the city versus moving to the Main Line to be closer to the practice facility. I called my realtor and found a four-bedroom brick-facade town-home in Rittenhouse Square. What sold me on the place was the home gym and that it had parking. It was perfect. My brothers roasted me for getting such a big place all to myself, but I reminded them we had a big-ass family, and they shut up. Assholes.

I found out the buyer had accepted my offer the day after the wedding. I had stepped out of the room so I didn't wake Veronica, but when I came back, she was gone. When she texted me asking what our cover story about our breakup should be, it crushed me. I wanted so badly to have something real with her, but she showed me repeatedly that wasn't possible.

"Having stability's good. But I want you to know that if you need to talk, I'm here. I know I'm your coach, and that probably feels weird to you."

I nodded.

"But I want you to play like you actually give a fuck about this game."

I nodded. "Right, yeah. I'll do better."

He gave me a quizzical look. "And whatever you did to fuck it up with that lady of yours, fix it. For fuck's sake, kid, I saw the way you played when she was cheering you on. This shit right here's not it."

I bit my tongue, not trying to explain that it didn't matter. None of it mattered.

He motioned to the door. "Go on, get out of here!"

I didn't say another word and took off for my dad's house. My younger brothers were arguing in the kitchen about something hockey related when I walked in. Dad stood at the counter drinking his coffee with an amused smirk on his face.

"What are you assholes hammering on about?" I asked.

"That headshot Eli took last night," Michael seethed with anger.

Right, that. Montreal played Pittsburgh last night, and one of the goons on the Miners hit our oldest brother in the numbers. I talked to Eli last night, and he seemed a little foggy, and we were all worried.

"He can take it," Dad said with a shrug.

The three of us whipped our heads around at him. "Dad!" Ayden cried. "You can't go all old-school hockey tough guy anymore. Concussions are serious."

"Why do you think I don't want to play professionally?" Michael argued. "That can be dangerous."

"That's not why you don't want to play," Dad scoffed. "You just like writing your kissing books."

I froze and stared at Dad. Michael self-pubbed his romance books under a pen name, but I didn't know Dad knew about it. His pen name was Mikey Holmes, so it wasn't like he tried too hard to make it different.

Ayden laughed his ass off at my expression.

"Wait...I thought it was a secret?" I asked.

Michael sighed. "Maja told on me."

Dad laughed. "Got me laid, so I don't care."

Me and my brothers looked at him in disgust and cried in unison, "EWWWWW!!!"

Dad laughed and then fixed me with a glare. "I have a bone to pick with you."

"Me?" I asked and put my hands up in surrender.

He glared at me. "Yeah, I was wondering why you've been in such a bad mood, and these two spilled that you and Veronica broke up."

Ayden mouthed, 'sorry,' and Michael shrugged.

Dicks.

"It's not your business," I explained. "Are you assholes gonna help me move the rest of my shit, or what?"

Dad held up a hand. "No, I want to know what happened. I should have known something was up when you didn't show up to her art show."

Art show? What art show?

"What are you talking about?" I asked.

Dad set his coffee down and went into the living room. When he came back in, he held a painting in his hands, one that was framed and ready to be hung. It was a painting of me on the ice.

"She painted this of you," my dad sneered at me. "So I want to know what you did to mess it up."

"What happened?" Michael asked softly. I never told them because I knew I'd tell my brothers the truth. They had a way of getting it out of you, even when you didn't want to.

"Nothing," I lied. "She couldn't handle having a boyfriend who travels so much."

My brothers nodded in understanding, but Dad crossed his big arms across his chest. He didn't buy it. He saw through me so much because he was right; I was exactly like him.

"Can we get going? I wanna get to unpacking my house," I tried to change the subject, looking at my brothers with a 'help me' look.

Dad grunted. "Take the painting with you. I bought it because you weren't there to support her. No wonder she looked so defeated."

That made me feel like an asshole. I never wanted to hurt her. We specifically set out for an end date because she didn't want to get hurt. She had set the boundaries.

"You need to talk to her. You're both miserable," Dad said.

"How do you know she is, too?" I asked.

Dad sighed. "Because she was a wreck when I went to her art show."

"Why did you go?" I asked. She didn't even tell me she had an art show. I'm not sure I would have gone had I known. My heart was still too raw to see her.

Dad sighed again. "Because I knew you fucked something up if I hadn't seen her in a while. You need to talk to your woman and fix this shit."

He walked out of the kitchen in a huff, leaving me and my two younger brothers staring at each other in confusion.

I sighed, and we high-tailed it out of there. It was a long day of unpacking and putting everything into the house. Ayden flopped on my couch in the living room and cracked another beer while I sat on the other end and instructed our baby brother on where to hang things.

"What about this?" Michael asked and pulled out Veronica's painting.

Why did she make a painting of me? And why did my dad buy it?

"Put it in one of the other bedrooms, so I don't have to see it," I grumbled and chugged some of my beer.

My brothers exchanged a look. Ayden punched me in the arm. "Dude, tell us what really happened between you two."

Michael set the painting down and sat on the floor in front of us. He crossed his legs underneath him and took a slice of pizza from the coffee table. "Man, tell us already."

"Fine, you assholes. It wasn't real," I explained.

"What wasn't?" Ayden asked, but Michael had his face in his hands.

"Goddamnit, Blaise. Were you doing like a fake relationship thing?" Michael asked and stared daggers at me. My baby brother wasn't one to let his anger show, so that was interesting.

I picked a piece of lint on my hoodie. "Yeah."

"Wait..." Michael trailed off. "I totally walked in on you two, and it didn't seem fake to me."

I gave them a cocky grin. "Oh, there was definitely a lot of sex, and that was real. But that was it."

Ayden looked between the two of us with a confused look on his face. "I still don't understand."

"Numb-nuts, they were only pretending to be in a relationship," Michael explained, drawing out every word. That earned him getting a pillow thrown at his head from Ayden.

"Why?" Ayden asked.

"To get back at her ex and go to his wedding with her," I explained.

"What did you get out of it?" Michael asked.

"Sex? Also, you assholes got off my dick about me being upset about Astrid."

Michael steepled his hands over his face. "Asshole, you never do a fake relationship."

"Why?" I asked and rubbed the back of my neck.

Michael shook his head. "Dude, two of my books have used this trope. You know what always happens?"

I shrugged. Ayden looked completely lost in the conversation.

"HEA!" Michael yelled.

Ayden narrowed his eyes. "Motherfucker, why are you talking in riddles?"

"Happily Ever After. All those couples fall in love, but they break up and realize they're ding-dongs and get back together. And get married and have a ton of babies," Michael explained.

"So what is it, asshole?" Ayden asked me.

I hung my head. "I fell in love with her."

"So?" they both asked in unison.

"So?" I repeated. "She only does casual."

Ayden grumbled under his breath and pulled out his phone. He shoved it in my face, and I saw myself looking at one of my social media profiles. He pointed at the photo I posted of us at the wedding. "You see this shit?"

"Yeah?"

"That looks like two people in love to me. Go talk to her," Ayden urged. He kicked me off the couch.

"What, now?" I asked.

Michael pushed me back onto the couch. "Not now. First, we need a plan."

"What if she doesn't feel the same way?" I asked.

My baby brother gave me a sympathetic look. "That's the risk you have to take. Do you love her?"

I nodded. "Yeah. I really do, Michael."

"More than Astrid?" Ayden asked.

Michael waved him away. "Fuck off; he didn't love her. He was just infatuated with her. What is it about Veronica that you like?"

I smiled. "I love that she's so talented but humble about it. I love that she doesn't care about hockey, but she tries to be supportive of me. Like wishing me a good game or being in the stands during a home game. Or listening to me bitch about what's off with my game. Even though she has no idea what I'm talking about. I want her to be the first person I see when I wake up and the last person I see when I go to sleep. I want to tell her everything, and I want her to realize that not everyone in her life's going to abandon her. That she's not the issue."

"Fucckkk," Ayden slurred out. "You love that woman."

Michael grinned. "Yeah, no shit. Anyone can see that."

"What am I going to do?" I groaned. "I miss her so much."

Michael ran to my kitchen, and I heard him shuffling around in the junk drawer. He came back with a pad of paper and a pen. "Okay, let's get a plan together to win Veronica back."

It may have been the alcohol, but goddamnit, did I love my nosy family. Also, having a romance writer for a brother was extremely helpful. He'd help me figure out how to win her back for good.

CHAPTER TWENTY-EIGHT

VERONICA

"WHO WAS SHE?" I heard a woman scream. She was so loud I heard her from the office. Cautiously, I walked out to the lobby and saw Seth sputtering with excuses to his new wife, who was red in the face and jabbing a finger at his chest. She had the baby in the stroller and was rocking it slowly while the baby cried her head off.

The shop had opened an hour ago and had been a little slow. It was a weekday, so that was par for the course. I locked eyes with my brother. 'What the fuck?' he mouthed, and I shrugged in response. We still weren't exactly on good terms, but since we hired Kelly and got an apprentice, Seth was going back to his old shop in a couple of weeks. Good riddance. I was hoping it could finally mend my relationship with my brother.

"Baby, let's talk about this outside?" Seth pleaded, but he looked guilty.

"No. I want all your friends and coworkers to know what a piece of shit you are. We've been married for two months, and you already found someone else. So I want to know who you've been fucking behind my back," she screeched at him.

He bent down to pick up his daughter, but Lily slapped his hand away. "No. I don't want you anywhere near my daughter."

Seth clenched his fists. "She's our daughter."

Olivia stood at the receptionist's desk, frozen in fear, and I didn't blame her. None of us seemed to know how to handle the situation. Guilt wrapped itself around my throat. I should have told Lily she was the other woman.

"Baby, it's not what you think," Seth tried to explain.

She held up the receipts. "So please tell me when you were in Vegas for a tattoo convention? Because I checked with the shop so I could do the taxes, and Liv told me you had to take sick time because I couldn't get off work and the baby was sick. When was the baby sick? And when was I working? Because you told me to quit so I could be a stay-at-home mom. Why did you need to stay at this luxury hotel? Or how about the work trip right before we found out I was pregnant? What was that?"

The guilt wrapped tighter around me. Could that 'work trip' have been when we went to Cancún for our anniversary? This man had shattered my heart, but I didn't want Lily to go through the same heartache I did.

"Come on, Lily. Let's talk about this at home," Seth urged.

She shook her head, tears running down her face, and my heart wrenched. I should have warned her. I should have told her who she was marrying. But I didn't want to butt in because I thought it wasn't my place, and now another woman got her heart shattered by this asshole.

She wrenched her ring off her hand and threw it right at his face. "Fuck you very much, Seth!"

He grabbed her hand. "Baby, please."

That's when Eddie put a stop to it. He put a large hand on Seth's shoulder. "Buddy, let's go for a walk."

Seth shrugged Eddie off. "Fuck off, man. This is between me and my lady."

"And you're interrupting our business. It's not a request."

Eddie wrenched him away. Lily picked up her daughter and tried to shush her. I walked over to her. "Hey."

She gave me a pained look. "Oh, I'm so sorry about all that."

"Do you want to come into the office with me? To talk?"

She nodded. She held the baby while I pushed the stroller down the hall. I gave her a water and let her settle into a chair.

She eyed me. "You changed your hair again."

When I got over Blaise, I decided it was time for another change. So I chopped my hair to chin length, got bangs, and went back to my natural chocolate brown color.

I ignored her question as I sat beside her. "Are you okay?"

She shook her head. "Not in the slightest. Can I ask you something?"

"Sure..."

"When did you and Seth break up?"

I cringed.

She sighed. "I was the other woman, wasn't I?"

I nodded. "I didn't know until he gave me the invitation."

"It's because of Rosie, wasn't it?" she asked. She bounced the baby in her arms, trying to get her to stop crying.

"I assume so. I thought maybe he had changed, that becoming a father made him realize what was important."

She wiped her eyes. "What did he tell you? About me?"

"Nothing."

She narrowed her eyes. "What do you mean, nothing?"

I sighed. "Lily, we were high school sweethearts. We were supposed to get married, and then a week before the wedding, he left."

Her jaw dropped. "You were engaged? Oh my God, and I invited you to my wedding. And asked you to watch my baby. You must think I'm a complete B-I-T-C-H."

I laughed at her spelling out the cursing again. Especially since she had been letting the f-word fly while she had been yelling at Seth. "No, Lily. I figured you didn't know."

She cringed. "Why didn't you tell me?"

I gave her an uneasy look. "Would you have believed me?"

She shook her head, and the baby fussed a bit. Lily repositioned her, and she seemed to settle. "I'm so sorry. And for causing a scene."

I put a hand on her arm. "It's okay. I'm the one who should be sorry. You looked so happy at the wedding. I didn't think it was my place to tell you."

"You really were engaged?" she asked.

I nodded.

She sighed and pushed her blonde hair out of her face. "Okay, okay, I can do this. You moved on and are happy now. I need to get a divorce and move on with my life."

My face must have crumbled at her words because her smile turned down into a frown.

"Veronica? You moved on with Blaise, and you look so happy."

I blinked back tears. "No."

What do you mean, no?"

"We broke up."

"Why?" she cried. "You two looked so in love at my wedding. I was slightly jealous because Blaise paid more attention to you than Seth did to me that night, and we were the ones getting married."

I wiped the tears from my eyes.

"Oh, honey, what happened?" she asked.

I was supposed to be comforting this woman who had just gotten her heart stomped on by the man she loved, not the other way around. But the tears fell despite me trying to keep all the emotions in. The baby had fallen asleep, so Lily gently tucked her back into the stroller.

I wanted to find the words, but I couldn't. Instead, I blubbered out gibberish while she 'momed' me, rubbing my back and telling me everything was going to be okay.

Is that what mothers did? I'd never know.

I wiped my face. "Sorry."

"Tell me," she urged.

"We hooked up last summer, but I don't do relationships."

She frowned. "Because Seth broke your heart."

I nodded and wrung my hands. I trailed my hands over the flower tattoo that covered up Seth's name. Her eyes widened. "Oh, Veronica. I knew he covered up your name, but you had his name tattooed too?"

I nodded. "Cover-up tattoos are my specialty now."

She squeezed her eyes shut. "I'm so sorry."

I shook my head. "It's not your fault." She opened her mouth to protest, but I held up a hand. "It's not. He did us both wrong. I walked away with my heart shattered, but you have your daughter to worry about, too."

"I know," she admitted softly. "But I want to know what happened with you and Blaise. You looked so happy."

"Lily, it wasn't real. We were just pretending."

Her eyes were saucers, and looking into her blue eyes reminded me of what it was like to look into Blaise's. Like when we had made love, and he looked deep into my eyes before he kissed me like he meant it.

"Because of me," she said sadly.

I shook my head. "Because of Seth."

"Can I admit something to you?"

"Sure."

"I think he did it on purpose."

"Did what?"

"I wasn't on the pill."

"Oh?"

She stared at me for a moment, and then my eyes got wide as I realized what she was getting at. I was on the pill, but sometimes he conveniently 'forgot' to put a condom on. He always pulled out, but I wondered now. What kind of monster did that? I clenched my hands into fists. I was mad for this woman, for her baby, and for what the asshole would continue to put her through.

I wanted to say something else, but the door to the office opened, and my brother stood there with a deer in headlights look.

Lily smiled up at him. "I'm sorry."

Alex shook his head. "I need to talk to my sister, but are you okay? Do you want one of us to walk you to your car?"

She shook her head. "I'm fine. Thanks though. I'm sorry about the disruption. I found those receipts, and he had been dodgy all week."

Alex nodded.

Lily gave me a quick hug and stood up. "Veronica, I think you should call him because you may say it wasn't real, but I know what I saw with my own two eyes."

Alex walked her out, and I sat back in the office and tried to bury myself in the bookkeeping, but then my brother came back into the office. He stared at me, but I pretended not to notice him.

"Talk to me," he urged.

I waved my hand at him. "No, go away. I have to figure out why these numbers don't match."

He took the papers out of my hands. "No. I said talk to me, sis."

"I'm still so angry with you. Now, do you understand why?" I sneered at him.

He nodded, running a tattooed hand through his short hair. "I'm sorry. I shouldn't have hired him. I thought you would have been okay with it."

"Are you serious?"

He sighed. "I'm sorry. Okay?"

I nodded. "He's a good artist. So I get why you did it. Still pissed, though."

"I'm sorry. But you've been in a bad mood since you and Blaise broke up, so let's talk."

"It wasn't real," I admitted.

He raised an eyebrow. "What wasn't?"

"Our relationship!" I exclaimed. Why weren't people understanding that what Blaise and I had was all a facade? The only things real were the feelings that crept into my heart. "When you hired that asshat, I saw Blaise at the desk, and I got this idea in my head that I could get back at my ex by pretending I dated that hot hockey player."

My brother nodded. "He's very hot."

I glared. "Hey, you're married."

"But I'm not dead. Eddie and I would both fuck him. We talked about it."

I made a face. "Can you please not sexually harass my boyfriend?"

He grinned. "I thought he wasn't your boyfriend?"

I groaned. "He's not. We were just doing casual until the wedding. Then when I woke up that morning, he was gone. I knew we had an expiration date, but it hurt."

Alex glared at me. "You're a liar."

"What?"

He pointed a finger at me. "I saw the way you two were when I walked in on you. That didn't seem so casual to me."

"It was. It had to be."

"Why?"

"Because everyone leaves me. It's better to protect myself than to have another person I care about leave me high and dry."

My brother's face fell, and he walked over to me and pulled me into a great big hug. I leaned into it.

"Hey, you know I'll never abandon you, okay? You're my baby sister, and I love you. I'm sorry I hired your dick-hole of an ex. It's not your fault, okay?"

"Then why does everyone leave me?" I cried.

Alex wiped my tears. "Oh, V, Dad died. He didn't abandon us."

"I'm not talking about Dad!"

He pulled back and sat down in the chair across from the desk. His elbows were on his knees, and he steepled his hands in front of his face. "Your mom... She was really sick."

That was the first time he ever said anything about my mom. Dad refused to talk about her. It was taboo to even mention her name.

"What do you mean?" I asked.

"She was a drug addict."

I nodded. I had a feeling that was the case.

"Don't be mad, okay?"

"About what?"

He sighed. "She wanted to come see you when you were twelve."

"What?" I shrieked.

"She was going through rehab and doing the twelve-step thing. Dad wouldn't let her see you, made me promise on his deathbed I'd always protect you from her."

"That wasn't your choice to make!"

He nodded. "I know. Dad was a good man, but he shouldn't have left that up to me. She reached out when she heard about Dad's death."

"What?"

He reached into his back pocket and pulled out his wallet. He produced a card and handed it to me. "I told her to fuck off, but it's your choice if you want a relationship with her. I had Tony look into her. She's been clean since then, living in bumblefuck PA, but she seems good."

Eddie's brother Tony was a PI. Of course Alex had him do a background check on my mother because he was trying to protect me. I wasn't sure I ever wanted to see her, so I was more annoyed than angry that he withheld this information.

"Why tell me this now?" I asked and crumbled up the card.

Alex sighed. "Because you've been a shit to work with lately, and I hate seeing you like this. It wasn't your fault. Your mom left because she had an addiction. Seth's an asshole, but Blaise wasn't. He made you happy."

I stared at my brother. "I can't."

"Yes, you can. You're gonna show him a big grand gesture and tell him how you feel, or so help me God!"

"What if he doesn't feel the same? Big grand gesture? What am I in a romcom?"

He tipped back his head and laughed. "Yes! Go to his game, wear his jersey, and then tell him you love him and want to have his babies."

"I don't want his babies," I muttered.

My brother laughed. "Yeah, you do. You'd have cute little babies, and I want some more nieces and nephews. I've heard that family's fertile, so you better hop to it."

"What about asshat?"

"I kicked him to the curb early. I feel terrible for Lily."

I nodded. "Me too. She seems nice. She didn't deserve that."

"Neither did you."

I ran my hands down my face. "There's only one problem with this grand gesture plan."

"What?"

"I don't have a ticket for tonight's game."

My brother looked at me like I just told him the sky was green. "Hoe! You know Eddie's baby sis is about to marry a Bulldog."

"Yeah?"

Alex rolled his eyes. "And one of your clients is a sales manager for the team."

I stared blankly at him.

"Oh my God, V, could you be more dense? Call Rox or Dinah, and figure it out! Just get your man and stop being such a shit to work with."

Before I could insult him back, he rolled his eyes and stormed out of the office. But he wasn't wrong. I had been extra bitchy lately. Because I missed Blaise. I missed the way he called me 'sweets' and the way he listened when I talked about a difficult client. Most of all, I missed waking up beside him.

So I pulled out my phone and called Roxanne Desjardins, hoping she could help me win back my man.

CHAPTER TWENTY-NINE

BLAISE

I taped up my stick and tried to focus on what I needed to do in tonight's game. It was the last game before the All-Star Break, which I wasn't in, so it would be nice to get a little vacation time. I should be a shit for saying that, but I planned on spending it trying to figure out how to get Veronica back. Michael and I had been brainstorming, but every time I thought of going to the tattoo shop to talk to her, I froze up.

"You ready for tonight?" TJ asked me while he laced up his skates.

I nodded. "Yeah. I am."

He grinned at me, but it was that devilish grin he got when he knew something you didn't. I wasn't sure what that meant. Noah elbowed him and gave him a stern look. What was that about? I tried to ignore them and went about my pre-game rituals.

We were playing the Montreal Saints again, which meant my brother Eli was in town. Since the All-Star Break was about to happen, my entire family was in town. That didn't happen a lot with us all in different parts of the country or in Canada.

I checked my phone and laughed at a text from my sister.

MAJA: You need to stay on your skates if you wanna beat Eli tonight.

ME: Thanks, coach!

MAJA: You know it!

I put my phone back into my cubby and walked with the rest of the team down the tunnel. TJ and Noah were doing their normal pre-game handshake, and TJ was trying to pump up the rest of the team.

I skated onto the ice and did a lap around the zone. I wristed a few pucks into the net for practice and was about to stretch on the ice when TJ nudged me.

"Dude, what?" I asked, annoyed.

He pointed to the glass where the WAGs usually sat. I glanced over and came face-to-face with my ex-girlfriend. No, my fake ex-girlfriend. She'd cut her hair, and colored it a muted brown. It looked different on her, not as wild and colorful as her normal hair. A wave of sadness washed over me because I wondered why she did that. The other thing I noticed made my brow furrow in confusion.

She was wearing my jersey.

We locked eyes, and she smiled at me and tapped two fingers against her heart, and then pointed at me.

I broke out into a big smile and skated over to the glass. I tapped two fingers against my heart and pointed back at her. She nodded and raised her beer in salute.

I felt a gloved hand clamp around my shoulder. "Oh, good, Roxie got her a ticket," TJ said to me.

"What?" I asked.

TJ grinned. "Come on, get ready for this game, okay? You can make up with your girl after we beat your brother."

The man in question skated over to me and gave me a big grin. "Did you and your girl make up?" Eli waved to Veronica, and she gave him one in return.

"I'm not sure..." I trailed off.

"Hey, she changed her hair," Eli commented.

"I liked it better before," I grumbled.

Eli shrugged and skated off to his end of the zone to talk to his teammates. I wasn't sure why Veronica was here, but my heart felt like it grew three sizes too big tonight. When I got back into the locker room before puck drop, I checked my phone. I smiled at a text from Veronica.

VERONICA: Your sister told me to tell you that you need to stay on your skates? I don't know what that means. But also good luck.

ME: I have so many questions.

VERONICA: Later, baby, okay? Win me a hockey game first.

ME: Yes, Ma'am!

I saw TJ and Noah grinning at me. I glared at them. "What do you two assholes know?"

They gave me, 'Who me?' looks and shrugged. Logan, who sat next to Noah, had a bemused look on his face. He ran a hand through his red hair but smiled. "I don't know anything, man, but if that lady makes you play better, I'm all for it."

I pointed accusing fingers at all of them. "All of you are dicks. All of you."

TJ and Noah smiled at me, and Riley gave me a shove to the shoulder. "Come on, big guy, let's go win this thing."

I amped myself up, and we all went down the tunnel again. I didn't know why Veronica was here at my game wearing my jersey, but it made me want to win the game even more. For her. And then I could tell her all the things I left unsaid. All the things I wanted to tell her the night of the wedding.

I was on the starting line-up tonight, and I grinned as the PA called out our names. I shuffled on my skates at center ice during the national anthem. But once the puck dropped, we were on it, with Noah getting possession of the puck right away. He brought it past the neutral zone into the Saints' offensive zone, and he fought with my older brother for the puck. Noah batted it over to Benny, who wristed the shot, but it went wide. We scrambled for the puck, but I was more interested in my brother's fancy footwork.

Eli got possession of the puck, but I checked him into the boards, trying to knock it out of his way. Our sticks smashed together, and we fought for dominance, but he beat me and got the puck back into neutral. My eyes cut across the ice, and I thanked the hockey gods Riley was a good defensive partner because he was already chasing after Eli while I hung back. I hustled down the ice, trying to get back into position and prevent the Saints from scoring. Eli sure did try, but while I was neck-and-neck with my oldest brother, Riley was protecting the slot in front of Metzy.

Eli passed to his teammate, who deked and then passed back to Eli, who slapped it towards the net. Metzy did some aerobics to keep the puck out.

We lined up for the face-off. "Do better than that, old man!" I chirped at my brother, who was currently facing off with TJ.

Eli's eyes narrowed at me, but he didn't let it rattle him. I faced the Saints d-man Samuelson. He was a big guy clocking in at six-foot-six and a lot of muscles. He had that whole enforcer thing going on, even though that shit had been going out of the game lately. He was also an instigator.

"You got a problem, Baby Holmstrom?" he snarled.

"Baby Holmstrom?" I laughed. "Is that the best you could do, bud?"

"Yeah, you're just coasting on your brother's talent."

I gritted my teeth against my mouthguard. He was trying to rile me up, and it was working. I was gonna prove to this city that it was *Blaise* Holmstrom they were cheering for, not Hal Holmstrom's kid or Eli Holmstrom's baby brother. Me. Samuelson was just trying to get under my skin.

"Is that why you can't block a shot to save your life? Surprised you're not riding the pine all season long," I chirped back.

He didn't have an answer because TJ knocked the puck back out of our zone and headed down the other end of the ice. I laughed in Samuelson's face and skated up the ice with my teammates. TJ batted the puck on his stick in the Saints' zone, trying to set up the play. Benny was getting hassled by Samuelson, and Noah was getting screened by another Saints player. TJ had to play selfish hockey here if we wanted to be the first to draw blood.

But he didn't because I was open.

I was wide open, and the Saints didn't notice because I wasn't an offensive-defenseman. I didn't take offensive opportunities all that often, but this one was golden.

It all happened in a millisecond. TJ passed it to me, and I slapped the puck. It wasn't a pretty goal. It hit the crossbar, but then the Saints goalie didn't know where it went until it was behind the redline and in his net. The siren went off, the lamp lit up red, and the arena full of Philadelphia Bulldogs fans were cheering my name. *My* name, not my dad's.

I skated over to TJ where we exchanged big hugs. I sped past the glass where the girls all sat and smacked the glass with my stick. Veronica beamed at me, and I tapped my fingers against my heart and pointed at her. Her lips turned up into a big smile and she repeated the action back at me.

I skated back to the bench with a grin that cracked my face. Seeing her here cheering me on and wearing my jersey made me come alive again. Like all these months without her, I had been dead inside. I had so many things I wanted to say to her, but I had to get my head in the game first.

I felt Coach tap my shoulder, his way of telling me I had done good. I chewed on my mouthguard as I watched my teammates set up the next play.

"Nice goal," Riley said with a smile.

"Did you know she was coming?" I asked.

He shook his head and nodded at TJ and Noah sitting next to him. "That was all these two."

"I don't know why she's here."

He nudged me as the shift change started, and we slid down the bench. "Because you love each other, and she wanted to do something about it."

I smiled when I saw my sister sitting next to Veronica. Maja had that wild look in her eyes when she got excited about hockey. She pointed to the players on the ice, and I could tell from a distance she was probably boring Veronica with all the hockey talk. But V was a good sport.

"Focus on the game, man. Then you can patch things up with your lady," Riley told me, noticing my concentration elsewhere.

I nodded.

It was good advice. I wanted to win this game for her, and then when it was over, I'd tell Veronica O'Malley I loved her, and I'd never ever abandon her.

CHAPTER THIRTY

VERONICA

The Bulldogs defeated the Montreal Saints 4-0. Blaise's sister explained that was a shutout. I wasn't prepared for Maja Holmstrom. She was nice, but holy fuck, that girl lived and died by hockey.

It was comical to watch her and Rox together. They were like two peas in a pod, yelling at the refs for missing calls and screaming for the Bulldogs. Maja was a Philly girl through and through, and despite living in Canada now, she'd always rooted for Philly. Rox was a diehard Toronto Wolves fan, but I didn't think so anymore. Not with the way she screamed for her man and her twin brother.

"You're gonna come to the bar, right?" Maja asked.

I nodded and pushed my now chin-length hair behind my ear. I was still getting used to having shorter hair. The other girls said it looked cute, except for Dinah, who saw it for the cry for help it was. I may have drunkenly told her what was going on last weekend.

"Come on," Dinah urged. "Let's head over to the bar. I'll drive."

"Okay," I agreed.

"Can I hitch a ride, too? My brothers are going to harass Blaise in the locker room and take too long."

Dinah laughed. "Sure. Come on."

The three of us got out of our seats and filed out of the stadium. Maja and I followed Dinah to her car, and she drove us over to Eileen's Tavern.

We lost Maja when we walked inside the bar, but I froze in place at the front door when I spied both Hal and Ayden behind the bar. I couldn't bear to show my face here after Blaise and I 'broke up.' The pain and the guilt had been too much.

Dinah gave my hand a squeeze. "Come on. Let's get a drink while we wait for the boys."

I nodded solemnly, but my nerves built up inside my chest.

Dinah bounced over to the bar, snagging the two barstools that had just opened up. She hopped onto one and immediately started chatting with Ayden. I took a breath and followed her, sliding uneasily onto the barstool next to her.

Hal walked over to me and set down a lager in front of me. He didn't ask my order anymore; he always knew what I wanted. That used to make me love this bar, but now it made the guilt twist in my heart.

"Hi, sweetheart. Haven't seen you in a while."

I took the beer, but he wouldn't take my money. Ayden snatched the bills out of my hand with a glare at his dad.

"I know," I said with a sigh.

"Hey, Veronica's family!" Hal argued and glared at Ayden.

Ayden glared back. "Then I'll make her pay double."

I laughed. Ayden giving me shit was a good sign.

"You cut your hair," Ayden said while he gave me my change.

"It's not you," Hal said with a scowl.

Ayden nodded in agreement. "It looks like shit."

"Wow...you guys sure do know how to compliment a girl," I said with a roll of my eyes. Did I mention Ayden was kind of an asshole?

"Stop being mean to my girlfriend," a deep voice spoke up behind me.

I turned around and came face-to-face with the man I had been heartbroken over. Blaise's blonde hair was getting longer, but he styled it so it was out of his face. His muscular frame was bulging out of the classic black suit he wore. People said men in suits were to women what women in lingerie were to men, and I had to agree. Because I wanted to tear the clothes off of him, even if I didn't deserve him.

"Blaise..." I started but then stopped because I didn't know what to say.

"C'mere you," he ordered in that soft voice that made me melt.

"What?"

"Kiss me already," he whined and pointed at his lips. He was cute when he was all pouty, and I had missed those puppy dog eyes.

Dinah barked out a laugh next to me at his whining, but I ignored her while Blaise bent down and slanted his mouth over mine. I melted into the kiss and probably would have been in a puddle underneath my barstool if I wasn't already sitting down.

He pulled away slowly and rested his forehead against mine. "Hi."

"Hi," I breathed back at him.

"Can we talk?"

I nodded.

"Finish your beer."

Dinah plucked it off the bar and handed it to Noah. "Problem solved!" she cheered.

"Go on you two," Noah urged.

I grinned at them, and Blaise helped me out of my seat and into my coat. He took my hand as we walked outside, and it was so nice holding this man's hand as we walked on the sidewalk together. This time not faking it for the people around us.

"Where do you want to go talk?" I asked.

"My place."

"Okay."

He led me to his car, where we lapsed into an uncomfortable silence. We had a lot to say to each other, but I wasn't sure where to start.

When I asked Rox to get me a ticket to the game and explained why, that was as far as I thought it through. My brother said I had to make a big gesture, but now I wasn't sure if showing up to Blaise's game wearing his jersey was enough. I didn't know how he was feeling, but he had called me his girlfriend in front of his dad and younger brother, so that had to count for something.

I let myself get lost in my thoughts that I hadn't realized we were heading into Center City. Wait...

"Blaise, I thought you said you wanted to go to your place?"

He ran a hand through his hair. "We are."

I cocked my head at him.

"I moved out of my dad's."

"You did?"

He nodded. "Yup."

"When?" I asked.

"Um...two days ago?"

"Two days ago?"

"I honestly forgot I put in the offer until the realtor called me the morning after the wedding that the buyer had accepted. But then you were gone when I came back."

"Oh," I sighed out, realization dawning on me of how I broke my own heart.

"And then you texted me asking what we were supposed to tell everyone."

Dammit. I had ruined it. It had been me who broke *his* heart. Not the other way around.

"It really hurt, V."

"I thought you left like everyone else does," I explained.

I didn't want to tell Blaise that Olivia picked me up that morning and I cried my eyes out all day. She plied me with chemically made junk food, and I cried because, for the first time, I found someone I thought I could love, but he left me like everyone else. Like my mom did, like Seth, like every friendship I had before I met Liv. Liv doesn't allow you to stop being her friend, which was what I loved about her.

Blaise pulled down a back alley and into the driveway of a townhouse. The house had a brick facade and a classic Philly style to it. I peered up and saw it had a rooftop deck. Rittenhouse Square was ritzy, and on Blaise's salary, he could afford it.

He cut the engine of the car, and we quietly got out of it together. He walked me inside his house, and it became clear he had just moved in because while he had furniture set up, everything else looked bare.

Blaise took my coat and hung it up in the closet while I walked into his living room. I froze when I saw the painting of him leaning up against the wall.

My painting.

The one his dad had bought at my art show after he asked why I looked so sad. Until I burst into tears, and Hal pretended like he knew how to handle when women cried. He doesn't, for the record. Which probably explained a lot about Blaise's sister Maja.

Blaise saw me staring. "Oh."

"You have my painting?"

He nodded. "Um...yeah, my dad might have thrown it at me after yelling at me to fix things with you." He shuffled his feet and looked towards his kitchen. "You want a beer?"

I nodded but couldn't speak. I wasn't sure what I should even say to this man. He walked into his kitchen, and I heard him grabbing beers. He came back into the living room and handed me a 611 Ale.

I took the beer. "Oh. This is what we drank at the brewery the last time we went."

He took a swig of his beer. "Yup."

"Blaise."

"Yeah, sweets?" he asked, but he wasn't looking at me. He was looking down at his beer and picking at the label.

"Do you know what I did the day after the wedding?"

He shook his head but still wasn't looking at me.

"Liv picked me up, and I cried the entire way home. Then I sat on my futon, ate a bunch of carbs, and cried the rest of the day."

His head snapped up, and my heart wrenched when I saw his eyes were shiny. "Why?"

I wiped at my face, now realizing the tears were welling

up in my eyes and a few had fallen. "Because I fell in love with you, and I wasn't supposed to."

He sat on his couch and put his beer on the coffee table. Then he patted the space next to him. "C'mere. Sit with me."

I went to him, putting my beer next to his and gingerly sitting beside him. He put an arm around my shoulders. "I'm sorry."

"What do you have to be sorry for?" I asked.

He caressed my cheek, and his thumbs wiped away my tears. "I never wanted to make you cry."

"It's my own fault. I fought so hard to guard my heart that when you did as I asked, it broke me."

His hand didn't move, but his eyes searched mine. "So when you woke up, and I was gone, you thought I was gonna let you go?"

I nodded.

"Veronica, I didn't want to. I wanted to keep you forever. I wanted our relationship to be real because I fell in love with you, too."

"So when I texted you, that hurt?" I asked.

He nodded. "I wanted to respect your wishes." He took my hand and placed it above his heart, right where I covered up the tattoo of his ex-girlfriend's name. "When I told you that you fixed my heart, I didn't mean my tattoo."

"Oh," I breathed out. "Blaise?"

"Yeah, sweets?"

I smiled through the tears. "I love when you call me 'sweets.' I may have rolled my eyes the first time, but I love it."

His thumb continued to caress my cheek. "What else do you love?"

"I love how your whole face lights up when you see me

on the other side of the glass. And that we have that ritual that's just ours. And how you don't laugh when I ask you a dumb question about hockey because I'm not into sportsball."

He chuckled. "Sweets, it doesn't matter to me that you don't know hockey like the back of your hand. I love that you try to be supportive. That you're there and you listen to me rant when something's off with my game. I love seeing you in my jersey."

"I want to be your girlfriend," I blurted.

"Yeah?" he asked, his voice dropping to a low whisper. "Not a fake girlfriend?"

I shook my head. "No, baby. I want it to be real. I want you."

A smile broke out across his face, and then he kissed me, pressing me into his couch. I didn't mind because my body needed him close. I needed the feel of him again. Then the jerk pulled back.

"Kiss me," I demanded.

He put a finger on my lips. "Shush, let me say what I gotta say."

"If it's not about how much you want to fuck me right now, I don't want to know."

He gave me an amused look. "No, sweets. I really want to be your boyfriend, and it was hard letting you go."

"I'm here, and I don't want you to let me go now."

He smiled at me and ran a hand through my hair. "I hate this hair."

I frowned.

"It's not you. I never want to be the reason you dimmed your light. I love you, Veronica O'Malley. I didn't expect it, and I wasn't looking for a relationship when I met you, but the past months without you... I've felt hollow."

"Worse than when Astrid broke up with you?" I asked.

He nodded. "She was my first love, but you might be my only."

I slanted my mouth on his again, pretty sure he might be the only man I ever wanted to kiss again. When I pulled away, he looked at me like I hung the moon. I don't think a man had ever looked at me that way. I thought Seth took my heart when he left, but I think this blue-eyed blonde giant had put it back together.

"You gonna give me a tour of your house?" I teased.

He shook his head. "Later. Tonight, I want to show you how much I love you."

I laughed when he lifted me up into his arms and carried me upstairs.

CHAPTER THIRTY-ONE

BLAISE

There was a weight on my chest when I woke up the next morning. The weight was a naked woman, and my cock was already hard against my leg at the feel of Veronica, my girlfriend, wrapped around me. Her hand was swirling across the red flowers on my chest.

I kissed the top of her head. "Morning, sweets," I whispered.

She tilted her head up to look at me. "Hi."

"Hi? That's all I get?"

She nodded into my chest. "Somebody wore me out last night, and I'm exhausted."

I grinned.

Last night after we talked and told each other how we felt, I spent a long time making slow love to her. It differed from our usual affair, but it was nice. Then I let her tie my hands to the headboard, and she rode me. We ended up in the shower for round three before collapsing onto the bed naked with damp hair late in the wee hours of the morning.

A memory surfaced suddenly. "We didn't use a condom in the shower."

She kissed the tattoo on my chest as she worked her way up to my neck and then to my lips.

"S'okay. I'm on the pill," she said, and she climbed on top of me. Now my cock was getting even more interested in her body grinding against mine. This woman was just as horny as me, and it was one of the reasons I loved her.

I frowned and raked a hand through my hair. "You sure that was okay? That wasn't very smart."

"Hey, it's okay," she reassured me. "You seemed to enjoy it."

That was true, but I always wrapped it up. I had no intention of doing her in the shower last night, but she was too much of a temptation. I kinda wanted to go without again, but my family was very fertile.

VERY fertile.

"I'm usually more careful than that," I explained. I never went bare with Astrid, ever, but if things went my way, Veronica would be the only person I ever did that with for the rest of my life.

"Baby, it's fine," she told me and nosed across my neck, giving me light kisses. "If you're so worried about it, pull out next time."

I grinned at that. I loved her calling me a pet name, especially now that everything between us was real. I opened my mouth to say something, and then my doorbell rang. I groaned because I had a feeling who was bothering me today.

"Who's that?" she asked, looking down from her perch above me with a disappointed look on her face. She was so cute when she was all pouty.

I gave her a look.

"Your family?" she exclaimed and climbed off me.

I sighed at the doorbell again. "Sweets?"

She was shrugging on her bra and already had her jeans on. Her whole face lit up when I called her that. I loved seeing that look across her pale face. I had missed that look for months. It surprised me when she showed up to my game last night in my jersey, but now we were together. I hadn't expected to ever see her again. I thought Michael and I would have to put our heads together and come up with something good to win her back. I didn't think she would try to win me back first.

"What?" she asked.

I got out of bed and walked over to her. I put my hands on her face and tilted it up to me. "Please don't let my family scare you away."

She kissed me quickly. "I'm not letting go of you again."

I kissed her again, sliding my hand to the back of her neck, but she pushed me away and put a finger on my chest. "Don't start what you can't finish, big guy."

"I love that you're a bigger horndog than I am."

She laughed and pulled her shirt over her head. "Do you want me to get the door while you get dressed?"

I shrugged on a pair of jeans. "Please. Wait, that's probably..." But she was already out of the room, and I heard her clomping down the steps.

I took a black t-shirt out of my dresser and pulled it over my head. I didn't want to deal with my family today, but with everyone in town, it made sense they wanted to see me. I would have rather spent the morning in bed with Veronica.

With a sigh, I ran down the steps, taking them two at a time, only to find Veronica and my sister-in-law Emily talking about the painting of me that was leaning against the wall.

"Looks a little bare in here," Emily teased, her French-Canadian accent coming through.

"He literally moved in!" Michael called from the kitchen.

Emily had a hand on her pregnant belly, but she smiled at me. "I like this one better."

Veronica arched an eyebrow. "Thank you?"

The other woman laughed. "Good thing."

Eli walked into the living room with his two-year-old daughter on his hip and son pretty much hanging on his ankles. Emily laughed when she took the baby, but the baby seemed more interested in Veronica's tattoos.

"You want to hold her?" my sister-in-law asked.

"Oh, I love babies!" Veronica exclaimed, and I watched as she took my niece, who immediately pulled on her hair.

"Simone!" Emily scolded.

Veronica smiled and gingerly uncurled the baby's fingers around her hair. "Happens all the time. You like my hair, huh, baby?" she asked as she bounced Simone in her arms until the baby giggled.

Something primal clawed up my chest at seeing my niece in her arms. One day that could be us. It was way too soon for me to think that, but my caveman brain had other thoughts.

"Uncle Blaise!" my nephew Alex cheered and jumped into my arms.

"Buddy!"

"Is that your new girlfriend?" he asked.

"She is."

"Uncle Ayden said you were a..." he dropped his voice to a whisper. "A dumbass."

Of course he did.

"Alex," Eli warned.

"I didn't say it!" My nephew tried to debate.

"Who's all here?" I asked.

"All of us!" Maja called from the kitchen.

We walked into the kitchen, and somehow, my large family was all gathered around my kitchen table. Okay, I might have bought it, keeping in mind how big my family was. Dad was brewing coffee while Maja and Julien searched my cabinets for cups.

"Hey, cutie," I said to baby Simone in Veronica's arms.

"You want her? You can keep her. She kept us up all night," my eldest brother joked.

I felt a nudge at my elbow and noticed Brendan, his husband, Adam, and my other nephews, Caden and Ash, sitting on the other side of the table. My whole family was in my kitchen. No wonder Veronica was holding the baby. It gave her an excuse not to answer questions from my nosy family.

"Hey man," I greeted Brendan.

Brendan smirked at me. "So, introduce us!"

Veronica handed the baby back to Emily, and she held out her hand to my older brother. "Brendan, right? I think you're the only one I haven't met yet."

Brendan smiled. "Saved the best for last!"

She laughed. "And Adam, the husband, right?"

Adam gave her a small smile. "You get used to the big family."

Dad and Julien came around to the table and dropped off coffee for everyone. Dad stopped to hug Veronica.

I sighed and ran a hand through my hair. "Why are you all here?"

"To annoy you," Ayden teased, and I felt him kick me under the table.

Dick.

"We wanted to meet your girl," Brendan explained.

"Well, most of you already know me. I'm a regular at the bar," Veronica said.

Michael shuddered. "Let's not remember how I met you."

"Learn to knock!" Veronica teased.

I put an arm around her and kissed her temple. I loved that she could dish it out to my siblings as good as they served it to her.

"Actually, it was my idea," Maja announced. "I figured with the All-Star Break, it was good to get the whole family together."

"When was the last time we did that?" Dad asked.

It had been a long time since all the Holmstroms were in one room. The silence didn't last as Eli and Ayden started arguing about a bad call on the ice last night, and then Maja started in by telling them they both were wrong. It didn't take long for my loud-mouth Philly family to be screaming at the top of their lungs. My new neighbors were gonna hate me.

I shook my head, and Veronica gave me an amused look. I hoped she understood my family was always this nosy, and she needed to get used to it.

I kissed her temple again. "Are you prepared for my family?" I whispered in her ear.

She nodded. "They're part of you. Plus, you haven't met my brother's side of the family. His Abuelita will give you the third degree."

"Can't wait to meet them, sweets."

"I love you."

"Love you too."

And of course, my asshole brothers ruined our nice moment by throwing balled-up napkins at my head. "Get a room," Brendan teased.

"It's my house, and none of you jerks were invited," I snapped.

Veronica laughed. "I mean, we could go back upstairs and..."

Ayden laughed. "I knew I always liked you, V."

"Why? Because I don't put up with your BS?"

The twins laughed, and Eli shook his head. "Pretty much. Welcome to the family, V. I hope we don't scare you off."

She squeezed my hand under the table. "I'm not going anywhere."

"So, are we allowed to say how much we hated Astrid now?" Maja asked.

"Wait, seriously?" I asked.

My siblings laughed.

"Sorry, bro. She straight up sucked," Michael admitted with a shrug.

"Yeah, we like V," Ayden agreed. "Even if she's got that whole goth girl thing going on."

"Goth girl?" Veronica laughed. "Black's classic."

"I love your tattoos," my sister told her.

Veronica beamed. "Thanks. Flowers are my specialty."

"Oh, you did the cover-up for Blaise, right?" Maja asked.

"Baby, show them." She turned to me.

I sighed and took my shirt off. Veronica's black, manicured fingernails ran over the red flowers on my chest.

"Oh, wow, it looks great," Maja cheered.

Veronica wrinkled her nose. "It's not perfect. I need to

do another session to get the colors right. They healed too lightly."

Veronica pulled her hand away, and I threw my shirt back on. "She does good work."

A blush ran down her neck, and I put an arm around her. I felt Veronica's hand squeeze my thigh, and it sent tingles down my spine. When Astrid broke up with me, I had been a broken shell of a man. I never thought when I had that one-night stand with Veronica, it would have led to something more.

I locked eyes with my dad across the room, and for the first time, I saw how he actually saw me. That he was proud of me. I grinned at him while I jumped in to save Veronica from Ayden's rant. She didn't need saving; my girl could go toe-to-toe with my brother like she was already part of the family.

"Love you," I whispered in her ear.

She laughed and swatted me away. "Needy."

"For you."

"Geez, can you stop being a horndog for like an hour?" Eli teased.

Veronica laughed. "He cannot, but that's okay. We have a lot to make up for."

"We do," I agreed and kissed her temple one last time and then let my siblings razz me some more. I didn't care. I was happy, I was in love, and everything was perfect.

EPILOGUE

VERONICA

AUGUST

"Oh my God, look at that baby!" I cried as Lily came into the house with Rosie in tow. My heart melted at seeing the little stinker.

Okay, I might have a touch of baby fever.

"Hey, V, thanks for having us," Lily said to me.

"Gimme that baby."

She laughed and handed off Rosie, who naturally grabbed at my hair, which was freshly dyed with red tips for the Bulldogs upcoming season.

"How are you? Really?" I asked her.

We had hired Lily to do our books at the shop, and she was so awesome at it that Blaise hired her to be his personal accountant. We had become close friends over the past several months. I still felt like her marriage crumbling was my fault, but she always reminded me that Seth had done both of us dirty. She was a sweet girl, and I might have been trying to matchmake her with one of Blaise's teammates. She deserved someone who would treat her right. I had my happily ever after, and I wanted her to get hers too.

She sighed. "Do you know what it's like having to move back in with your passive-aggressive mother after getting pregnant, married, and now in the middle of a nasty divorce?"

I cringed as I bounced Rosie in my arms.

Lily sighed again. "Sorry, didn't mean to unload on you. I got into another fight with my mom on the way over here."

"Lil, you know—"

She held up her hand. "V, I'm so grateful for how much you and Blaise help me, but I'm not moving in with you."

I frowned.

Blaise and I had talked about that a lot. I felt awful about Lily's situation, and Blaise was such a big brother, he couldn't stand to see Lily and Rosie struggle. We had three empty bedrooms, but Lily's pride got in the way.

"The offer still stands, you know."

She gave me a sad smile. "I know, but I'm fine. Right, Rosie? We'll figure it out."

The baby cooed at me and yanked on my hair again.

"Rosie!" Lily scolded and took her baby back.

I didn't mind, though; I loved Rosie. Between her and Logan's nephew Liam, my biological clock screamed at me, 'make a baby, already!' I hadn't expressed that to Blaise yet because I just moved into his house last week. We talked about wanting kids, but I didn't think we were ready yet.

"How was the move?" Lily asked.

"Good. It's nice when your boyfriend's one of six because you can rope in big strong hockey players into helping you move all your stuff."

Lily laughed. "Remind me to enlist your boyfriend whenever I have to move again."

I beamed. "I can arrange that."

"Where's Blaise?"

"Outside on the deck tending the barbecue," I explained.

Blaise planned this get-together as a housewarming party since he never had one when he moved in, but he said it was official now that I was moved in, too. Plus, training camp started soon, and then it would be pre-season, and then I'd lose that hunk of a man for days at a time when the new season kicked off. It was one last hurrah before it all got underway.

"Come on," I told her and walked outside onto the rooftop deck, only to stop in my tracks at seeing my hot boyfriend holding Liam.

"What's wrong?" Lily asked.

I grimaced. "I have really bad baby fever."

She tipped back her head and laughed. "Oh, you can keep mine tonight if you want so you can get zero sleep."

I watched Blaise as he listened intently to whatever Liam was saying to him. Logan smiled, grateful for a slight break. Blaise ruffled Liam's shock of red hair and set him down when he saw me coming outside. He strode over to us, and Rosie grabbed for him.

He smiled as he took the baby, holding her against his chest.

Ow, my heart. I couldn't wait to see him hold our baby like that. The very nonexistent one.

"Hey, thanks for coming, Lil," Blaise said to her and then bounced the baby in his arms. "And for bringing this little stinker. Who's Uncle Blaise's favorite?"

I had to put a hand over my chest at the sight of this

big broody hockey player baby-talking and holding the tiny girl in his arms. God, if that was our future, I could not wait.

Blaise bent down to kiss my cheek. "Hey, sweets."

"Hey, baby."

"Blaise, when are you two gonna have a baby?" Lily asked.

I glared at her.

Blaise looked like a deer in headlights. "I don't think any time soon."

Lily looked at me with a mischievous smirk. "You might want to reconsider that."

Blaise started to ask her what she meant, but then she took Rosie back and walked over to take a seat beside Logan. Hmm, an interesting choice there.

Blaise nosed across my neck. "What's she talking about?"

"Nothing," I insisted. "Baby, don't burn the burgers."

"I won't," he told me, but he insisted on kissing my neck.

I bit back a moan. This man was insatiable, but so was I, and I loved that he made me melt with every touch. He could be needy sometimes, too, like the fact he had been begging me to move in with him for the past three months until I finally relented.

I pushed him away. "Baby, we have company. You can have me later."

"Do I get to tie you up tonight?" he whispered huskily against my ear, and I felt his dick poking against my stomach.

"Maybe, but you need to get that thing out of here."

He laughed as he adjusted his shorts. "Sorry, sweets, you know what you do to me."

"Horny!" I teased.

He reached a hand up and caressed my cheek, his thumb sliding across my bottom lip. "Don't be a brat."

"You like when I'm bratty."

"Fuck yes, I do."

"Get out of here before we have to escape upstairs, and you burn the food for everyone. I need to check on the mac and cheese."

I darted back into the kitchen before he could say anything else. I loved my boyfriend, but I didn't need to get all hot and bothered in front of our friends. I checked the baked mac and cheese and started working on the salad.

I turned my head at the sound of the back door opening, and I smiled at Lily coming in with her little girl in her arms.

"Hey! Did you relax for like thirty seconds?"

She jostled Rosie onto her other hip. The baby started crying, and Lily sighed. Lily recently weaned her off breast-milk, and her soon-to-be toddler was cranky lately.

"Honey, you need help," I said.

She bounced her daughter again. "Hang on, I'm gonna put her down for a nap in the guest room. She was up all night last night; she's probably cranky."

I waved her off as I whirled around the kitchen, making sure we got everything done. Max ended up coming inside and saw me looking stressed.

"Oh gosh, tell me what you need," she offered.

I shrugged and took the mac and cheese out of the oven. I let it cool while I instructed Max on what I needed last-minute touches on. Dinah mentioned Max was a whiz in the kitchen. Maybe I should have enlisted her sooner.

Lily came back into the kitchen. "Okay, what do you need from me?"

I poured her a glass of wine and handed it to her. "Drink this and relax. Max is helping."

Lily slumped into one of the kitchen chairs and drained her glass. Max and I shared a concerned look.

"Everything okay, Lil?" I asked.

"No."

"What's wrong?" I asked.

Max bit her lip, and I could tell she felt uncomfortable.

"This single mom thing's hard."

"You looked pretty cozy with Logan," I teased. "Noticed you decided to sit next to him when you got here."

She shook her head. "It was the only open seat. We were just commiserating about how hard it is. I can't believe he's raising a kid. He's so young."

I laughed at her. "Um, so are you."

I handed Max platters to take out to the backyard, and I think she was grateful to get the escape. I sat down next to Lily and pulled her into a big hug.

"Thanks, I needed that," she said.

"I could tell. Listen, Seth straight-up sucks, but you know Blaise and I are here for you. I'll babysit whenever you need. You have a team to lean on. And you can still move in here."

She shook her head. "Thanks for the offer, but no. I can't do that. Some days it's just hard."

"I can't even imagine, but you're so strong, and your little girl's gonna grow up kicking ass and taking names."

She wiped her eyes. "V, I'm glad you don't hate me and that we became friends."

"I could never hate you; you didn't know. Worked out for me, and it will work out for you someday soon."

She sighed. "I hope you're right."

I knew I was right. I saw the way she and Logan looked

at each other today. If that wasn't love at first sight, I didn't know what was. They might need a push about it, though. And yes, Logan was exactly the teammate I had in mind for my friend. He was a gentleman, and he knew how to take responsibility. They were both single parents, too; it was a perfect match.

The rest of the afternoon went off without a hitch, and by the time we were crawling into bed, I was too tired for anything but sleep. I laid across Blaise's chest, and he played with my hair.

"Sweets?" Blaise asked.

"Hmm?"

"I want a baby."

I looked up at him in surprise. "What?"

He sighed. "Sweets, we see Lily's little girl and Logan's nephew all the time, and I want that. I want to hold my own baby in my arms and give them the world."

When we got back together, we talked about wanting kids eventually, but we weren't in a rush. So this was a surprise.

"Okay..."

"If you're not ready yet, that's okay."

"Blaise, I have baby fever. And every time you hold Rosie, I think about what a good daddy you're gonna be. It does something to me."

I felt his chuckle vibrate across my whole body, and then he shifted me so I was straddling his thick thighs.

He reached up and caressed my cheek. "Yeah, what does it do to you?"

"Makes me want to have a baby with you. I want to see you holding our baby in your arms."

"How long have you felt this way?"

"A while..."

"You want to start trying?" he asked.

I nodded.

He pulled back and reached over to the bedside table. I thought he was about to pull out one of my vibrators. Instead, he pulled out a black box.

"I guess I should give you this then, huh?"

"What, a cock ring?" I joked because I was a brat.

He slapped my ass. "You're asking for punishment tonight, huh, brat?"

I nodded. "Spank me. It's the only way I'll learn."

"Veronica, stop distracting me!"

I laughed. "Okay, what do you need to give me?"

He opened the ring box, and I gasped at the massive rock he offered me. The ring had a round aquamarine gemstone at the center, but a halo of tiny diamonds surrounded it. The band of the ring was also encrusted in tiny diamonds. It was so flashy, but it was perfect, and he remembered I said I loved that Dinah and Fi had unique gemstone engagement rings instead of a traditional diamond.

"Veronica O'Malley, I planned this to be romantic as shit—"

"Yes!" I squealed, not letting him get in another word.

"Let me ask!"

"The answer's still yes."

That got me another slap on the ass. "Will you let me ask, you brat?"

I shook my head and laughed as he slid the ring onto my hand. I pulled my hand back to examine it. Something had never felt right about the ring Seth had gotten me. It was fine, but this ring felt right to me. And it wasn't just because Blaise paid a fortune for it. Or that it was a gigantic rock on my hand. He listened to me, and he knew aquamarine was my birthstone. He was so thoughtful about what to buy me.

"We don't have to get married to have a baby, Blaise," I told him.

"I know, but I want you to be my wife."

"Okay, let's have a baby and get married."

"Don't you need to stop taking the pill?" he asked.

"Yes, but practice makes perfect."

He grinned, and he flipped me over so I was underneath him. "I am *very* good at practice."

He kissed me, and I melted into him, knowing that with Blaise, I was finally getting everything I ever wanted.

ACKNOWLEDGMENTS

I don't know how to tell you all how much I love this book and The Holmstroms. I know I said Benny and Rox were my favorite, but I lied! It's Blaise and Veronica!

Huge thanks to my betas on this one once again! Becky, Chris, Jim, J Lynn, Kat, and Sophie. You all help me so much with each and every one of my books.

Big thanks again to Charlie Knight for editing this one and championing my work. Can't wait for the next one.

Look out for Lily and Logan's book in the near future!

ALSO BY DANICA FLYNN

PHILADELPHIA BULLDOGS

Take The Shot

Score Her Heart

Against The Boards

The Chase

Game On

Risky Play

MACGREGOR BROTHERS BREWING COMPANY

Accidentally In Love

Trapped In Love

Temporarily In Love

THE MURPHY BROTHERS

Protecting Her

Capturing Her

ABOUT THE AUTHOR

Danica Flynn is a marketer by day, and a writer by nights and weekends. AKA she doesn't sleep! She is a rabid hockey fan of the Philadelphia Flyers. When not writing, she can be found hanging with her partner, playing video games, and reading a ton of books.

www.ingramcontent.com/pod-product-compliance
Lightning Source LLC
LaVergne TN
LVHW091114080826
845145LV00008B/1907

* 9 7 8 1 9 5 7 4 9 4 2 5 8 *